The Slither Queen

by

Tamera Lawrence

The Slither Queen

Contact Information: info@thewildrosepress.com

Cover Art by *Teddi Black*

The Wild Rose Press, Inc.
PO Box 708
Adams Basin, NY 14410-0708
Visit us at www.thewildrosepress.com

Publishing History
First Edition, 2025
Trade Paperback ISBN 978-1-5092-6043-0
Digital ISBN 978-1-5092-6044-7

Published in the United States of America

Dedication

This book is dedicated to my mother, Muriel E Hicks, may she rest in peace.

Chapter One

Philadelphia, Pennsylvania

A wind-swept rain pelted the streets with ardent affection as if trying to rid the asphalt of every possessive stain. Barely fit for human habitation, the deteriorated buildings shuddered beneath the icy onslaught.

Stepping from the shadows, a young woman appeared. A thin blanket covered her huddled form, damply molded to her narrow shoulders like a second skin. Beneath the shroud, she blocked the raindrops from touching the wailing bundle, which she held tightly to her chest. She shoved her index finger into the infant's mouth to still the ceaseless cries.

Desperation echoed in Lustra's heart as she inwardly cursed. Damn it! How could she be so lost? All her life she'd known these streets, and now here she was like a stranger in the midst. The alleys between the buildings appeared dark and indistinct. It was after midnight. Shivering, she stood in the middle of the street, undecided, and slowly pivoted, scanning the area. Across the street, a shadow developed into a man as he moved into view. Beneath the hood of his jacket, his face lifted, dark eyes piercing her, twisting deeply into her soul. Water dripped from his mangy beard as he held his stance.

"No!" Catching her breath, she reversed course, opting to go toward the distant traffic light. As she approached, she recognized a thrift shop. Finally, she knew her location.

Lustra had been staying at a local boarding house, a refuge for battered women who were hiding from their abuser. Although she wasn't exactly abused, she was in a crisis and hiding from her unborn child's sire, Blake Howard. Another resident had given her an address of a church affiliation who might be able to help her, so she had taken her chances and had previously met with a minister, who listened with rapt regard as she told him everything about her life, especially the past nine months. She revealed all that she saw, all that she had done, and all the things she couldn't explain as she tried to purge her soul free from its demons.

The newborn had arrived earlier than expected. She guessed she'd been in her eighth month, closer to ninth. It was hard to know for sure without prenatal care. But she couldn't have risked going to a doctor, let alone a hospital. Blake would've been expecting that. She had been moving around the city, living in shelters, the streets, and occasionally with a newfound friend. Now, she was out of money and had tapped out all her resources. The baby needed supplies. Perhaps adoption could work, even though it was a depressing proposition, but in reality, she had nothing to offer her daughter.

Blake's minions prowled the city, a known fact to her, and she had foolishly thought she had outsmarted him. But as soon as the baby had arrived, odd things began to happen. Strangers stalked her and most likely reported her every move back to Blake. Just thinking of the man was terrifying.

Fearing the shadows that followed, Lustra rushed into another alley and tripped over a curb. For a moment, the baby's face was revealed, staring at her with the bluest eyes Lustra had ever seen. Quickly, she recovered the infant. The massive stone church came into view, and she hurried around the building, glancing behind her. No one was in sight. Above her, the glistening raindrops reflected against the stained-glass windows. The muted light within gave her hope. She yanked on the side door. It was locked.

"Please," she begged, catching a sob. "Please, someone answer."

She banged on the door, her fist stinging from the abuse. A week ago, Father Mallard had met her at a local coffee shop, listened to her crazy story with rapt ears, nodded in understanding, and never judging her tale. He said he'd help her and to return when she was near delivery. He had claimed he would make plans for her, keep her safe, and find a place for her to go.

Abruptly, the heavy door opened. Father Mallard stood before her wearing his vestments, a sad expression on his hawkish features. His thinning hair revealed a sheen of sweat, eyes averted.

"Please, please," Lustra cried. "You must help me. Help us."

The priest shuffled to the side, pressing against the door jamb. "Come in, child."

Grateful tears stung Lustra's skin as she entered the vestibule. She followed the beckoning priest into the sanctuary. Wooden pews lined the chamber and candlelight diffused the room. At the front of the church, a huge golden cross manifested the light, instantly calming her.

The preacher moved toward the front rows, strides urgent. At the altar, the man pivoted around, soberly facing her, swallowing the lump in his throat. For a moment, he appeared as if ready to give a sermon but then his eyes changed to wonder as the air charged. It crackled in frenzied energy. Lustra stilled, heart lurching in her chest even as a whimper escaped her.

Blake's evil allure touched her before an actual visual.

"No!" she cried. "You can't be here!"

Lustra scanned the room. Mysterious silhouettes appeared, blocking the exits. She held her baby closer to her heart and silently prayed for help.

Blake Howard stepped out of the shadows, a smile of revelation in his handsome, carved features. Tall, dark, and deadly, he moved down the middle aisle toward her, dressed impeccably in a tailored suit.

"Hello, Lustra." Blake's voice was deceptively soft and alluring as he approached.

"You betrayed me," she cried to the minister, who shifted to one side of the room, watching the procession. "How could you betray a desperate mother and an innocent baby? We needed you. You were supposed to help us. You said you would. You're a man of God!"

Lustra's words were his undoing. The priest glanced away, appeared shaken.

"Do you really think he's a man of God?" Blake cruelly laughed. "Perhaps not your God. He is a shaman, a dark priest. He'd been planted just for this occasion, but I will say he did enjoy your confession, every juicy detail." His gaze traveled to the moving bundle beneath the blanket. "Now, I want my daughter."

"No," she said, voice barely audible. "Leave her be."

Blake smiled, bringing an alluring dimple to his jaw. His murky eyes brightened. Reaching Lustra, kindness filled his features. "Enough of this nonsense. If you're a good girl, Lustra, I will let you come with us. The baby needs fresh mother's milk. I admire your spirit in protecting her. Nothing compares to a mother's love, and I appreciate that. You may still be useful to me and can stay with your daughter for a time."

"You're lying to me," she said. "I don't believe a word you say."

"What choice do you have?" His long fingers reached out, beseechingly. "I own you. Own her. You will simply disappear if you don't accept my offer. I can't have you causing trouble. Your ramblings have been noted. No one can help you. My patience is at an end."

"You have already destroyed me." Defeat filled Lustra's features. All her efforts to protect her daughter had failed. "You have taken away everything I have ever cared about."

The priest stepped forward, positioning himself next to Blake. The man reached for the newborn; palms outstretched in a plea. "Let me look at the baby, Lustra, and make sure she's unharmed. I won't hurt her. I just need to see."

"No," Lustra said, tucking the baby closer to her. She retreated a few more steps, eyes sweeping the church. Dark spirits stood in the corners; anticipation crackled the air. She raised her eyes to the cross hanging above the altar, a silent plea in her heart.

"We can do this the easy or the hard way," Blake said in a silky voice. "In the end, you know you will lose. Stop fighting me. We need to see the baby is unharmed."

She cringed. That seductive tone had once lured her into his lair. How blind she'd been. Her vision blurred with tears as her body heaved in exhaustion, the weight of the world on her shoulders. She was spent, mentally and spiritually. Even as Blake waited, she accepted defeat. What was the use in fighting anymore? She'd been on the run since her delivery. She was losing blood and growing weak. Her gaze met his, the man she once loved, in some ways still loved. But the handsome façade was only a cloak for the darkness in his evil soul.

Wearily, she lifted the blanket, revealing a perfect baby with dark, downy hair. The baby was partially wrapped in a towel.

"Beautiful." Blake's smile deepened. "The mark. Does she have it?"

The imposter moved closer to the baby. He snared her tiny left hand and turned it over. A half crescent moon marked the baby's wrist in a red puffy display.

"She has it," the man said to Blake. A reverent smile lifted his lips. "Be praised."

"Be praised indeed," Blake said. "Will you come with us, Lustra?"

Lustra's breath caught as her options faded. The decision was only a moment in the making, but it felt like an eternity. Hell and damnation awaited her. She would suffer the consequences, but her innocent child wouldn't be alone and at their mercy. Her daughter's angelic face caught her gaze. Love swelled in her heart as all doubts fled. There wasn't a choice to make. She couldn't abandon her child. Wouldn't abandoned her child.

Blinking through her tears, she nodded, whispering, "Yes."

"Good girl," Blake replied. "I knew you wouldn't let me down."

Chapter Two

Rachel Garth stood before her selected group of campers, ranging in age from six to fifteen. As their camp leader, she had bonded with the kids during the past week. Second Chance Camp was a place for troubled kids. Once a camper herself, she was now an employee, helping others deal with their difficult lives. Many of the children were in danger of falling through the welfare cracks. The system was often broken. With parents not involved or even incarcerated, many kids were stuck in foster care or group homes. Many of the children were from the city, and the camp was an opportunity to experience nature and to just have a bit of fun. The camp was not only a temporary haven for the kids, but it gave them a chance to be heard without fear of repercussions. It was a place to discover nature, a friend, or yourself. She herself had found that part of her at the camp and so much more.

Goodbyes were never easy. It was the most difficult part of Rachel's job.

"Come here," she said, stretching out her arms. "Group hug."

The girls came to her, and she pulled them all together and squeezed tightly. "I'm going to miss you all so much. Remember—you are not alone. If you ever need me, I'll be here. I might even find a few of you back at camp next season."

After a few tears and some laughter, the girls finally broke apart, moving toward the pavilion area where their baggage was being sorted and then loaded into cars or vans. The first week of summer camp had both its rewards and downfalls. Rachel had counseled and led the girls in their daily activities and grueling therapy sessions. It had been all too easy to see the hidden pain in each child's heart—a natural gift she employed. It had been an emotional journey, reflecting on her own turbulent childhood, but her own troubled past helped to aid in her task. She herself had been a foster kid, moving through the system. Some of it had been good, a lot of it bad. The worse part was acknowledging her biological mother had never done anything to rectify the situation, and over the years, she'd given up hope and frankly, barely cared.

Michael, another team leader, approached, his lanky arms laden with sleeping bags and pillows. The tall blond team leader paused and said, "Don't look so glum. You can manage this."

"I'm trying, but I didn't know I would grow so attached already."

Michael shrugged, giving her a sympathetic smile. He moved toward a distant van, struggling to balance his load.

Sighing, Rachel leaned against a wooden post. The parking lot was quickly emptying, the noise dying down from the now missing human element. Michael was right. She had to get a grip on her emotions, or she would be a mess, maybe even regress from her own personal progress.

Dreamily, she stared at the sky. Clouds formed in the distance as a stir of wind swirled through the trees.

Abruptly, something jabbed her hand, tearing her from her musings. She lifted it, scanning her skin. A bloody smear trailed from the scar on her wrist, zigzagging along a pathway to her palm. How odd. Her inner wrist held a half-moon flaw. It was usually white and slightly puffy, but now a small dot of blood had squeezed out of a tiny hole. Like a balloon, it filled under her skin, bubbled to the surface, and broke, trailing over her flesh. Yuck. Had something bitten her, perhaps a spider?

Quickly, she dug in her jeans pocket, grabbed a crumbled tissue, and shoved it against the wound. She glanced around to see if anyone had noticed. There were only a few souls in the distance. How embarrassing. Maybe she'd nicked herself and never felt it, which wasn't surprising since the scar held little sensation. She wiped her hand as best she could with the cloth, blotting the hole. The seepage slowed. Washing her hands became her next priority. She walked toward the distant bathroom, shrugging off the injury, returning to her earlier musings.

For the most part it had been a wonderful week, uneventful considering the camp's history. She had enjoyed working with the kids, the campfires, and fun competitions. The only problem was Gabe Richards wasn't there. She had met the other team leader the prior year when she had been a camper herself, just shy of her eighteenth birthday. At first, she'd resented the camp's intervention into her own life. Hated it, in fact. But she had always been drawn to Gabe like a moth to the flames. He had been kind to her, and she had to admit, she had fallen for him—hard. She'd thought he had felt the same, but now she had doubts. After all,

Gabe was supposed to be working at the camp, and he was nowhere in sight. She had no clue to his whereabouts.

The previous year, her life had been so crazy. It was still, but now she understood why and exactly what she was. She was a guardian, a changeling, something newly discovered while at the camp. It was terrifying but also exhilarating. She was still learning about that part of her—her serpent. The previous summer, Gabe and the other guardians had known her physical state before she had ever known, but it was a path she had to walk alone. She'd always felt different, odd, but as she approached her eighteenth birthday, the sensation had spiraled out of control. It wasn't just physical. She had been missing stretches of time, mentally and physically.

During her time at camp, she had discovered several of the team leaders held a secret pact, including Gabe. It had been by accident, or perhaps not, that she'd come across the group in the woods, hands clasped beneath the moonlight. They were performing a ceremony. It had been creepy and yet compelling. A ritual had been taking place—a ritual involving her, though she had no way of knowing that at the time. The group had been undecided over her fate within their lair. Hands clasped, they were in the vortex. Their eyes were void, energy surrounding them. A cloud of something indiscernible engulfed them. So, she ran.

That night, she had thought she would end up dead and that they would kill her. She had witnessed something bizarre, something out of this world and yet she had been utterly drawn to it. Terrified, she stumbled in the darkness, fleeing along the path, and then Gabe was there, in her way. She'd thought he'd strike her down as she swore not to tell their secret. But he did something unexpectedly; he kissed her. Oh, that magical kiss—one that calmed her. She sighed. The changes in her body began thereafter. Her inner serpent had made herself known. She was a beast, beautiful and strong, changing at will deep in the night. It was horrifying yet exhilarating.

Over the course of that time, she had discovered something else—a choice. She could follow the ways of the dark serpents or join the guardians, destined to protect changeling children from evil sects. She'd followed her heart and claimed the title of Guardian. Now here she was, doing what she loved the most.

Inside the bathroom, she turned on the faucet, dipping her hands into the cool water. Last time she had talked to Gabe, he was somewhere in Maine on a mysterious mission. He'd been elusive, secretive. She tried to reach him in her mind, but he had shut down their telepathic bond. The question was—why? What was he hiding from her? Was he okay?

Rachel missed him. He was always in her thoughts, especially at night. Sometimes she felt him in her mind, something she resented at times. But then he'd send her warmth and love. But she wasn't sure if it was the kind of love she craved. They were guardians, spiritually connected in their cause. There was a natural love between them, but she wanted more. She was part human, a teenager. There was no way she could just shut down her emotions. And she didn't want to. She liked that part of her life. She had come to grips with her flaws, her accomplishments, her imperfections, and her beautiful serpent. She didn't think she needed to be sorry about it. It helped make her who she was. She was a work in progress. They all were.

Rachel prodded her wet scar. The blood had stopped. She pressed a paper towel against it and then shoved a couple of towels into her pocket for good measure.

Exiting the bathroom, Rachel paused, gazing in the distance. It was quiet. Serene. The past week had been so peaceful, so different from last year when she had come face to face with one particular serpent, an evil beast who'd wished to corrupt her, but she had refused his offering. She, Michael, Gabe, and Ariel had united against him and his kin, and they won the battle. But the war raged on. Dark Serpents were on the rise and seeking mixed human hybrids for mates but not just any mixed breed but a woman who could reproduce an heir, capable of definitive power. She herself had the ability to bear this kind of offspring and was now, and probably would always be, a target.

She had her gifts and knew her purpose. She had chosen the path of enlightenment. It had given her some protection against evil schemers. She was coming to love her serpent life. Now that she knew who she was, her objectives were becoming clearer. She was still learning to deal with her inner serpent and the path she'd chosen.

Michael came toward her, Tina by his side. Amongst the other human counselors, they were the only three serpent guardians at camp. No one was sure where Ariel, a prior employee, was working or living. The elusive guardian had disappeared, apparently preferring solitude. Ariel's absence didn't surprise Rachel. They weren't exactly the best of friends—both had been rivals for Gabe's affections. Or at least it seemed that way. Ariel claimed it wasn't so. That Gabe and she were only best friends. The other woman had a way of making Rachel feel inadequate—a feeling she hated—so she strived to prove Ariel wrong. It helped mold her purpose.

Rachel had worried there would be trouble with dark serpents at the camp. Thankfully not as yet. She supposed it wasn't that surprising since so far none of the campers had been of serpent blood, so there really wasn't a threat to any young changelings. But a new week would begin, and with it, new children would arrive, perhaps of serpent blood. Things could change rather quickly. Sure, she could oppose them, fight them off. She wasn't exactly alone. She had Tina and Michael. They could also call for backup, but from the little experience she'd had, it was a daunting task.

"Aren't there any stayovers?" Rachel asked Michael. "All the campers have left?"

"Not this week," Michael said. "Maybe next. We're on free time until tomorrow."

"Not exactly free time," Tina reminded him, brow arched. "Till after the cabins are clean."

"I work in the stables, remember," Michael told the pretty blonde. The two could have been siblings so similar were they in appearance. "I'm done for today. And I've already finished my work. I think I'll take a dip in the pool while you ladies get to cleaning."

"That's not fair," Tina said, pouting. "You can help us."

"Perhaps if you ask me nicely," he said, teasing her. His blue eyes twinkled mischievously. "I might think about it."

"Please," Tina begged, tugging on his arm. "Then

we can all go swimming."

Rachel closely watched them. Was there something more going on between the pair? The flirting was obvious. They seemed perfect for one another. A hint of jealousy reared inside her, not of Michael and Tina, but envy they had one another. Gabe was so far away from her—in mind and in spirit. She hadn't seen him for over two months. She hated thinking of the obvious reason as to why he would stay away. It hurt.

Rachel felt lost without Gabe. He had been her rock. Still was. She was lonely. True, there were other camp leaders at the camp, but most were newcomers and humans. She felt disconnected from them, ever alert to her secret life. Perhaps it was better that way. When Gabe was around, she could only think of him.

"We better get started, you two," Rachel said, walking away. Over her shoulder she added, "Tomorrow will be here before we know it."

There was something refreshing about being in the yellow cabin by herself and tidying up the rooms. Rachael swept and shook out the carpets, cringing at several nasty spiders hiding in the corners. She had to laugh at her fear. Of all the things she had faced last year, a tiny spider somehow could evoke her fears.

She pulled open the thin curtains to let in more light, which instantly spilled into the room. Then she cracked open the screens. Warm air filtered in, stirring her hair. The cabins didn't have any air conditioning, the only drawback from camp.

"Ahhh," Rachel cried. She jerked her hand toward her chest, cradling it with her other hand. She gaped at her wrist where the old circular scar marred her flesh. Once again, the scar was throbbing. Pulsating.

Normally colorless, the defect was now red as if filled with blood. It felt hot, scorched as if she had been burned.

"Not again," she said.

Rachel raced into the bathroom and spun the cold-water faucet. As the water flowed, she shoved her wrist beneath the stream. Cool water barely made a dent in the pain. It took some time, but the sizzling faded. When she finally removed her wrist, it appeared normal.

Strange. Rachel wrinkled up her nose, probing her scar with her finger. She had the scar since she had been a little girl—compliments of one of her mother's many boyfriends, or was it her mother? Her memory was fuzzy, but she remembered an elderly man holding down her arm and the searing hot burn against her wrist. She had assumed it had been a cigarette or something poker hot. She had screamed in pain. It had hurt for days afterward, inflamed and bloody. Then it had blistered, itched, and had trouble healing. Now years later, it was just a blob of flesh on her skin. Ugly. She hid it as best as she could. It was easy to just turn her wrist when hiding it or to wear long sleeves. Why her mother had let her be burned, Rachel hadn't a clue. But then nothing her mother had ever done surprised her. The woman was a drug addict. She only cared about her fix, not the two daughters that had been taken away by the state. She hadn't seen her mother in years. And Stacey, her sister, had been adopted and lived in New Jersey. Now and then, they wrote to one another, but she barely remembered her little sister. She could only hope she was happy with her new family.

Rachel rubbed her fingers against her temples.

Something snagged her mind. A memory on the tip of her thoughts. But a wall was blocking it. With the threat of a headache adding to her troubles, she shoved away her past. It was time to energize her spirit. She longed for the night, the moon, and the scent of the earth beneath her.

Chapter Three

It was a beautiful night filled with bright stars and a full moon. Before she even reached the clearing, Rachel felt the blood pounding in her veins. A fever broke her brow as her body became aware of the subtle existence of life around her. From the tiniest of insects to the earthworms hidden in the soil, she was aware of everything all at once. It took a moment for her to get her bearings, enjoying the essence of life. It was her favorite part of being a serpent.

There wasn't much to say when Rachel approached Tina and Michael. The ritual of bathing in the moon was as natural as breathing itself. Tina and Michael were standing in the moonlight. An aura surrounded them. The air was invigorated, crackling with energy. Silently, she took Michael's and Tina's hands, forming the circle. Electricity raced through their bodies, circulating between their fingers in a heated current. They lifted their arms and bathed in the moonlight. The vortex opened above them, an endless void of light and beauty that seemed to stretch for eternity.

The visions were the best of all. The brilliant array of colors illuminated the sky above them. Misty figures and spirits were in the vortex. Voices blended together yet no words could be discerned. Rachel gave in to the sensation, becoming one with the others. It was breathtaking, enlightening. Peace filled her with intense acceptance and love.

Sighing, Rachel luxuriated in her euphoria. Time and earthly matters slipped away.

A baby cried out, shrill and loud. It pierced through her soul. Something blazed against Rachel's wrist, burning, jabbing as hot claws dug into her flesh.

"Ahhh," Rachel cried.

She yanked her hands free from the others, the circle now broken. A shock of electricity raced up her spine. Dizzy, she lost her footing and face-first fell onto the hard ground, holding her wrist to her chest. The burning subsided.

Michael and Tina stared down at Rachel, confusion in their features.

"Are you all right?" Michael asked, kneeling beside the fallen teen. He grabbed her arm, concern in his features.

"Rachel?" Tina moved to Rachel's other side, just as worried. "What just happened?"

"I don't know," Rachel said, allowing Michael to help her stand. Her body trembled in the dewy night. Emotionally, she was drained, desolate, and lost. Her wrist still throbbed. "That was weird." She stared at the source of her pain. Once again, her scar was red and swollen. If she didn't know any better, she'd think she'd been burned again. It was so odd. And yet the pain had already subsided.

"Didn't you hear it?"

"What?" Michael's brow scrunched.

"The crying."

"No. I didn't hear anything unusual." His gaze snagged Tina's. "Did you?"

"No," she replied. "I was enjoying the tranquility,

and then my hand disengaged."

"It was a baby's scream. It was so terrifying and then my wrist began to burn." Rachel shook her head in disbelief. "It was awful, like reliving a nightmare." She left off the part that the nightmare was more of a memory.

"Did it come from the vortex?"

"No," Rachel said. "Somewhere else. It was hard to discern."

"So, it crossed over the spiritual realm," Michael said, frowning. "Whatever happened obviously affected you physically. Mentally. I felt you beside me then you were ripped away from us. And that happened before you even let go of our hands. I never experienced anything like it."

"Not ripped away, exactly," she said. "I was somewhere else, just for a moment." She twisted her wrist, considering her scar. "I'm trying to remember."

"Your wrist. Let me see it." Michael grabbed her arm, steadying it. He tried to take a closer peek. "A scar?"

"It's nothing," she said, pulling her hand away. "An old wound that sometimes bothers me."

Michael frowned, shaking his head. "Why wouldn't it heal then? We heal naturally."

"I don't know," she said a bit too quickly. She had asked herself that same question many times over. As serpents they healed quickly, carrying over to their human form. The wound was from her youth. She couldn't explain it or even know who to ask about the healing process. But she had instinctively known not to draw attention to it. Perhaps Gabe would know what was happening. But she didn't relish the idea of showing him her flaw. Who would?

"The baby was scared," she said, changing the subject. Intense danger had filled her mind. It wasn't the first time she felt danger. It was second nature to her. But somehow it was different and hard to distinguish. "I don't know who she is, but she's lost. Afraid of something. How could you not hear her cries? It was so loud."

"I heard nothing," Michael replied. His frown deepened. "It's so strange."

"Neither did I," Tina said, sharing a worried glance with Michael. "But you said she. It's a baby girl, so that's a start. Perhaps you were singled out for a reason, possibly a mission and it's for you, and you, alone. Sometimes it happens that way."

"Well, it never occurred before." Rachel didn't know if she should be pleased or worried to suddenly be chosen for a mission of sorts. And how could a baby choose her anyway? That didn't make sense. She doubted their scenario.

"The vision was only for you," Michael explained. "We didn't hear the baby. Perhaps the spirits are sending you a message. Go into the vortex alone. Maybe, it will happen again, and you can figure it out. Try to connect telepathically. The answer is there. You only need to look for it."

"Ugh. I don't know if I want it to happen again." Rachel sighed. So much for a peaceful evening beneath the stars. "Okay. Will you wait for me?"

"Of course, "Michael said. "I and Tina will be right here beside you."

"Catch me if I fall." Rachel closed her eyes, drawing in the night air. Her lungs filled with the fragrant breeze. She lifted her hands, stretched them high, asking for the vortex to open. It did, spread above her in a shimmering cloud. Energy surrounded her, lifting her spirits. Billowing and endless, the vortex appeared murky. Smaller than usual. Something was off. Where were the spirit guides? Suddenly, she was alone. Expectantly, Rachel's mind floated, seeking answers. She called out for enlightenment. Seeking answers. Nothing happened. Rachel concentrated harder. Blanketed her mind from outside influences.

Rachel envisioned a baby's face. It came into view. At first, the image was blurry but then one of the sweetest faces she had ever seen filled her mind. A natural blush stained the baby's cherub face. Dark, downy hair was barely visible. Rachel's wrist pulsated. It took all of her efforts not to respond to her physical pain. A moan escaped her. She moved closer, gazing into the baby's unbroken blue orbs, absorbing the infant's essence. Suddenly, she blended with the baby's spirit, becoming one with the child's innocence, feeling nothing, being nothing. Words failed her. She became childlike in her thoughts, regressing. But then sounds emerged. Voices and humming engulfed her, the words foreign. She became cold, afraid, and so alone. There was no way out.

Noises resounded around Rachel, throbbing in unison. She opened her eyes, seeing through the infant's orbs. At first, everything was fuzzy but then a man's face appeared, his coal black eyes observing her. His hot breath stirred against her skin. Intense evil shook her core. Confusion filled her with terror as his scowl deepened. She knew not what he was, only he was someone to fear.

The voices lulled her as shadows slipped into her mind. All hope faded into oblivion.

Rachel screamed.

Chapter Four

The ritual continued as the voices rose together in unison and recited the ancient verses. The chant crested and then repeated as the battle for the baby's soul continued. The child was unresponsive, staring up at them curiously at first but then the infant's eyes faded from blue to black. Her tiny body went limp in defeat. The baby opened her mouth as if she were crying but not a sound emerged. Slowly, the baby's eyelids closed. She slept.

Excitement filled the room. Blake Howard held his breath. Success at last. Intense satisfaction filled his soul. Giddy with sensation, he mentally shook himself, remembering where he was and quickly continued with the ritual. The baby's birthmark, which was shaped like a crescent moon, changed into the Mark of the Serpent—a black symbol reminiscence of the shape of a snake.

The others around Blake soften their voices in awe. This was a monumental moment of victory. This child was theirs to command. Someday, she would be a mother to the coming leader—the ruler of all beasts. The baby would be carefully and artfully raised, and he, Blake Howard, would be by her side, commanding her in the ways of the Ophites, sharing her power and glory. She'd be the vessel for bringing in a supreme being with untold powers.

The voices hushed as the room became expectant.

A soft sob erupted, breaking the silence. Lustra. Blake glared at the woman, who couldn't keep the misery out of her eyes. The baby's mother sat in the corner, apart from the rest of the people in attendance, twenty-five in all. She noticed him and froze. Terror entered her features as she quickly tried to compose herself. Tightly, she clasped her hands in her lap, bowing her head in submission.

He would deal with Lustra later, Blake decided. He'd like to drag her from the room, but that would interrupt the proceedings. The baby's mother had been a thorn in his side since day one. His use for her was almost at an end. He was tired of her tears and begging.

The gathered group leaned forward in their chairs, eagerness in their features, eyes glowing in fevered excitement. Several forked tongues slipped between their gaping mouths as the inner serpents could barely contain themselves.

"It's finished," Blake said, his tone humble.

As Blake said the words, the baby stirred in her sleep. He leaned over her, a ready smile on his lips, ready to welcome her into his lair. The baby woke, but now staring at him through the infant's blue eyes was the face of a young woman, spiritual and ghostlike. It wavered and strengthened. The woman's aura surrounded the baby, encompassing her tiny life force with an invisible shield. The infant stretched out her tiny arms and yawned as if not a care in the world.

"Get her out of here!" Blake turned to Lustra, startling her into action. He picked up the infant, shoving her into her waiting arms. "Take her." He then lifted his fist, shaking it toward the ceiling, yelling,

"Everyone, get out!"

Cursing and twisting around, Blake slammed his fist into the stone wall. Blood oozed between his fingers. Humans and serpents fled the room. Blake then grabbed Sow, his chief commander, by his upper arm, dragging him toward him. He seized the man's shirt, dragging him until their noses almost touched. "Listen to me, carefully. I want you to take five or six serpents with you and bring me that woman."

"What…what woman?" Sow asked, his voice barely a squeak.

"Rachel Garth. Bring her to me…alive!"

Chapter Five

Sunday brought a new wave of kids to camp. Rachel half-heartedly greeted her current charges, but she couldn't get the infant girl out of her mind. Who was the baby? She knew so little about the child. The baby was in a desolate place, surrounded by dark serpents. But there had been someone else around the child—a woman who rang with uncertainty.

The camp was filled with children of varying ages. Rachel now had eleven girls in her cabin. She handed out their team shirts and it wasn't long before they were all dressed in their yellow attire. The first few hours were just getting to know the girls and settling into camp life. Dinner was a lively affair. The new camp director was Thelma Stuart, an elderly woman who was a barrel of fun but cared deeply for the children.

After dinner, they had their first campfire. Singing and roasting marshmallows, the kids seemed to enjoy the atmosphere, but Rachel could still see the pain behind so many eyes. It was a gift of the spirit that was both bitter and sweet—the gift of knowing.

After settling in with the girls for the night, Rachel grew restless. The cabin was overly hot. Oppressive. She couldn't catch her breath or still her racing heart. The night called to her. Kathy, another team leader, also resided in her cabin due to the considerable number of girls. Rachel walked over to the twenty-year-old, one year her senior.

"Do you mind if I go out for a walk?" Rachel asked Kathy, who was busy working on a crossword puzzle with a puckered brow. Kathy was a bit reserved and took her job seriously. The woman wore thick glasses, no makeup, and kept her hair pulled back in a single ponytail.

"Sure," Kathy said. "The girls are asleep. If I need you, I'll pull the bell rope."

"Thanks." Rachel slipped into the night. Her eyes quickly adjusted. She went a short distance and hid behind a large boulder, ditching her clothing. Sighing, she rolled her eyes toward the moon and changed. With a burst of adrenaline, her serpent burst free. It was a defining moment when she met her other half and released her. After that, instinct took over and she was speeding through the forest, reveling in the scents and musky earth. She moved toward the lake, staying low in the grass. She traveled to the other side of the large body of water to a desolate area that was rarely used due to the thick marshy undergrowth. Here she found a perfect spot and settled down to stare out at the water. Crickets belted out their ballads along with the occasional burping frog.

The moon dipped its blush over her, and she luxuriated in its beams. But as peaceful as it was, her thoughts remained on the mysterious infant.

In her serpent's form, she concentrated on the baby.

"Prisca." The name entered her thoughts. It meant *ancient*. She envisioned the tiny face, studied it to memory.

Deeply rooted in her mind, she searched out

Prisca's location, but a wall blocked her meditation. A noise broke her from her concentration. The feeling of intense danger filled her, and she had stupidly allowed herself to be in a vulnerable position. The dark serpents were still miles away, but they were traveling fast, coming toward the camp. It was only a matter of minutes.

"Michael," she called out, warning him telepathically. "Where are you?"

"I know," he replied. "Don't do anything. I'll be right there."

"They're coming for me," she said, the knowledge disclosed to her. "There's no time. I've got to move and lead them away from camp. We can't take any chances with the kids." Already, Rachel was moving away from the camp, traveling northward toward higher ground.

"No!" Michael said. "It's too dangerous. Come to me so we can team up. I'll get Tina. There are too many."

"It's too dangerous," she replied. "I will lose them underground and circle back. You need to stay with the children and protect them."

Rachel blocked Michael from tapping into her mind. There was no way she was backtracking toward him and risking the safety of the camp. She stopped and waited a moment, discerning the dark serpents' direction. It was working. Already, they were moving north behind her, following her, confirming her earlier assessment of her being their target. She moved toward Cannon Run Summit, a place of many caverns and deep tunnels. She would try to lose her scent in the earth and hide until morning or at least till she deemed it safe.

Trees passed her in a blur. Rachel crossed streams

and fields. In the distance, the bottom of the summit stood out in the moonlight. Quickly, she slid up the rough terrain, crossing logs and moving over larger boulders. Instinctively, she found the first cavern's entrance and slid into its cold, dank depths. She could sense the dark serpents closing in on her. She went deeper into the earth, burrowing through twisty tunnels of soil and rock. She barely felt the abuse she dealt her serpent's form. The adrenaline and need for survival had taken control.

Rachel burst out of a cave and moved away from the entrance. She only needed to travel another half mile to be at the top of the summit and be able to enter the deepest of the caverns that led to miles and miles of underground tunnels. If she could reach the maze of passageways, she could shake the serpents or at least fend them off one by one.

She was about quarter of a mile from the entrance when colliding sounds echoed in the night. Trees snapped. Rocks and leaves were tossed aside.

Anxiously, Rachel moved faster, resisting the urge to call Michael for aid. She still had a chance. She rounded a bend. The entrance was hidden between two huge boulders. She aimed for the portal.

Something hit her with tremendous force. Her body rolled, crashing into a tree trunk. Stunned, she faced the first of the evil serpents. He was ugly and gray. A jagged lightning bolt stood out on his forehead. She recoiled quickly, her inner serpent enraged by the abuse.

Rachel engaged him in battle. They locked together, fangs snapping. He was strong, but she was angry. Her anger gave her the added thrust of adrenaline. Quickly, she rolled him into the death position, squeezing and striking her fangs deep into his heart. He stilled. She shook him off as another serpent approached.

This serpent was older but wily. He too held the same marking on his forehead. She felt him studying her as if how to approach her. The serpent behind him was younger, at least twenty feet in length with coal-like skin glittering in yellow diamonds. He was eager to engage in battle.

"What do you want, old one?" she hissed telepathically.

"You. Come willingly, and you might live."

"No," she said. "I am enlightened, a Guardian. Go and leave me alone."

The old serpent considered her. She could sense his hesitation.

"If you don't leave, I will kill you," she warned. "The choice is yours."

Ignoring her words, the old one moved to the side, allowing the younger serpent to pass him. Furious, Rachel's serpent met him head on. The air filled with their battle cries. The younger one was strong but lacked direction. It was easy to maneuver him. He fought recklessly trying to frighten her off with hideous sounds of his rage. She laughed at him, goading him to foolishness. Within several minutes, she had him pinned and silenced his heart.

Two other male serpents appeared, bigger and more seasoned than the younger one. They both had the same black, gray color with silver triangles decorating their coats. They both bore the lightning bolt symbol between their eyes. They were heavier serpents, a bit slower but incredibly strong and cunning.

Rachel hissed trying to decide her next move. There was no way she could defeat them on her own. They held the power of the warrior serpent, something she lacked. Her gaze moved over them, making eye contact. Dancing from side to side, she tried to beguile them, something that came naturally to her.

The older serpent laughed at her as Rachel hissed in rage. She dashed toward the cavern entrance but one of the beasts sank his long fangs into her tail. The pain filled her with intense heat as she was dragged toward the offenders.

Suddenly, the air electrified. She felt Gabe's presence before a visage. His anger at her abuse consumed him. His fierce battle cry gave heed, and she turned her head to see Gabe's serpent attacking the other serpent, which had bitten her. The dark serpent's neck dripped with his blood loss.

"Go!" Gabe told her telepathically. "Hide. Now."

She stiffened at his command. Who did he think he was ordering about?

Abruptly, Michael's serpent joined Gabe, and the pair finished battling the twin serpents. The older serpent disappeared. Rachel wanted to give chase, but she was exhausted. She slithered toward the cavern's entrance to watch the outcome of the battle.

It was a nasty clash, but Michael and Gabe were young, strong, and sly. They both took an opponent and prevailed, killing their challengers, dragging their withered bodies farther into the woods where they would disintegrate.

Gabe's serpent approached Rachel, his fury washing over her. "What were you thinking, Rachel?

Michael told you to wait for him. Why didn't you call out to me for help?"

As miserable as she felt, his telepathic words enraged her. "You have closed me off from your thoughts. You haven't talked to me in weeks. I didn't think you would come..." The words hurt to express. In that moment, she knew the true extent of her pain. She thought he hadn't cared anymore, that he had moved on without her.

Gabe coiled, studying her for a moment and then turned toward Michael. "And you...why didn't you come sooner?"

"Because I told him to stay at the camp," Rachel replied. "Don't you dare yell at him."

"She blocked me from her mind and took off," Michael said. "It took some time to figure out where she'd gone."

"I will deal with Rachel," Gabe said. "You can return to the camp."

Michael didn't reply but left them, disappearing into the trees.

"How injured are you?" Gabe came closer, slithering around her form, his gaze trailing over her skin. "You need to spend some time healing."

"How can I do that?" she answered. "There isn't any time. I need to return to camp. I have a job. A responsibility..."

"Had a job," he said. "Not anymore. A replacement will be sent to take your place as a counselor. These dark serpents have come for you, and we need to find out what they wanted. Since they failed in their mission, others will come in their place. It's not safe for you at the camp right now and you could endanger others, including your foster family."

Gabe's words hit her like a weighted stone. Not to counsel the kids. Not to work at the camp. Not to go home to see her foster parents?

Not replying, she glided into the cavern, found a cavity that glistened with limestone, and twisted into a tight coil, laying down her head. Gabe followed her and coiled beside her, his large head lying beside hers.

"I'm sorry," he said telepathically. "I didn't mean to snap at you. I know I have been absent."

"You don't owe me any explanations," she said. "You have done your good deed and saved me. You can leave if you wish. I'll be fine."

"You are so stubborn," he said. "I said I was sorry."

Rachel didn't reply. It hurt having him so near. She had missed him so much and now that he was finally with her, she felt only worse. He only was there because he was responsible. He only came because he would protect any of their kind, even to the death. He was honorable and good, something she struggled with at times.

"I'm not that good," he said reading her thoughts and responding.

"Don't you dare read my mind," she said. "I'll block you."

"You can try," he said. "But I will always find a way in."

"That's not fair," she said, assessing him. "You block me all the time."

"To keep you safe," he replied. "That's the only reason."

Gabe's serpent was magnificent with his sleek

amber coloring with gold motifs. Over twenty-five feet in length, he was muscular and supple. Her serpent's blood rushed with excitement having him so close.

"I can keep myself safe," she said. "Despite you thinking otherwise, I have my own gifts."

"We are on the same team," he said. "Remember? We work together. None of us are alone in this fight. Why do you insist on trying to manage things on your own? Haven't you learned anything by now?"

Rachel thought about his words. Her tail throbbed but the healing had begun. She would have to stay in her serpent's form to heal overnight. In her human form, she wouldn't be able to manage the injuries.

Gabe's snout nudged her head. "You need to sleep, and then we'll talk in the morning."

"You don't have to stay with me." She wanted to let him off the hook but, in her heart, she wouldn't be able to bear it if he left, something she would never admit.

"I'm not going anywhere," Gabe replied. "Sleep."

Chapter Six

Gabe scrutinized Rachel as she slept, her beautiful golden serpent a marvel to behold. Her rational thoughts were closed off, safely tucked away but her lurid dreams slipped into his mind as he telepathically probed for answers. Her nightmares replayed their recent battle. Fear surrounded her visions—misgivings and vulnerability. Guilt ate at him for his intrusion into her private thoughts. She would be angry, but he was seeking answers to who or what was after her. He had been having visions of his own, visions of destruction and death. Danger surrounded Rachel. She had no idea how connected they really were or how hard it had been to stay away for so long.

Sighing, Gabe moved away from her, left the cavern, and went out into the night. Situated on a rocky incline, he studied the landscape below the summit, searching for danger and any human life. He and Rachel needed clothing, and he didn't intend to leave her for long. For higher vantage, he ascended a tree, scanning the countryside with razor-sharp vision. In the distance stood a farmhouse and with a bit of luck, a full wash line with a load of laundry attached.

Perfect.

Gabe lifted his head, alert to any immediate dangers. Finding nothing alarming, he quickly left the trees and traveled the hilly terrain toward the farm.

****

Rachel awoke to the sound of Gabe's serpent moving restlessly beside her. She shifted her serpent's head, studying his powerful form before he'd notice her.

"I felt you leave me," she said telepathically. "Where did you go?"

"I went to get clothing," he replied. "When you're ready, we'll leave the summit, and I'll take you to my car. I left the clothing down below."

"Your car? You were driving…"

"I had just entered Pennsylvania when I felt danger surrounding you. I am glad I'd been so close. If I had been farther away, I don't know if I would have gotten to you in time."

"I would have managed," she said, tilting her head. She didn't care if he knew she lied. She was still furious with him.

"You're healed." He ignored her claim, approached, and then stopped by her tail. "The damage wasn't that bad. It could've been much worse."

"Why did the old serpent have scars?" she asked. "What would have caused such damage to his skin?"

"Fire sometimes causes such damage," he explained. "A serpent will heal from melted skin, but sometimes the healing process has trouble leveling out beveled flesh."

"Sounds painful," she replied, averting her gaze. Perhaps that was why her wrist never healed. It had also been a burn of sorts. "However, I don't have much pity for him."

"He's old and has seen many battles."

"Yet he didn't fight. He fled like a coward."

"He was called by his leader to return to his lair, probably to give a report on what just occurred. There wasn't any use in his death. He was merely a messenger."

"How do you know all of these things?"

"In time, you will know them too," he said. "Just like you notice the inner turmoil in humans, you will pick up the aura of a serpent. It goes both ways, so you need to learn to outthink your rival. If he knows your weaknesses, you will be more vulnerable. You are a young serpent, just a babe really. Give yourself time to grow."

Rachel stiffened, swallowing her bitter reply. She didn't want to be considered a baby who was weak and needed a lot of support.

"I didn't mean literally." His words filtered in her head.

"Stop reading my thoughts," she hissed. Angrily, she swept by him and out of the cavern, finding her way through the foliage. She didn't care if he followed. Her emotions were at an all-time high and his reading her thoughts only made it worse. The sun was just about to rise. Shadows played with the beckoning light.

"Rachel." Gabe followed her. "Will you stop being so sensitive to my every word?"

She snapped her head around, facing him. "If you'll stop prying…"

"Okay, okay." He moved past her, starting down the hillside. "I'll stop. Just stop arguing with me. Follow me. I want to be human again and then get breakfast. I'm starving."

Chapter Seven

Blake's fury was heard throughout the mansion. Maids scurried out of sight. Doors slammed shut and voices erupted in the library.

"Insolent fool," Blake screamed at Sow. "How dare you fail in your mission. You only had to bring me back a simple woman. Period!"

"She is not just a simple woman," Sow said. "She is strong and cunning. She has special forces around her, protecting her. And then there are the other guardians. They were strong and will do anything to safeguard her."

"I told you it wouldn't be so simple," a woman said. She moved past the six men gathered around Blake. "Is it such a wonder that Rachel is so special? So strong. Why are you surprised by her talents? Her bloodline is strong."

Blake considered the large warrior, rubbing his jaw. "Rachel has a hold on Prisca that has to be broken. Her lineage means nothing to me. I will think nothing of killing her."

"But Rachel has connected with Prisca," the woman said. "Even death might not break its hold. You need only to bring the females together to get what you want and then if you want to kill Rachel, so be it. The choice is yours."

Blake paused. "The idea has merit. I need to know

that Prisca is mine—her future intact. I want Rachel tethered, one way or another."

"So, do I," Ariel said, nodding. A slight smile carved her mouth. "Soon."

Chapter Eight

Gabe led Rachel to a thick grove of pines. On a large rock, a pile of clothing lay neatly folded. They separated, each changing back into their human forms.

Rachel groaned as she dressed, the cool air assaulting her exposed skin. Her body ached and her legs and feet were bruised. She drew on a pair of faded gray shorts and pulled on a black cotton shirt. It wasn't much, but it would have to do until she got her own clothes or found something better.

From beneath the trees, she walked out of the shelter to find Gabe already dressed and waiting for her. Her heart reacted just looking at him. His dark hair had grown past his ears, lying errantly across his neck. His blue eyes stood out in the rising sunlight. He looked striking in his white T-shirt and cutoff jeans. Unlike her loose outfit, his fit him as if tailored for his size.

"I'll find you some shoes," he said, staring at her bare feet. "My sneakers are in my car."

"And how far away is it?"

"About two miles north of here."

"Great," she said, shrugging her shoulders.

Gabe grabbed the bottom of his T-shirt and ripped off a long strip. He then tore it again into two pieces. "Sit down on that log."

Surprised, she sat down on an old stump while Gabe knelt by her and quickly wrapped the material

41

around her feet. His fingers on her skin were like a gentle balm.

"It's better than nothing," Gabe said, standing to survey his task. "The asphalt will be hot."

"What about you?" She stood, nodding toward his bare feet.

"I'll be fine," he said. "I can manage it."

Rachel began lifting the bottom of her shirt, revealing her taut stomach. "You could rip a piece of my shirt and wrap up your feet…"

Gabe's eyes slid over her skin as he swallowed. "No." He yanked down her shirt and turned away. "I'll be fine. Let's go."

Rachel followed him down the rest of the slope and onto the roadway. They made quite an interesting pair, like two souls down on their luck. They only needed a stick on their shoulders with a handkerchief holding their supper. She smiled at her musings.

Gabe slid his gaze toward her, lingering on her mouth. "What's so funny?"

"Nothing," she said. "Just thoughts. How are your feet?"

"Fine." He reached over and grabbed her hand, interlacing their fingers. Without talking, they walked side by side for a time. Warm energy flowed between them.

Rachel allowed the sensation Gabe's touch evoked to spread through her body. It felt so right between them. Her chestnut hair blew around her shoulders as she shielded her gaze from his. Shyness overtook her thoughts as she tried to make sense of her feelings for him.

"Where are we going?" she finally asked.

"We're going to see Steve Westfield—or more importantly, Ace."

"Ace?"

"That's his nickname," he said. "We need his help to find out more about the serpents who attacked you. I need to know about their markings and their lair. We need to know what we're up against and how to stop them."

"I just thought they were dark serpents like the others?"

"No. They're different, but I'm not sure what's making them different." He paused, shrugging his shoulders. "We need to know."

"And where is this Ace?"

"Maine."

"Really," she said. "But that's where you just came from."

"How do you think I know him?"

"Are you going to tell me what your mission had been about?"

"Not right now," he said. "In time…"

"Why are you always so secretive with me?" She pulled her hand from his. "You never trust me."

Gabe stopped walking, face sober. "I do trust you. You have to trust me and that I know what is best for the both of us."

"You're impossible." She kept walking, staring straight ahead. Her emotions were in chaos. Hot angry tears spiked her eyelashes.

"Hey, Rachel," Gabe called and then ran to catch up with her. He grabbed her arm, forcing her to look at him. "What's wrong?"

"I didn't ask for this crazy life," she said, yanking

away her arm. "I didn't ask to be a guardian or to be enlightened. No one really gave me a choice. Sure, I got to choose which side to be on, but now what? Sometimes, I just wish I could go back. Be just a human with all my imperfectness." She sniffed, wiping an angry tear. Embarrassment at her outburst spread through her. "I'm sorry. I didn't mean that. I don't know what has gotten into me lately."

Gabe pulled her into his arms, holding her close, her head tucked beneath his chin. They stood locked together, each lost in their own thoughts. "Don't be upset, Rachel. I'm feeling more like a complete jerk."

"Good," she said against his shoulder. "You should feel bad for making me worry about you for months while you just go about your way without a care in the world."

Gabe lifted her chin, staring into her eyes. "I love the way your eyes change color. Sometimes they're blue and sometimes chocolate brown. And I do have a care in this world. I care about you."

Gabe lowered his head and kissed her. Her worries and fears faded in his feathery touch as her heart thumped in bliss. She sighed, pulling him closer, her body molding to his. Their kiss deepened, arms intertwined.

A car horn broke them apart. Someone yelled from the open window. "Get a room!"

Chapter Nine

An old blue 1979 Camaro which had seen better days sat alongside the dusty roadway. Gabe grabbed the hidden keys from the rear tire and opened the trunk, grabbing his socks and sneakers.

"Your car, I presume?" Rachel arched a brow.

"For the moment," Gabe replied. "It's a classic. Don't begrudge it. Here. These are my extra sneakers."

"They'll never fit me," Rachel said, taking his offering. The worn black and white sneakers had seen better days.

"I'll shove some material in the toe area," Gabe explained. "That way when we stop for breakfast, you'll have something to wear into the restaurant."

"I'll look ridiculous wearing these things. They're huge."

"You'll look cute," he said, tapping her nose. "It's the best I can do now."

Unimpressed, Rachel slid into the front seat and set the sneakers on her lap. The car smelled like Gabe's unique scent. The interior was worn but clean.

Gabe slid behind the driver's seat and smiled at her. "What do you think of my ride?"

"It's pretty cool," she said, staring at the gearshift. "You can drive stick?"

"Can't everyone?"

"I can't," she said.

Gabe turned the ignition key, revving the engine for show. He put it into gear, pressed down the gas pedal, and squealed the tires, an impressive burnout following.

"Show off," she said, holding onto the seat.

They traveled north as the sun rose in the sky, but Rachel was torn with regrets. The faster they ate up the miles, the more she missed the camp and her foster parents.

"Shouldn't I call the camp to let them know I won't be back?" she asked. "It doesn't seem right to just abandon them. They'll think I am a terrible employee."

"Michael will oversee it," he said, glancing at her. "I know you're disappointed, but this was unexpected. We need to find out what we're up against. Your safety comes first and then there's the safety of the kids to think about."

"But what if the dark serpents try to get to my foster family to get to me or worse, Stacey? I don't even know exactly where she is living, but they could track her down."

"I think your sister will be okay," Gabe said. "They know you left the area. I doubt they will bother your family. For what? You're not there. They'll just track you. There was something about their markings that stands out. They are from a unique sect, something unusual."

Rachel thought about his words. "I had a vision when I was in in the vortex. It was of a baby girl. Her name is Prisca, and she is in trouble. These serpents have something to do with her. I can feel it."

"Any idea where Prisca is at?"

"No. I can't seem to locate her in my mind. She is in a desolate location and heavily guarded. I feel like I am meant to help her, but how can I when I don't know where she is?"

Gabe made a right-hand turn into the parking lot of a small diner. He shut off the car, and for a moment he was silent and finally turned to her.

"A lot of this is new to you, Rachel. You will learn to trust your instincts and allow them to guide you. I really think Ace will be able to help us. He has been around for many years and has knowledge of cults and diverse sectors. He should be able to tell us who these dark serpents are and where they're from. It might link us to the child."

"I hope you're right. This baby girl is helpless. I am afraid for her. She is innocent and on her own.'"

"She's not helpless." He paused, thoughtfully. "That's why she has chosen you to help her."

"Chosen me?" Her mouth dropped open. "But how?"

"There is a connection between you both. A link. It will be revealed to you." He opened his car door. "That's how it works sometimes. Let's eat. I'm starving."

****

Rachel observed Gabe as he ate a hearty portion of pancakes. He hadn't been kidding when he said he was starving. When was the last time he had eaten? He paused to look at her. Whenever he met her gaze, butterflies fluttered in her stomach. She had missed him so much. And now that he was here, nervousness had overcome her.

Gabe had said he cared about her but what exactly

did that mean? Again, he and Michael had put their lives on the line for her. She was so grateful they both cared. She hated not knowing where her future was headed or what was in store for her. She wanted the same self-confidence that Gabe exuded. She wanted to be like Ariel, strong and sure. She wanted to be equal in their eyes, not someone they had to look after.

"Eat, Rachel," Gabe said, pointing his fork toward her scrambled eggs. "We've got a long drive ahead of us. I don't know when we'll stop again."

"Where exactly are we going?"

"Mount Kineo," he said. "Maine."

"I've never been there," she said. "What's it like?"

"It's really beautiful." He downed his glass of orange juice. "Peaceful. You'll like the terrain."

"When will we get there?"

He glanced at his watch. "Not till later tonight and that's if we don't make any long pit stops."

She sighed, considering the bleak restaurant and its lack of customers. She crossed her arms on the table, listening to the waitress singing a tune behind the counter.

"Hey." Gabe reached over and grabbed her hand. "It will be all right. Stop worrying so much."

"I can't help worrying," she said. "I feel like I have a bullseye on my forehead. I don't want to put anyone in danger."

"That's why we're going to see Ace."

"Does he know I'm coming?"

"I told him about you," he said. "He's been anxious to meet you."

So, Gabe had already spoken to this Ace about her. She wondered what he'd said. Why was this man so special to Gabe?

"If you're not going to finish your eggs, then I'll eat them."

"Go for it." She slid the plate toward him. "I don't have any money, Gabe. I don't have any of my things, my pocketbook, or my bank information. I do have some money in savings. If I could just get my ATM card…"

"Forget it, for now," he said, polishing off the eggs. "I don't want anything electronic linking directly to you. I got you covered."

"I'll pay you back," she said. "I promise. I don't want you to have to pay for me."

Gabe stopped eating, considering her, a slight frown marring his lips. "Whatever happened to the adventurous Rachel, who took on some really nasty serpents? Now you're worried about owing me a few bucks…"

Rachel glanced away and swallowed. Unease spread its ugliness over her. She rolled over her wrist. "I need to show you something. It's here on my wrist. It's my scar…"

Gabe grabbed her hand, pulling it closer. He studied the white puffy lines. "I never really noticed it before. How did you get the marks?"

"I don't know," she admitted. "Someone burned me when I was a little girl. I have a memory of an elderly man holding down my arm. My mother wouldn't let me look as he did whatever he did. I remember the smell and the pain. What kind of mother does that to their daughter?"

Gently, Gabe touched the circle. A frown marred his face. "It's odd."

"When I connect with Prisca, it turns red…like it's pulsating with blood."

"Why didn't you tell me this sooner?"

"Because it's ugly," she replied. "And it just happened a day or two ago. Who wants to show someone their ugly scar?"

"It's important to tell me everything," he said. "Everything. Don't hold anything back from me. We're the same, you and I. We're on the same team, and we don't keep secrets from one another."

"I didn't look at it like it was a secret. More just like an embarrassing deformity."

"There is nothing deformed about you," he said. "You are beautiful just the way you are. Special in every way." He lifted her hand and kissed her scar. "And your eyes just turned blue."

****

The sun dipped lower in the sky. Rachel shifted in the car's bucket seat, trying to find a comfortable position. Guilt ate at her. She couldn't drive a stick shift, so she couldn't give Gabe a driving break, but he didn't seem to mind. He had turned on the radio and was singing to every tune that echoed throughout the car.

"I would think being a guardian you would have a beautiful singing voice," she said, laughing. "Apparently, I was wrong."

Gabe glanced at her. Wind slipped through the open window, stirring his dark hair over his unique eyes. "I haven't heard you sing…"

"Because I sound awful." She sat up in the seat, sick of inactivity. Her butt was numb, and she wanted a shower. A stick of gum would be nice.

In the distance, the lights from a country fair lit the evening sky. A huge Ferris wheel and several other rides stood out. The fairgrounds became more colorful as their car approached. People of every age milled around, standing in lines for tickets or food.

"Let's stop at the fair for a few minutes," Gabe said. "I want a cold drink. We both need a break, and it looks like fun. We can both stretch out our legs."

"Are you sure? Maybe we should keep moving."

"We'll be fine," he said. "You're being way too quiet and depressed. Let's just pretend we're out on a date."

"A date?" His words slid over her, an intense longing in her heart. If only they were normal teens out on a date. What a different life she could lead. She shook loose her errant thoughts. "I don't know how long I could walk in those sneakers." She wiggled her sock-clad feet, frowning.

"I'll figure something out." He drove the car into the stone parking lot. A guard directed him to park behind another row of cars.

"Just wear the sneakers for now," he said, shutting off the engine. He got out, walked around the car, and opened her door. "Here, I'll try to make them fit better and help you put them on."

She slid her feet out of the car and sat awkwardly, grass poking her bare ankles. Gabe grabbed the right sneaker, checked the rags he'd earlier stuffed inside, and slid it onto her foot. He pulled the ties tightly and created a neat bow.

"Okay, servant," she said, handing him the other shoe. Teasingly, she lifted her other foot, repeating the same actions. She grabbed his offered hand and stood.

51

"I look like a duck," she said, gawking at her oddly huge feet. "People are going to stare. I hope I don't walk like one."

"It's just for now," he replied. "Come on. It will be fine."

They followed other patrons into the main area of the fairgrounds. Scents of hotdogs, popcorn, and french fries lingered in the air. Screams erupted from several rides. Gabe noticed a small booth with sandals, yanking her into the entrance. "Pick out a pair for your feet."

Rows of sandals with various adornments were lined along a shelf. A brown pair with tiny beads caught her eye, appearing around her size seven. Indecisive, she chewed her lip. Twenty-five dollars. A bit steep.

Gabe noticed her regard, grabbed the sandals, and pulled her to the side. He knelt by her feet, untying the right sneaker. "Try it on."

"But…"

"Stop worrying about the cost." He pulled off her sneaker and sock, sliding the sandal onto her foot.

"Stop reading my thoughts." She touched the top of his bent head, his soft hair filling her palm. He lifted his eyes, sheepishly smiling. He pulled off her other sneaker.

"I can do it myself," she said, quickly bending down to dress her foot.

"Do you like them?" Gabe asked. "They fit perfectly."

"Should I even reply?" she said, giving him a gentle shove. She twisted her foot. The sandals were pretty. She wished she could paint her toenails. "You already know. Perfect."

"Are you going to pay for those?" the clerk asked,

eyeing Rachel's feet. One brow arched upward when the woman noticed the sneakers lying in the grass.

"Of course," Gabe said, pulling out his wallet.

Once outside, Gabe tied the sneakers' laces together, shoved the socks inside, and threw them over his shoulder. He grabbed her hand and headed toward the portable restrooms. A line of trash cans stood nearby. At the first can, Gabe shoved his sneakers amongst the garbage.

"Sure you want to do that?" she asked. "You might miss them."

"Not in this lifetime," he said, grinning.

The crowd was typical of a fair with people milling about with their kids and a lot of babies in strollers. Teenagers stood around in small groups, joking and laughing. Gabe grabbed Rachel's hand and pulled her to the ticket booth, where he purchased a ride bracelet for each of them.

"Beautiful," Rachel said, holding up her wrist with the paper bracelet. "And yellow, my favorite color."

Gabe laughed at her antics. "Let's ride a few rides and then the Ferris wheel."

"I'm afraid of heights," she said, laughing.

"Liar." He grabbed her hand, tugging her along. "Let's go."

They spent the next hour riding various attractions. They rode on the bumper cars, the tilt-a-wheel, and the super slide. Gabe was right. It was what she needed. She had never laughed so hard or enjoyed being with him more. She was the center of his attention, and she loved every minute of it.

"Now the fun house," Gabe said, rushing her along.

They were ushered into a two-seated car that drove

on a track inside a darkened tunnel. "This looks familiar," Rachel said, leaning against Gabe's arm. He slid his arm around her shoulder.

The car bumped along and came to a doorway. Above them a huge snake stared at them with glowing red eyes. Rachel squirmed at the image, even though it was fake. The reminder was nerve wracking after what she and Gabe had gone through the previous night. The car went up a short hill and then drove along a curved track. Monsters popped out of hidden doors and lights flickered. Unexpected noises shrilled. The car dipped and pushed through an exit door.

"What a rip off," Gabe said, climbing out of the car. "It lasts what, a minute or two?"

"I liked it," she said. "But you're right. It was too short."

"Hungry?"

"Sure," she said, following him to the food stand where they ordered hotdogs, fries, and sodas. They sat at one of the picnic tables to eat.

"Are you having fun?" Gabe asked. "You look like you are."

"Yes." She bit into the juicy hotdog. "Thanks for the food. I was starving."

Chapter Ten

Her huge bedroom with its ornamental moldings and oversized furniture didn't impress Lustra. A white marble fireplace sat against the middle wall with etchings of tiny cherubs chained to serpents carved into the stone. Two oversized chairs with decorative pillows stood on each side of the fireplace. A huge bouquet of fresh roses adorned the middle of the mantel, spreading its heady scent.

It was a room meant to pamper any woman, a room meant to seduce. A built-in vanity held perfumes, makeup, and head adornments. The closet was filled with beautiful clothing, furs, and shoes for any occasion. An armoire held fine silver, gold, and pearls. The adjacent bathroom was marble and gold with thick, plush carpets.

As she studied the bedroom's décor, her belly turned sour. Why had she been so blind, so taken in by Blake Howard, a man almost three times her age? What once had seemed like a fairytale come true had ended when reality struck. She knew what Blake Howard was and the minions that served his wicked purposes.

The serpent's lair beneath the beautiful mansion was sinister and frightening. It was rumored to be a portal that ran into a darker realm beneath the Earth's surface. Serpents lived in this realm, which had never given in to their human forms. She had seen one such beast. The sight of him alone had her quaking in fear despite being under Blake's protection at the time.

But now...

She swallowed hard. Her precious daughter was in the hands of these monsters, who wanted to change her into what...?

She had to save Prisca. But how? What could be done? Her mind slipped to the ceremony when the baby had somehow resisted the invasion into her tiny soul. Her precious baby had outdone the serpents. There had been a light around Prisca, a protective aura. She was so afraid to hope for a miracle...but still hope filled her heart.

If only she could escape with the baby. If she could just find a way.

A knock sounded on the door. Before she could move, it was thrown open by a male servant and a large blonde woman entered the room, holding a tiny bundle.

"It's time for her to eat," Ariel said. "I thought I'd do the honors and bring her to you."

Eagerly, Lustra grabbed her baby, holding her tightly. She closed her eyes, grateful for the time she got to spend with her daughter. She laid the baby on the bed, searching for any signs of abuse or changes. But Prisca gazed up at her with pure innocence. One tiny fist found its way into the baby's mouth.

"Leave us," Lustra said to Ariel. "I nurse her in private. Blake gives me an hour with her."

Ariel stood beside Lustra, staring down at the baby. "So, you are from Philadelphia?"

"What difference does that make?" Lustra said. Hatred for the cold-hearted woman seized her.

"Do you know a woman by the name of Leah?"

Ariel moved closer, eyeing down the smaller woman. "She goes by many names, but that is her birth name. Leah Sanction."

"No," Lustra replied, glancing away from the penetrating stare. She cried out as Ariel seized her throat, jerking her close.

"Don't try to fool me, harlot," Ariel said. "You are related to her. A distant cousin. Have you seen her in the past few months?"

"No," Lustra said, trying to shake her head.

"Don't lie to me."

"No, I haven't. I swear." Lustra tried to twist away. "Leah runs the streets. Her mind is gone. I don't see her anymore."

"Streets? What streets? Where?"

"Camden, New Jersey. Along the waterfront..."

After a long pause, Ariel released her grip. "Very well. I believe you."

"Why is she so important?" Lustra asked, rubbing her throat. "What is she to you?"

"Never mind," Ariel hissed. "She is only an end to a means. You already wasted ten minutes of your time with your daughter. I suggest you get to feeding her. Tonight, there is a full moon. There is a special guest arriving to meet Prisca. Another ritual will be performed. And this time, you will not be allowed to attend." Ariel turned around and left the room.

Lustra lifted her baby and wept.

****

As night fell upon the huge mansion, guests began to arrive to bear witness to a great awakening. Prisca was to be honored and revered as her fate would be sealed and impenetrable to any outside influences.

Witnessing the transformation was a once in a lifetime opportunity for members. A huge feast would take place afterward. Prisca was destined to be a future vessel, once her serpent reached full maturity, and she would one day give birth to a serpent with extraordinary powers, none which had ever been present since ancient times.

Beneath the mansion lay a sanctuary and the entrance to an underground cave, where the serpents would congregate and pledge their allegiance to their leaders. That evening, the entrance to a hidden world would be revealed, opening for a time the annual passageway for the arrival of an ancient lord.

The cave's entrance flickered in firelight, a blaze fed with primeval wood. Carvings of the sun, moon, and stars were revealed in the interior along with ancient symbols. Incense filled the air as the people gathered around the stone ceremonial table. At the head of the table, a huge marble serpent was coiled, poised to strike. In the flickering firelight, the snake appeared to move, its eyes crimson, captivating.

The group in attendance were dressed in black ceremonial robes with their heads covered. Each wore a heavy chain laden with the medallion of a golden serpent. The patrons spoke in hushed tones, huddled on the stone benches surrounding the ancient table.

Blake Howard entered the room, dressed in the same garb as the others but his head remained uncovered, revealing his dark, neatly trimmed hair. His eyes were black, glowing with fierce intensity as he scanned the room.

"Welcome, my brothers and sisters," Blake said to the crowd. "I am pleased to see so many coming to this most special occasion." He paused for effect and then motioned with his hand. A woman entered the room, holding a swaddled baby. She slid back her hood, revealing her identity.

"Thank you, Ariel. You will be truly blessed." Blake took the squirmy baby from her arms and gently laid her on the stone table. The infant quieted, opened her blue eyes to gaze at the fierce serpent above her.

Blake stood at the foot of the altar. Humbly, he bowed his head and then lifted his hands in praise toward the statue. "Noble Nag, we beseech you to come."

A shaman came forward out of the darkness. The elderly man wore red ceremonial garb. Feathers adorned his long gray hair. His face was haggard and old, eyes barely slits. Between his brows, a long lightning bolt scar stood raised and throbbing as blood pulsated beneath his skin.

Beside the table, a wooden bowl had already been prepared with herbs, leaves, and plants. The shaman picked up the bowl, stirring it with a wooden tool. His eyes never left the infant as he began chanting and humming.

The onlookers joined in the same chant. All eyes turned to the baby, who calmed down and became trancelike. She wore a white lace ceremonial gown, her blue eyes fixated on the serpent above her. The shaman walked around the table and dipped his finger into the bowl he held. He drew the shape of the serpent onto Prisca's forehead, leaving a wet crimson image.

"Mana. Mana." The shaman repeated the name, each time with urgency. He turned the baby's hand to reveal her unique marking. Over the crescent moon, he drew with his finger the sign of the serpent. "Mana. Mana." The shaman's eyes rolled toward the marble serpent. "We beseeched you, Nag, serpent of ancient visions. Hear our prayers."

Blake closed his eyes as rumbling excitement filled his senses. His serpent longed to be free. He wanted to hunt, to fight, to be free of his human form. The others around him were also restless. The ancient words stirred up their primitive need to join the dark forces and be one with the murky bowels of the Earth.

The baby's eyes turned black. It was happening again. Blake held his breath. The powerful shaman would be able to manage any interference from Rachel. They were ready for her should she try to intervene. Nothing could stop them now.

Chapter Eleven

On their last ride of the evening, Gabe and Rachel got onto the Ferris wheel. After the safety bar was secure, the attendant hit the lever and their seat moved a few feet in the air while more passengers were addressed.

"I really don't like riding a Ferris wheel," Rachel said to Gabe. "The spinning bothers my stomach, and I'm afraid the seat's going to fall. I don't like it when they just stop moving it like this."

"It's not so different than being in the trees," Gabe said, shrugging.

"But I'm not in my serpent's form," she said. "I'm a little afraid of heights. If you hadn't talked me into it, I would never have gotten onto this ride."

"It's the last ride anyway. We only have a few more hours left to get to our destination." He laid his arm behind Rachel's shoulder, pulling her closer. "I just wanted to spend some time with you."

Rachel sighed and laid her head against his chest. When he nuzzled her mouth, she lifted her face for his kiss. Gabe pulled her closer as the seat gently swayed. The chair moved higher as more passengers got onto the ride. It wasn't long before they were at the top.

"I hate when it's not moving," she said, against Gabe's lips. She avoided looking down.

"Rachel, look at the view. You can see

everything."

Rachel followed Gabe's regard, looking downward. People appeared like ants, automobiles matchboxes. A little fearful, she turned her attention to the stars above her. She located the constellation Orion. The moon was huge and golden, drawing her inner serpent's delight. A yearning to be in the vortex filled her but not tonight—tonight she would just enjoy being a human out on their pretend date.

A brilliant star caught Rachel's regard. So strange, it was brighter than the moon. It filled her vision until two golden dots blocked her sight, blinding her to everything but its smolder. She blinked, trying to break the spell, to see. Her fingernails dug into Gabe's arm as she struggled to speak. Darkness closed around the edges of her vision until the image grew pinpoint. The starlight held on, sucking every part of her into its heated embrace. Obscure words filtered into her mind, becoming a chant. Time stopped. She was floating now as the physical world faded away. She tried to make sense of the words cresting in tempo but couldn't discern their meaning. Danger surrounded her. She was afraid. She telepathically called out to Gabe, but it was as if a wall had been installed, the connection void. The chanting crested as her memories faded into basic need. Suddenly, she longed for her mother, to hear the soft beating of the woman's heart.

The starlight changed into a face of an old man. He was ugly, his breath foul. The man's face was etched in wrinkles, his tone gray in color. The bolt on his head pulsated the blood of the serpent as the feathers that adorned his skull danced as if alive. He was speaking to her. She couldn't discern the words, but then they clarified.

"I see you now," the man said. "Rise, Mana. Rise and be free. Death and destruction to all who oppose you."

****

On the seat beside Gabe, Rachel began to convulse. Her head moved backward, her mouth agape, eyes colorless. She struggled to breathe, gurgling. She slumped to one side.

"Rachel!" Gabe said, pulling her against him. She was as if a ragdoll. Was she having a seizure? "Rachel! What's the matter with you? Wake up!"

A guttural noise erupted from Rachel's throat, her body stiffening. Blood oozed from the scar of her upturned wrist. It pulsated as if alive. Something wormlike slithered beneath her skin.

Rachel's shirt ripped across the shoulders as her body elongated and contorted.

"Rachel, no!"

There was no stopping her. Gabe was shoved against the metal barrier as she altered into her golden serpent. He had little time to think as the safety bar bent and broke free, dangling from one bolt. The chair dangerously shook as her movements sent it to a climax. Rachel's sandals fell to the ground below.

"Stop, Rachel!" Gabe yelled, trying to grab her as half of her serpent's form hung over the side. "Don't fall." But she effortlessly slid from the cramped seat onto the metal casings of the ride, twisting her body around the metal frame. The ride started to rotate.

People on the ground noticed the twenty-foot snake, pointing upward, and screaming, "There's a huge snake on the ride!"

"Rachel, come back!" Gabe hung over the seat, reaching for Rachel. She hissed at him, turning toward the ground. Despite the spinning force of the ride, she moved toward the middle of the frame. The Ferris wheel sped up as she used her tail to hold on, twisting and turning.

"Stop the ride!" Gabe screamed to the attendant.

When she got near the ground, Rachel let go and fell, landing hard onto the earth. She quickly coiled and hissed at the stunned spectators. She rammed her head into a man who was trying to snap her picture and then she was moving toward the center of the fairgrounds. Anyone in her way, she knocked down, daring anyone to stop her. People screamed, running in fear.

When the Ferris wheel stopped near the ground, Gabe had no choice but to jump from his seat, which was several feet in the air. He landed with a thud, rolled to his feet, and raced after the fleeing serpent. Along the way, Rachel was leaving a path of destruction. Tables and booths had been overturned. Injured people were sitting on the ground. Stunned, he ran for the edge of the fairgrounds. Rachel was now in the parking lot. She was bowling through people like they weren't even there. He changed directions, hoping to cut her off before she hit the open field.

Gabe grabbed Rachel just as she was entering the grassland. He jumped onto her form, wrapping his arms around her thick neck, but she wasn't having any of it. Furiously, she twisted and shook him off until he was holding onto her tail. In seconds, he was flung onto his back. She hissed, whipped around, and pinned him down with her head. With his chest nearly crushed, he struggled to breathe.

"Rachel!" He struggled to speak and changed to telepathic but to no avail. "Turn back to human!"

Rachel bared her fangs, curling the slant of her mouth. Intense hatred filtered over him, washing him in bitter acid. Her eyes were black and lifeless, reminding him of a shark. Something was wrong. This beast was not Rachel. The knowledge jolted him.

With no choice, Gabe altered into his serpent's form. Rachel's hold was broken as she struggled to hold him down. Just as his serpent made his showing, she attacked him, ramming her head into his. He was stunned by her newfound strength.

Sirens wailed in the distance, as flashing lights moved closer. Gabe fended the serpent off, trying not to injure her, but she was trying to hurt him. She gnashed her teeth against his throat trying to coil and squeeze him. He managed to break free.

Rachel's serpent broke loose and sped off to the nearby tree line. He followed her, glad they were leaving the vulnerable fairgrounds. He lost sight of her as she disappeared into the woods. When he rounded a bend, she dropped from a tree and landed on him, hissing in impressive rage.

"Stop it!" he said telepathically. "What is the matter with you? Get control of yourself!"

No response.

Again, he was forced to defend himself. She was determined to injure, maybe even kill him. When she nicked his throat, he coiled around her, tightening his grip. She struggled to break his hold. He bent her neck toward the ground, holding her hostage. She hissed and thrashed in fury.

"Rachel!" He shook her, screaming into her mind.

"Snap out of it! Come on."

She tried to bite his face. He took his head and rammed into hers. Her fangs receded. He hit her again, but not as hard and this time she went limp. Her head fell onto the ground, her serpent's form collapsing. Releasing her, he called again into her thoughts. "Rachel?"

"Gabe," she replied, telepathically.

"Stay here. I'll be right back." His form quivered in relief as he made his way back to where he'd first altered into his serpent. He'd never been so afraid. Rachel had scared the heck out of him. He'd no time to figure it out. They needed to move from the area. In the field, he found his ripped clothing, grabbed it in his mouth and moved into a thick coppice of trees. After dressing in what appeared more like rags, he headed to his car. Vehicles were still leaving the scene. Lights flashed from numerous police cars arriving. He grabbed his keys from his pants and unlocked his car. He drove down the street, parking alongside the roadway where he'd left Rachel. He grabbed a blanket from the back seat and walked into the woods. She was still in her serpent form. He feared she'd attack again but she was limp and unmoving. Dogs barked in the distance.

"We've got no time! We need to go. Change into a human, now!

"Look away," she said into his mind. She grabbed the blanket with her mouth, tugging it away from him. He pivoted around as she altered and a moment later, she had the blanket wrapped around her human form. He faced her. She was pale, body trembling from head to toe but it was her lost expression that held him.

"Hold on," he said, remembering where they were.

He scooped her up in his arms and headed out of the woods. After depositing her into the car, he got into the driver's seat, started the engine, and hit the gas pedal, yanking the stick shift. The wheels screeched, flinging rocks as the car moved down the roadway.

"What the heck just happened back there?" he said, gawking at her. "I've never seen anything like that."

"I don't know," she whispered, tucking her chin. Her wild hair hung over her face, hiding it from his view. "I just don't know."

****

After traveling about a half mile, Gabe veered the car into a vacant lot. The rundown building was boarded up and obviously had not been used for some time, but it was the perfect place to hide for a few minutes. He drove around the building and parked, shutting off the motor. Silence fell as his thoughts circulated.

Rachel was curled up in the seat, appearing as vulnerable as a child and hardly like the remarkable beast which gave him a run for his money. She clutched the blanket to her throat, shivering, teeth chattering.

"I can put on the heater," he said, reaching for the key to restart the car.

"No," she said. "I'm not cold. It's just my body's response to what I just went through."

Gabe laid his head against his seat, exhaling in a long draw. He had never been so terrified. Rachel was becoming everything to him. If he'd lost her…Swallowing the lump in his throat, he struggled with what ifs. After a moment, he exited the car and walked around to her door, opening it. Miserably, she stared at him with huge blue orbs. He knelt on the ground, touching her cool face.

"What happened back there?"

"I…I don't know," she said. Tears brimmed in her lashes. "I was so lost and afraid. I couldn't speak and all forms of language had left me. I was in a primitive state. My serpent was wild and terrified of something just before I blacked out. Whatever took control over me, I couldn't stop it. The next thing I knew, I heard you calling my name. I can't remember any more."

He opened the glove box and grabbed a clean rag. "Here. Your wrist is bleeding again."

She held out her hand, twisting her wrist. Sure enough, her scar was pulsating, seeping blood. Gabe secured the rag around it, tying the ends. "Does it hurt?"

"No," she whispered. "But I can feel my blood rushing in my veins."

"I wish I had ice."

"What is happening to me?" She pushed a strand of hair behind one ear. "What if it happens again? I could hurt someone."

"But you didn't hurt anyone," he said. "You just wanted to get out of the area. Think, Rachel. What was the last thing you remember in your human state?"

She closed her eyes, tucking her head. "I was staring at the sky, the stars. I was looking at one strange star when it began to change, grow brighter. It surrounded me. Became me and then darkness. I wanted to call out, but I didn't know any words." She paused, pressing her palm to her mouth. "I remember now. I wanted my mother's arms. I wanted her scent and her warmth. I was scared." She opened her eyes, revelation seizing her. "It was Prisca. I'd connected with her and felt her fear. I was cold and alone. I heard voices, chanting similar to before, and then I faded away, became her. Prisca is just a baby. It was she that changed me and took control. For a space of time, she controlled my serpent. How can a baby be so powerful? How would she even know how to protect herself? She knows nothing yet of the world."

"It's not the human baby," Gabe said. "It's Prisca's inner serpent. As tiny as she is, she wants to survive. Her serpent's instincts had taken over. Somehow, she has bound herself to your serpent. I have never seen anything like it, and yet Prisca is not of age to decide her path. These people that are holding her are trying to take away her free will—her very soul before she can grow up and decide for herself which path to take. But Prisca's serpent is defending her."

"But what does that have to do with me?"

"She has chosen you, Rachel," he said, curling his hand over hers. "To protect the babe, to be her guardian."

Chapter Twelve

From the altar, the shaman picked up Prisca, holding her up so all could see. Whispers and ahs followed. Then he wrapped the blanket around the baby, nodding to Blake to release the Ophites in attendance. With Blake's command, the room exited quietly.

"How could this happen again?" Blake said, staring at the moving bundle. "How could it be possible? I never saw anything like this in one so young."

"Prisca has ancient blood, and with it, ancient gifts that we can't even begin to understand," the shaman explained. "She is special, indeed. No matter, the outcome wasn't predictable or unexpected. Don't worry. Indeed, we have claimed Prisca as ours. In time, she will submit to your will."

"But her soul force has left her body," Blake said. "It fled into the vortex. Without it bound to her body, she is lost to us. What good is this physical form when we don't have the complete package?"

"No matter," the shaman said. "Prisca will be easier to control this way. Physically, she will still grow to maturity. Her serpent will remain intact, and we can use her for future purposes. Prisca is like an open book. We need only fill in the blanks. After all, it's what she can do in the future that is important. She can breed a supreme being unlike any other, one that can lead all beasts. Until the time of her maturity, you will prepare her serpent for this honorable task, teach her our ways."

"But what of her human side?"

"When the time comes, we will try and reunite the two. If Prisca refuses to join us, then we will not allow her human side to reunite with her serpent. Her soul will stay forever lost and with it, her humanity."

"But what about Rachel?" Blake asked. "I felt her presence in the room tonight and her interference. What should I do about her?"

"Find the woman and kill her. No reason to take any chances. Prisca's future will remain uneventful and stay on target." The shaman paused, rubbing his jaw. "Or…capture this Rachel. She is of age. Despite what she tells herself, she is not fully committed to the Guardians. There may still be hope for a reconciliation. Why have one when you can have two?"

"Indeed." Blake paused in thought. "Yes, indeed."

Chapter Thirteen

Ace's appearance wasn't exactly what Rachel had been expecting. The man resembled a mountain hermit, with his long gray beard and baggy clothing. He lived off the land, traveling along Maine's rocky mountainsides and jagged coastline. The drifter preferred Mount Kineo's solitude and the shores of Moosehead Lake.

After a brief introduction, Gabe and Ace disappeared into the inky night, leaving her solo. She tried, without success, to engage Gabe telepathically, but he'd effectively shut her out, so she sat on a rock and waited. There wasn't much to do except stare at the portable grill, which held a steamy pot of what smelled like vegetables and meat.

Ace and Gabe returned, each quiet and avoiding her questioning brow. Ace disappeared into his tent, while Gabe stirred the food in the pot and then filled a bowl. He grabbed a spoon, plopped it into the stew, and handed it to Rachel, but she shook her head. Shrugging, he sat next to her on another rock and began to eat the mixture. She waited for a moment for him to speak, but he continued with his meal, obviously troubled over something.

The flap of the tent moved as Ace walked out, appearing solemn. He considered Gabe, then turned his gaze upon Rachel before speaking. "You both can rummage through my things and look for supplies. There is a duffel bag with clothing. I can't vouch how clean it is but you're both welcome to it."

"Thank you," Rachel said, hugging the blanket more tightly about her.

Gabe stood and cleared his throat. "I'll go take a peek." Without waiting for a reply, he ducked into the tent, leaving Rachel with Ace.

"You are just like Gabe described," Ace said. He sat on the boulder across from her and stretched out his legs. "Beautiful. Cunning. A special aura surrounds you. You have strong instincts and strong spiritual protectors."

"Well, where were my protectors earlier tonight?" Her words were bitter, but she was tired and drained. "No one helped me. I felt very alone and afraid."

"Sometimes we must help ourselves," Ace said. "Sometimes we must reach the bottom of a pit to find our way back out."

"I didn't help myself out of any pit," she said. "I had no control over myself or my serpent. Maybe, I'm destined to just stay in that pit you're talking about, and I'm a lost cause. I have no memory of the ordeal. It scares me to think of what I was capable of doing."

"Nonsense, child," Ace said. "You are overwhelmed, as to be expected. There is so much you have to learn. Let it come to you. We grow in knowledge when we are in distress. It helps clarify things. There are always answers to our questions, be they good or bad. There is a purpose for what you are experiencing. Lessons are necessary for growth. It doesn't mean you were abandoned. You are learning necessary survival skills. Despite what you think, your serpent kept you safe tonight."

"You make it sound so easy." She lifted her head, studying him. "Something is wrong with me. I can't learn if I can't remember. Most of what happened is a blur." She swallowed hard. "Gabe said you might know what to do."

"I know your story," Ace said, expression blank. "Gabe has been filling me in on what's been happening to you. He's been worried."

"How could he have told you? We only just arrived…"

"How do you think?" Ace straightened. "Gabe speaks to me telepathically, the same as you. He confides in me, and I keep his confidences."

"So, you're a serpent," she said. "I couldn't tell. Either you conceal it well or my discernment has been damaged. Gabe never said a word one way or another."

"Well, now you know." Ace shrugged as Gabe came out of the tent with clothing in his hands.

He dropped it onto Rachel's lap. "I think this will fit."

"Thank you," she replied.

"Go into the tent and change, Rachel," Ace said. "Take a few minutes for yourself. Rest if you want to. There are sleeping bags inside. Help yourself. When you're ready, we will sit and talk and find out what's been going on."

"Can you help me?" She said the words softly, afraid to hope.

"I will try." Ace threw a log into the fire, energizing the flame. "No matter what, you're not alone. We are here with you. We'll figure it out together."

Rachel blinked, uncertain. Ace gave her hope. He was right. She wasn't alone. She could count on Gabe and now she had Ace to rely on. She turned and entered the tent, eager to get changed and find out some much-needed answers.

****

Despite the overwhelming longing to cuddle up in a sleeping bag, Rachel left the tent. There was no way she was going to sleep without any kind of answer. She also feared turning back into her serpent against her will. She had no idea when it could occur again. It was a frightening reality. Ace was nowhere in sight, but Gabe was poking a stick into the firepit.

"How are you feeling?" Gabe paused, eyes sweeping over her.

"Okay, I guess." She shrugged, pulling the blue hoodie closer around her face. The night air was cool, and she was glad for its warmth along with the matching sweatpants. "I feel kind of numb inside. I guess...I'm just a bit scared. Some guardian Prisca chose to protect her."

"Sit next to me." Gabe patted the boulder next to his. After she sat down, he reached out and touched the bump on her forehead. "Does it hurt?"

"A little," she said, wincing.

"You didn't have a chance to heal in your serpent's form. I'm sorry; I hurt you."

"Apparently, you didn't have a choice." She swallowed hard at the implication. She couldn't remember their battle. "Why do you think I attacked you?"

"I think Prisca was frightened," he said. "You were seeing me through her eyes, and I was a stranger to

Prisca. Her serpent doesn't know who she can trust. She was just lashing out." He grabbed her hand, pulling her against him. "It wasn't you attacking me. Prisca's hold on you didn't last long. Have you since felt her?"

"No, and I'm worried. I feel like I let her down."

"That's why I brought you to see Ace," he said. He squeezed her hand and kissed her fingers. "He has mentored me for many years. You can trust him."

Abruptly, Ace returned and sat down across from them. He held a book in his hands and began paging through it. He stopped at one section and turned the book toward them.

"Is that the mark you saw on the dark serpents' foreheads?"

Gabe studied the image, glancing at Rachel. "Yes. That's it. It looks like a forked lightning bolt."

"I thought so," Ace said. His attention settled on Rachel, then lowered to her hand. "May I see your wrist?"

"Yes." She held out her wrist, which was still wrapped in rags. Gabe helped her unwrap it. Her scar was bloody, swollen, and raw. "It heals and then it bleeds again. I don't know why it keeps happening."

Ace sat closer, grabbed her wrist, and leaned down to inspect it. His brow dipped low as his concentration held rapt. "What happened to your mark?"

"You mean my scar?"

"No, child. I mean your serpent's birthmark."

"I don't know what you're talking about." Confusion filled her features. "I was burned as a child. It's just a scar."

Ace paused, nodding slowly. "Someone tried to burn off your birthmark."

"No, that can't be right," she said, stomach clenching. Her temples pounded as her memories became fuzzy. "My mother's acquaintance held down my wrist and he burnt me with something...maybe a cigarette. It was child abuse..."

"How old were you?"

"I was really young," she replied. "I think maybe three or four."

"Who is your father, child?"

"I...I don't know. My mother never spoke of him." Helplessly, she absorbed his words. She knew so little about her past. "Do you know who he is?"

"No."

Ace closed his eyes. His finger traced over her swollen skin, mentally probing. His face lifted as he sharply inhaled through his narrow nose, then released his breath. Time ticked away as he stilled and became trancelike. Finally, his eyes opened, and he nodded in understanding.

"Your bloodline is from a very old sect of ancient serpents," Ace said, his words exact. "Your father was a powerful serpent. You are a descendant of Mana, a fearsome queen of the underground world. She was once a powerful serpent who'd reigned since early man. Her bloodline runs through your veins."

"No." She shook her head, stunned by his words. "That can't be. It's just a scar."

"Your birth mother attempted to hide you from those who seek you now. They are the Ophites, an evil underground sect who seek the darker forces. When you were a child, a ritual had been performed and your mark had been sealed with fire. Thus, the reason you have a scar on your wrist. Your mother had this done to hide you from the sect and it worked for a while. But your Mana is still beneath your skin, still part of you. This is your connection to them, to the baby. You have gifts, child, gifts that you haven't even begun to explore. With age your wisdom will come."

"But my mother was an addict. She didn't care about me or my sister." She swallowed the knot forming in her throat. "She only cared about herself and knew nothing about my serpent. She abandoned me and my sister. What kind of mother does that?"

"A desperate one," Ace said. "You don't know what your mother knew. If she tried to protect you, then she had some idea. She wouldn't have stood a chance against them. Make no mistake. Your mother has serpent blood in her lineage, perhaps just a trace and not enough for her to change. She might not have known it. Sometimes it skips a generation. You wouldn't have been born a changeling otherwise."

Miserably, she hugged herself and thought about her mother, the way the woman had been afraid at times. She remembered how her mother would hang heavy blankets on all of the windows and excessively locked the doors. At the time, she'd thought it was her mother's fear of the police or of child services. Could it have been something else?

"Rachel," Ace said, breaking into her thoughts. "I know this is a lot for you to take in. You are a young serpent given the task that not even a warrior would relish, but believe me when I say Mana runs in your veins. You haven't even begun to tap into it. You have so many spiritual gifts left to reveal. The Mana in you is great. You have chosen the enlightened path. You must overcome your fears and believe in yourself. Only then will you achieve your greatest potential."

"I am not great," she said. "A baby took over my serpent, and I couldn't control myself. A baby? I attacked Gabe. That doesn't speak of greatness. That speaks of defeat. Prisca easily overcame me. Perhaps I am as cowardly as my mother for she failed me and my sister." Bitterly, her voice broke as tears brimmed in her eyes. "That's how much she cared."

Ace smiled sadly. "You have a lot of pain in your heart, Rachel. I can see that now. You must forgive your mother for abandoning you. You must forgive yourself for thinking it was your fault."

"I didn't say that," she said, denial in her eyes.

"You didn't have to," Ace said. "It's written all over your face."

Chapter Fourteen

Lustra couldn't take it anymore. Here it was morning and still no one had brought Prisca into her room to be fed. She'd banged on her bedroom door, screamed, and begged someone to bring her daughter. Minutes had turned into hours.

Something terrible had happened to her daughter. She felt it in her heart. Had the ceremony been successful? Was her daughter corrupted forever by Blake and his evil serpents?

The thought brought terror to her mind. Her innocent baby, so helpless against this crazy cult. She had prayed for an intervention, prayed somehow her child had been protected again. She had spent most of the night on her knees, pleading and promising God that she'd change her ways, whatever would work.

Abruptly, her door was unlocked, and Blake entered the room, clad impeccably in a dark suit and tie. He handsomely smiled, his features striking, just like the cat that ate the canary.

"So, I see you're awake, my dear," he said in his warmest tone.

"Where is my daughter?" she asked, rushing to him, clawing at his arm. "What have you done to my baby?"

"She's fine." He reached out and touched a strand of her long strawberry blonde hair. "I forgot how beautiful you are, Lustra. You have given me a great gift—a daughter of Mana."

"She is no daughter of Mana. She came from me. From me!" She pressed her hands to her belly. "She is my daughter. I want to see her. Please...If you ever cared about me don't keep her away. Please bring her to me. Let me see her!" She began crying, falling onto her knees. Her fingers twisted into his coattail. "I'm begging you. Please."

"Very well," Blake said, relenting. "I will let you visit her. It might be good for Prisca to see her mother. I will take you to her, but you need to get your emotions in check. Prisca needs exceptional care and can't be disturbed."

Confusion marked Lustra's features as she got to her feet, but she held her tongue. Blake was giving her what she wanted. She wasn't giving him a reason to deny her now. She moved to the doorway, following him into the extravagant corridor. It was strange being allowed out of the room but here she was walking down the large marble hallway filled with gilded portraits of people in all stages of dress and history. What a deceiver the mansion held. It appeared glamourous, the elite lifestyle, but it was anything but good. It was all a lie.

At the end of the corridor, Blake knocked on a large double door and then opened it. "We're coming in."

A nurse in a white uniform greeted them, her eyes narrowing in on Lustra. "Good morning, Mr. Howard." The woman ignored Lustra.

"How is everything going?" Blake asked the woman, voice held low.

"Prisca is being a little handful," she said. "She won't eat anything. She is being very nasty and tried to bite me."

Blake laughed and then laughed harder at Lustra's confused expression. "Come along, my dear. Prisca might be happy to see you. Perhaps your presence will calm her down."

They entered an adjoining room. It was very dim. The curtains had been drawn to keep out the sunlight and the air was humid and warm. A large glass bed reminiscent of a hospital bassinet sat in the middle of the room. A small heating lamp was clipped to its side.

Blake stood over the glass enclosure, staring down at its occupant. He tilted his head, seeking out Lustra, who hesitated by the doorway. He waved her over. "Well come here, Lustra. You wanted to see your baby. Here is your chance; see her."

Lustra slowly approached the enclosure, her heart beating furiously in her chest. Something was terribly wrong. She was almost afraid to look but her eyes couldn't turn away. Her mouth dropped in horror.

"That…that is not my baby," she said, choking out the words. "What kind of game are you playing?"

"No game." Blake grabbed her arm, jerking her forward. "Don't frighten her. Prisca is still confused. She has simply changed into her more natural state."

"No!" Tears filled Lustra's vision. "It's not possible. None of this is possible."

"Oh, it's possible," Blake said. "She is stunning. I never saw anything like her."

"No!" Lustra said, her words becoming a scream. "No! No! No!"

Chapter Fifteen

Exhausted, Rachel had fallen asleep while leaning against Gabe, the firelight playing softly over her features. Gabe tucked her body against his side, her head lolling against his chest. He wanted to wake her so she could sleep properly but she was already in her dream state, and he wanted to take advantage of the opportunity to find anything to help their situation. Gabe closed his eyes, sharing in the tormented dreams emerging in Rachel's mind. They were always the same—Rachel being chased by dark serpents. Sometimes she prevailed...other times she fled and hid. Sometimes she called out to him.

"I'm here," he'd whisper in her mind, and she would still. If only he could slay all her demons and keep her safe. He'd never thought he would feel so strongly for one of his own. Her torment was his, and he was terrified by Ace's revelations. Was Rachel destined to always be the object of evil intentions? Was their entire existence always going to be filled with death and destruction? Would there ever be any peace for them? Any hope of happiness?

Gabe knew the answer. It was their curse, their cause, and their blessing. Perhaps to be just a human was better in some ways. People had no idea about the spiritual battles that surrounded them every day, the forces that protected them from themselves at times.

Serpent children were the most vulnerable. Seedlings in the making. That's why guardians intervened but only when necessary.

Ace returned, added another log to the fire, and sat. He shook his head, pointing a finger toward Rachel, who was still asleep. "That girl is stubborn."

"I wish Rachel would have eaten," Gabe said. "She barely ate breakfast and didn't have much at the fair. After all she's gone through, I'm worried about her health."

"And you have a right to be worried," Ace said. "The Mana is strong in Rachel. She needs to have an equally strong human resolve to control the beast within her. On her own, Rachel is enlightened, setting her own path so her human side is safe but this child, Prisca…might now be corrupted; the baby's Mana can be very dark and telepathically merge with Rachel. I fear Rachel, in her serpent's form, might go feral again unless she finds a way to control both serpents."

"How? I saw her when this happened, and I can tell you that Rachel becomes feral. There is no reasoning with her."

"Tomorrow night, the moon will be at its fullest," Ace said. "Rachel's serpent will want to be released, be reenergized, and she needs to do this. Rachel must seek out the baby in the vortex in her serpent's form. Yes, it could backfire, and the baby's serpent might telepathically take control again but if Rachel is prepared for this…" Ace paused, tapping his chin. "Rachel's serpent must take the role as leader. Now that the Mana has been roused in Rachel, Prisca's serpent might be drawn to it. The simplest solution is to find the physical baby and rescue her, mission completed.

Prisca's serpent will release its hold on Rachel when the baby is safe. It's the only real solution, but for now, Rachel needs to show Prisca's serpent who's boss."

"And if Rachel can't do this?" Gabe said the words, hating the question.

"Rachel must win this battle, or she and the baby could be lost to us." Ace shook his head. "Rachel might need to be locked away for her own good until we find a solution."

"No," Gabe said, flinching. Beside him, Rachel's nightmares had returned. He felt her inner serpent restlessly longing to be free. He ran his hand over her hair, frustrated. "So, what do we need to do? What's the plan?"

"Rachel must seek a higher authority and get divine help to protect her soul and Prisca's. In seeking out the baby in her serpent form, Rachel will in effect calm the Mana in Prisca's serpent, who might release her grip, knowing Rachel has taken the role of her guardian, because in the end, that's what Prisca's serpent wanted all along."

"But isn't that dangerous for Rachel to tempt fate by going into the vortex as her serpent?" Gabe said. "I think she should be in her human form. What if Prisca's serpent takes over in the vortex? What could happen?"

"Rachel cannot let this happen, and she will be prepared this time," Ace said. "I see no other choice for Rachel. She can't hide from this. She needs a resolution. We might never find the physical baby. The only way to remove the baby's hold on Rachel is to take charge. Period. After that, the only recourse is to try to find the human baby and rescue her."

"A difficult task," Gabe said.

"Rachel is the key to ending this nightmare. Trust that she can manage this. She will need a lot of support. I know you want to protect her, but she needs to lead this journey. She must follow her path."

"Okay."

"Tomorrow night she begins this journey," Ace said. "The sooner, the better before the Ophites strike again. Prisca is only one of Rachel's problems. They will come for her, and we need to be one step ahead of them."

Gabe slumped in defeat. He pulled Rachel closer as she moaned.

"I know you want to protect her," Ace said. "But this is a battle Rachel needs to fight. When the time comes, you can join in the war."

****

Rachel woke to the breathtaking view of Moosehead Lake and the surrounding landscape. It was so peaceful and serene. The air was filled with the scents of dampened earth, pine, and fragrant flora. A gentle breeze swirled her hair around her shoulders. She yawned and pushed away her sleeping bag. She'd barely remembered Gabe carrying her the previous night and tucking her into its confines. She only knew he had watched over her all night.

Gabe's tall and physically fit form came into view along the shoreline, catching her regard. He was seemingly deep in thought. She studied him as he walked. His dark hair hung over one eye as he stopped to skip a stone across the water. She sensed the weight of the world on his being, the fear in his heart. And it was all her fault. She was always bringing trouble his way. No doubt, he probably wished he'd never had met her.

As if reading her thoughts, and she frowned at the implication, Gabe lifted his head and met her stare across the distance. Although they weren't touching, Rachel felt his probe penetrating right through her thoughts. She caught her breath, feeling him touching her mind. She didn't bother trying to hide her thoughts from him. Gabe knew her too well. In her human form, she could barely see into his mind. She supposed it was Gabe's special gift or perhaps she was as infantile as everyone pointed out.

Slowly, she stood and walked toward him.

"Hey," she said, moving in front of him. Embarrassed by her rumpled clothing, she tried to smooth out the wrinkles along her shirt. She had to look a mess. She longed for a toothbrush, deodorant, and just to comb out her hair.

"I hope you don't cut your feet on a rock," Gabe said, staring down at her toes.

"I seem destined to not have any shoes," she replied, smiling. "Next time I see a good sale, I will have to fill up my wardrobe."

Gabe nodded, picked up another stone, and skimmed it across the lake. Rachel bent and found a flat stone. She mimicked Gabe's movements, but her stone fell into the water.

"Here. Watch me." Gabe threw another rock, which skimmed the water's surface, bouncing three more times before disappearing into the lake. "It's all in the wrist."

She followed his movements, and her stone skipped twice before sinking. She tried several more times, enjoying the quietness between them.

"It's really beautiful here," she said. "I can see why you like it."

"When I was a teen, I spent a lot of summers up here fishing with an uncle of mine," Gabe said. "That is where I met Ace. My uncle had a small cabin near here and Ace had done some work on the place. It wasn't until later that I learned Ace already knew who I was and what I was. He helped me to find my purpose."

"He's been really nice to me," she said. "I'm glad he wants to help me. But I'm not sure if he can."

"He thinks you can help yourself," Gabe said. "But we can talk to him later about it. I thought maybe you would like to go into town and get some clothing, definitely some shoes. We could get a bite to eat."

"I would settle for a toothbrush," she said. "And mouthwash. A shower would be second best, but I'm hungry too."

"Good," he replied. "I'd rather get some real food than eat one of Ace's questionable dishes."

"I thought you liked his cooking?" She lifted her brows, teasingly. "You certainly didn't have any trouble last night."

"Desperate is as desperate does," Gabe replied. "And right now, I am feeling rather human and want something appetizing."

Gabe and Rachel entered a general store, which sold fishing, boating, and camping supplies. The local mart was small but cozy, reeking of northern hospitality. Rachel picked out a few articles of clothing, some toiletries, and a pair of hiking boots. She kept a mental note on how much Gabe was spending on her, fully intending to reimburse him when she could.

They had breakfast at the local lodge, which had a

breath-taking view of well cultivated gardens, patios, and the mountainous countryside. The murmur of lively chatter filled the room, giving a sense of family and peace.

"This is so beautiful," Rachel said to Gabe, buttering her toast. "I feel like I'm on vacation. This place must be something in the fall. Everything is so perfect and fresh. I could stay here and forget about all of my troubles."

"Our troubles." Gabe held his fork midair, staring intently at her. "You're not in this alone. I will be here with you every step of the way."

"I know." Warmth from his gaze filled her with hope. Slowly, she smiled. "You are being way too serious. Why are you so worried?"

Gabe didn't answer. He cleared his throat and shoved his fork into his eggs.

"Talk to me," she said, suddenly feeling cold. "Why do you hide everything from me? If you know something, then you need to tell me. You're not alone; remember your speech to me?"

"I just wanted us to enjoy today," he said, shrugging. "I want to put our troubles away for now."

"Why can't we talk about tonight? Are you worried I will turn on you again?"

"Maybe," he replied. "We are dealing with something that I have little knowledge about. These serpents holding Prisca are relentless and unpredictable. They are part of the Ophites, a dark, dangerous sect. They hate the humanity inside of them and instead want to create a new breed of serpent. They thirst for dominance and want to rise in power."

"So tell me about this Mana?"

"Mana was once a serpent queen," Gabe said. "Or so it was claimed. In ancient times, she ruled in the deep recesses of the Earth. The story goes that she had born twelve sons, who all met misfortune or were killed, but before they died, a few of these sons had taken human mates, selected half breeds that bore lineage to Mana's origins. The purpose was to spread the bloodline, creating future breeders. Mana hated humanity, hated the divine intervention that protects them and promises redemption. The Ophites have taken up Mana's cause and want to enslave mankind both body and soul—to rule—"

The waitress came to refill their drinks. They paused in their conversation, lest they be overheard but Gabe's words had set the mood with his dire predictions.

"That is some powerful stuff," Rachel said. "And Ace thinks this Mana's blood runs in my veins?" She shook her head, smiling. "No way."

"Why not?" He leaned back in his seat. "Why not you?"

"Because I would probably have chosen another path," she said. "I love my human side. It sounds like the Mana in me would hate that. Believe me when I say, there is nothing special about me. I am a simple girl who likes simple things."

"But you have been enlightened," he said. "Ace said your Mana has been suppressed by your choices. Prisca has opened the door for your Mana to reemerge. Prisca also has Mana in her blood. Your serpents have merged together, even for a few minutes and in some ways became one. This is dangerous."

"If that were true, then Prisca's Mana was stronger

than my free will," she said. "She simply snuffed me out telepathically. She enslaved my serpent, and I lost control."

"But you came back," he said. "You had broken through her hold. So, there is a way."

"A way? I don't even remember coming back. The hold was broken; that was all. I didn't do anything." Rachel shoved away her plate. "So much for having a peaceful day."

"I'm sorry," he said. "Having a peaceful day was my original intention but tonight the moon will be full. You and I will both need to prepare. We need to get ready if Prisca's serpent awakens in you. Perhaps you should suppress your serpent until we can learn more about Prisca. I don't know how much time we have."

"Prisca is a baby," she said. "A baby. She is only a few months old. How can her infant serpent do these things?"

"Prisca is a baby. It's her serpent who is confused, and her survival instinct is directing her. She can't defend herself in her infant form, and she is desperate."

Rachel thought about his words. "Then Prisca made a poor choice. I could barely fend off a few serpents the other night. If you and Michael hadn't come, I would probably be dead right now."

"You managed yourself," he said. "You fought well. Give yourself credit."

Rachel glanced away, staring out the window. People were dining out on the porch, laughing, enjoying the sunshine, planning their day. She envied them. Tears stung her eyes as she blinked them away. She rubbed at her blurred vision. No wonder a baby chose her. Prisca probably saw another infant.

When Gabe grabbed her hand and squeezed it, she held on tightly but continued to stare out the window, blocking her thoughts and hiding her face from his all-knowing perception.

Chapter Sixteen

After searching the Camden Waterfront, Ariel nudged Paula with her elbow, eyes narrowing in on their target. "There. See if that's her."

Stealthily, Paula Eden moved toward a woman, who leaned against a graffiti covered wall, partially slumped over, chin to chest. Stringy brown hair hid her features. In the shadows, people passed by the woman, never giving her a second glance.

"Leah." Paula prodded the woman, who was skin and bones, wearing a short flowery sundress. No reaction. Paula looked over to Ariel, who made a shoving motion with her hand. "Leah Sanction!" Paula repeated. Then she kicked the female with her foot.

The woman mumbled something and lifted her head, squinting in the sunlight. "What…what did you call me?"

"Leah Sanction. Is that you?"

"Who's asking?"

"Are you her or not?" Paula knelt and grabbed the woman by the hair, knotting it in her fist. She yanked the strands off her forehead, revealing her face. "Answer me."

"I could be," the woman said, then cackled. "I will be whoever you want me to be."

"I need the truth," Paula said, grabbing her chin, squeezing. "Look at me when I'm speaking to you."

"I…I'm trying," the woman said, blinking. Several of her teeth were missing or chipped. "Hey, are you that woman from that news channel?"

"No," Paula said. Disgusted, she glared at Ariel, who was keeping watch for any interference. "I need to find Leah. Are you her or not?"

"Depends on what's in it for me," the woman replied. "A girls' got to eat."

"I can see what you eat," Paula said, poking her finger against one of the many track marks in the addict's forearms. She glanced at Ariel. "She's dirty."

"Mosquito bites," Leah said, shrugging. "Who are you to judge?"

"Whatever you want to tell yourself," Paula said. "What's your name, woman?"

"Right now, it's Lucky Me."

Ariel walked over to the pair, shoving Paula aside. She placed her hand on the woman's head and closed her eyes, searching. Moments later, she snapped, "It's her."

"What do you want me…me for?" All humor fled Leah's features. Alarmed, she said, "My, you are some big tough girls. What are you, about six feet tall?"

"We want you to come with us," Ariel said. She held out a twenty-dollar bill. "We will pay you for your time."

"I…I ain't for sale," Leah said. She stared at the bill, swallowing. "I don't know what you think I am, but I ain't for sale."

"We just want to talk," Ariel said. "Nothing more."

"Talk?" Wariness entered Leah's eyes. "About what? I don't know you people. Why'd you want to talk to me? No way. Get lost."

"We want to talk to you about Rachel," Ariel said.

"Rachel." Leah squirmed, eyes widening. She scratched her head as if trying to remember. "I don't know any Rachel."

"Yes, you do. She's your daughter." Ariel grabbed Leah's skinny arm, hauling her to her feet. Paula took her other arm.

"Let go of me," Leah said, struggling against their grip. "You people are crazy."

"I can't believe you are her mother," Ariel said, gazing into Leah's face. "What a disgrace. No wonder she's got so many issues."

"Rachel is gone," Leah said. "She's not around here anymore. Probably dead. Good riddance."

"Rachel wants to see you," Ariel said. "And we are going to take you to her. Now just shut up."

"She's dead," said Leah. "You're a liar."

"She's not dead!" Ariel said. "She's very much alive. Now start walking and don't make a fuss."

"And if I do?"

"Then I'll break you in half," Paula said, gripping Leah's arm tighter. "Now don't get us mad."

The women prodded Leah along to an adjacent street to a waiting black limousine. The rear door opened, and they shoved Leah inside. Paula climbed in behind her, while Ariel got into the front passenger seat.

"You are sure it's her?" the driver asked, gazing into his rearview mirror.

"It's her," Ariel replied. "She's as crazy as a loon. Her mind is practically gone. Stick to our plan and take her out to Paradise Farms. We'll deal with her there."

"Sure thing," the driver replied. "But she sure is stinking up the car."

Chapter Seventeen

Enchanted Villa was a little bed-and-breakfast that boasted a sign reading, "The best coffee in town." Gabe paid a small fee so that Rachel could use one of their bathrooms to bathe and change her clothing. After taking a hot shower and drying her hair, Rachel walked downstairs with Ace's clothing in her hands. She moved into the quaint foyer, where Gabe sat by the large bay window.

"Feeling better," he said, noticing her. "You sure look a lot better."

"I like the outfit," she said. She wore a white blouse and cargo pants. "Finally, something that fits me." She held up her foot. "And my boots are impressive. I feel almost human again."

She followed him outside and onto the wide porch, which held rocking chairs and buckets of flowers strategically in place. A welcoming breeze scented the air, mixed with freshly trimmed lawn and the abundance of plant life. "This place is so peaceful."

"It's always been this way," Gabe said. "People treat each other like family around here." He grabbed her hand, moved down the staircase, and walked along the front sidewalk. They paused next to a large gazebo. "I lived here for a time. My uncle took me in after my parents' deaths. At the time I thought it was a dull place to live but now it suits me."

"I lived in some pretty awful places," Rachel said. "My mother never had any money. Often, we were homeless, lived in motels, or if she had a good spell, an apartment. She'd find new boyfriends. Couldn't keep a job. But I remember her drugs and how she'd scrape together whatever money she could get to buy more. Every day, I never knew what she was going to do next. It was an awful way to live."

"Sounds bad," he said.

"I didn't realize just how bad it was at the time," she said. "It was life to me. Normal. I can barely describe how it was. I took care of Stacey. She was just a baby. I learned how to feed and bathe her, change her dirty diapers." She paused, shaking her head. "When we had diapers. My mom had a few cloth diapers. They'd have to be washed out in the sink. I had to learn how to safety-pin it in place. I certainly pricked my finger a few times."

"But you survived," he reminded her. "Stacey is with a loving family. You're stronger because of your past."

"I don't feel very strong," she said. "Ace says I have this Mana's blood in me, and now I have Prisca to contend with. I confess that I am really freaked out. I'm scared to have this responsibility. I could fail."

"You can manage it," he said. "Or Prisca's serpent wouldn't have chosen you."

"What if her serpent was wrong in choosing me? What if she put stock in the wrong person and I fail? How am I supposed to live with that kind of failure?"

"You won't fail," he said. "Ace said you have gifts into which you haven't even tapped. You are special. You have Mana in your veins. Use Mana's strength and make her authority work for you."

"You mean accept her power and let it come through me?"

"Perhaps," he said. "But you must control it and make it your own."

"Show Prisca who is in control?" She considered his words, both puzzling and intriguing. A flicker of hope lit deep in her mind.

"Something like that," he replied.

****

The afternoon succumbed to the evening shadows. Rachel and Gabe returned to Ace's campsite and went on a long walk by the lake, holding hands and just enjoying being together—something encouraged by Ace. They sat by the lake for a while, watching people fishing or boating. They discussed Second Chance Camp, recollecting the better times they'd shared.

"You must miss being at the camp," Rachel said to Gabe. "The kids just loved you. You were such a natural with them."

"I do miss it," he said. "I was planning to work there this summer, but I couldn't get away from the other issue I'd been dealing with. Believe me, I wanted to be with there with you, Tina, and Michael." He lifted her hand, kissing her skin. "Okay, I confess, mostly with you."

"So, are you going to tell me why you weren't there? You've been very mysterious." She leaned against his sturdy arm as they walked.

"There's a boy who had and still has some issues," he said. "He's five years old and is destined to be a serpent warrior. He'd been in and out of foster homes since his birth. He doesn't speak, and I needed to try to reach him." His fingers squeezed hers. "His name is Brian. Although he doesn't use words, he does cry and make other noises. I've been working at Brian's school. Although his teachers meant well, they have trouble dealing with his temper tantrums, his rage, and for the most part, they want further assessments."

"Sounds like a hurting little boy," she said.

"You've no idea. Brian is so gifted. I was able to reach him telepathically and see the world through his eyes." Gabe's body tensed, pausing by the edge of the water. "I saw into his past and what he'd gone through. People have abused him over the five short years of his life, and he had no way of asking for help. His anger is his way of lashing out. I made a few calls and hopefully there'll be justice for Brian. He needs a lot of therapy, but I do believe he could have a brighter future."

"That poor boy," she said, bitterly reflecting on her own past. She could relate to Brian's story on so many levels.

"But the amazing thing, Brian spoke to me telepathically. It was a breakthrough that made an enormous difference. I've spent months collaborating with him at the school and the teachers were amazed at his progress. He's become more manageable and is actually very bright."

"Where is Brian now?"

"A couple have taken him in. They deal with special need children and are good people. Brian was fortunate. I will track what goes on."

"Are you going to see Brian again?"

"In the future," he said. "I must wait until he comes of age. He has a destiny to fulfill, and he will have his choices to make but for now, he is safe."

"See, that wasn't so hard to tell me," she said. "I thought it was something else…"

"Like another girl," he said, laughing.

"I didn't say that." She turned her head away, hiding the truth from his prying eyes.

"I know everything about you." He reached up and ran a featherlike touch over her jawbone. "You are like an open book at times."

"So you assume." She lifted her chin, meeting his steady gaze. Her heart flip-flopped. Oh, how she could drown in those striking eyes. "You didn't know of the Mana in me."

"True," he said. "But I always knew there was something different about you. You were never a typical serpent. I figured in time it'd be revealed to me. I thought I'd just wait it out. After all, who doesn't like a good mystery?"

"So that's what I am." She held her breath, scanning his face for the truth. His eyes intensified as he looked unabashedly at her and then a secretive smile followed. "So what have you figured out about me so far?"

"Well for one thing, you have a crush on me," Gabe said, shrugging.

"Oh, you're such a jerk." She shoved his solid chest. "You are so conceited."

Gabe grabbed her hand as she tried to flee, pulling her toward him. Breathlessly, she laughed and tried to escape. They ended up falling into the grassy bank. Her breath caught as he rolled her over and tickled her.

"Stop," she cried, laughing. She rolled into a ball, but he pulled her back, using his weight to straddle her.

"You know what else I know about you?"

"What?" She stilled as he became more serious.

"That you can't resist my kiss," Gabe said, placing his hands against both sides of her head. He leaned down, inches from her face.

"Maybe it's you who can't resist mine," she said, pouting her lips. "After all, I come from a supernatural being called Mana, kind of like a great-great grandmother. I bet she had been really beautiful."

"If she looked like you, then she had to be." He grew quiet, thoughtful.

"Stop being so serious," she said, breathlessly. "You're looking at me like I'm about to die or something."

"I don't want anything to happen to you." His words were soft. "I don't think I could take it."

"Just shut up and kiss me." She slid her arms around his neck and pulled him down, pressing her mouth against his. Their playfulness diminished as they absorbed one another, exploring each other's mouths.

Gabe rolled partially off of her, breaking their kiss. He rose up on his elbow, gazing down at her. His fingers trailed a path across her partially exposed belly. Beneath his trail, her skin quivered. She bit down on her bottom lip, expectantly waiting.

"It'd be so easy to continue." Gabe ceased his movements, drawing his hand away. "But now is not the time. It's not that I don't want to…"

"Shh," Rachel said, pressing her fingertip to his mouth. The warmth she'd felt had disappeared into reality. "It's okay. Let's just go back to the campsite. We don't need to talk about it right now."

Relieved, Gabe stood, held his hand down to Rachel, and helped her to her feet. Slipping his hand into hers, they headed toward Ace.

Chapter Eighteen

Night descended like a thick blanket, bringing with it a sense of doom. The limo drove down a long, winding driveway, passed an abandoned farmhouse, and continued toward the rear of the property. A small barn sat in the distance, surrounded by a thick grove of trees.

"Where are you taking me?" Leah demanded, addressing her kidnappers. "Let me go."

"Shut up," Paula said. "You haven't shut up this whole trip."

"You got no right keeping me hostage," Leah said. "What do you people want from me anyhow?"

"Are you sure we need her?" Paula said to Ariel. Disgust held her features. "It seems like a waste of our time. I could do away with her now and do the world a favor."

"She is extra security," Ariel said. "In case anything goes wrong."

"What are you talking about?" Leah said. With trembling hands, she shoved her wild hair out of her eyes. "What are you people going to do to me? You have no right to hold me against my will. That's called kidnapping, and it's a crime. Want to go to jail?"

Neither woman responded nor looked concerned over Leah's dire threat. The limo parked beside the large bank barn. Under the overhang, hanging lanterns threw light into the murky shadows.

Abruptly, Ernie, the obese driver got out and disappeared around the building, leaving the women alone.

"Couldn't he wait a few more minutes?" Paula said in disgust. "That man drives me nuts."

"We don't need him," Ariel said. She exited the limo, walked around the auto, and yanked open the rear door, revealing Leah inside. "Get out."

"Why?" With her question ignored, Leah struggled to move, but Paula, who was situated next to her, gave her a shove. With no choice, she climbed out, holding the door for support. "Where the heck are we?"

Paula came out next and shoved Leah as she passed. Her gaze swept over the gangly drug addict, lip curled in disgust. "Now what?"

"Go see if they're ready for this woman."

"What's to get ready?" Paula rolled her eyes and walked toward the barn.

"You said something about Rachel," Leah said, confronting Ariel. "Where is she? Is she in trouble?"

"When isn't Rachel in trouble?" Ariel said, smirking. She shut the limo's door. "I still can't believe you are her mother…"

"What's that supposed to mean?" Leah crossed her arms defensively.

"Nothing, I suppose," Ariel said. "It doesn't matter anyway."

"What did you expect?" Leah said. She pulled her skinny frame upright, trying to look eye to eye with Ariel. "A super freak?"

"You're pathetic," Ariel said. "Don't get close to me. I don't know what diseases you might be carrying.

105

What a waste of human flesh."

"I ain't carrying a disease," Leah retorted. Anger filled her face. "I guess there must be something special in me to give birth to a girl like my Rachel."

"You're not special." Ariel shook her head, snorting. "It had to be a crazy kind of bad luck."

"It's ready," Paula called from the barn's entrance. "Bring her in."

Ernie appeared from around the building, scratching his two-day-old chin stubble. He moved toward the barn in a slow gait.

"Let's go," Ariel said, shoving Leah ahead of her.

"Is Rachel inside?" Leah asked, wide eyed. "Is she one of those things?"

"You mean a serpent?"

"Yes." Leah tilted her chin toward the moon. "I know about that serpent stuff, ever since she was little. It's gonna be a full moon tonight. You better hope my daughter doesn't get mad that you took me. You got no idea who she is."

"I know who and what she is." Ariel gripped the frail arm as they walked. "That's why you're here."

"You don't like her, do you?" Leah smirked. "I can tell. You can't even say her name without hatred spitting out of your mouth. She must have really done something to piss you off. What did she do? Take your man? Stole something? She's certainly prettier than you."

"Shut up." Ariel's fingers dug into Leah's bone. The addict yelped. "You don't know anything."

"I might not be that special," Leah said, deliberately dragging her feet. "But I can see petty jealousy when I see it, and you got it written all over in your ugly attitude."

"Shut up," Ariel said, jerking Leah along. "Walk!"

"Truth hurts, don't it, girly?" Leah laughed, rewarded with a hard shove in her shoulder.

"When is the last time you saw Rachel?" Ariel opened the barn door, pushing Leah inside.

"I don't know." Instantly, Leah sobered. "She was just a girl. I wish I could have done better by her, but her being what she was didn't give me a lot of choices. People were after her. She needed protection. I was afraid she would change into that snake thing. At night, I locked myself into my room…"

Ariel rolled her eyes. "Pathetic…"

"Who are you to judge?"

"I don't want to hear your sad tale," Ariel said. "I don't care."

Inside the barn, a stall had been converted into a cage with bars that ran from floor to ceiling. Bales of hay sat inside the corners.

"You got to be kidding me," Leah said. "You're caging me up like a rat?"

"It's probably nicer than what you're accustomed to, too," Paula said, moving into the light. She smirked. "You're out of the weather. We might even throw you some scraps. It's going to be your home for the next few days, so get used to it."

"Think you can manage her?" Ariel said to Ernie. "She'll be yelling soon for her fix."

"You can't do this to me," Leah cried, trying to yank out of Ariel's grasp. "This is abduction. You got no right."

"I gave myself the right." Ariel pushed her through the stall doorway and shoved her into a haybale, slamming shut the door. "And there's nothing you can do about it."

"Lock it," she said to Ernie, who stood with crossed arms, watching the exhibition. "No one is to know she is here or talk to her. No one."

"I understand." He walked over to the makeshift cell. Leah had gotten to her feet, cursing and making threats as she tried to open the door. "You better behave, lady." He grabbed the heavy chain and locked it tight.

"Let's go." Ariel turned around with Paula trailing her.

Chapter Nineteen

Filtered smoke rose from the pungent campfire. The fresh scent of frying fish scented the air. Ace hummed as he worked over their meal, long metal tongs in hand. Rachel and Gabe sat next to one another, quiet, each in their own thoughts.

"Another minute and we can eat," Ace said, studying the couple. "My, you two look gloomy. I could have better company with the frogs."

"Just thinking," Gabe said quietly. His hand found Rachel's, fingers intertwining. She leaned against his arm. Beneath his skin, his serpent surged in need, eager for the night. He also sensed Rachel's restless serpent and her apprehension.

They each ate a portion of fish, chips, and drank iced tea. When Rachel was finished, she got up and walked away toward the river. Gabe watched her go, wanting a private moment alone with Ace.

"She is really something," Ace said, watching Rachel walk away. "But her insecurities are holding her back. If only she believed in herself. It would make all the difference in how she proceeds in all of this."

"What do I do?" Gabe ran his hands through his hair. "I've never met a serpent like her. She is different, unique. She's enlightened and yet, I fear for her. She is so vulnerable at times, lost. And I confess, my serpent is wary of her. Anxious. A sense of doom keeps hitting me. Should I fear Rachel's serpent?"

"It's the ancient Mana that has risen inside Rachel," Ace explained. "There is both evil and good. It goes against Rachel's bloodline to have joined our Guardian cause. In a way, her Mana's freedom is compromised. Prisca's serpent has managed to tap into something ancient they both share. It has fed Rachel's serpent, a memory of sorts, almost like primal instinct. Rachel's serpent remembers freedom. No constrictions. No commitments. She's had a taste of her own power and perhaps she liked it."

"Can it be reversed?" Gabe stood up, stricken.

Ace sighed, pausing in thought.

"Ace. I need to know," Gabe said, grabbing his arm. "Can Rachel be corrupted? Can she be lost to us?"

"Rachel, the human, no," Ace said. "But Rachel's serpent…perhaps. It could be almost a Jekyll and Hyde situation. Good versus evil. You need to free Prisca's hold on Rachel, thereby giving Rachel full control of her Mana. The baby needs to be found. The only way to do that is for Rachel to merge with Prisca again and take over her serpent's will. The baby's serpent knows her location. This needs to happen tonight." Ace shoved a piece of fish into his mouth. After a moment, he said, "The spirits will help guide her."

****

The moon loomed brightly above the lake as the night deepened. Gabe and Rachel stood by the water's edge, both lost in thought.

"Gabe, what are you going to do if I lose control of both serpents?"

"Run," he said. His tone was teasing, but his eyes spoke of his fears.

"Seriously." She turned and placed her hand on his solid chest. The steady beat of his heart beneath her palm was reassuring. "I don't want to fail."

"Then don't," he said, capturing her hand. "Make sure you stay you."

"I'm not sure how to make that happen."

"Last time, you weren't prepared for what happened to you," he said. "This time you are. You need to keep your wits about you."

"What if it just happens?"

"Rachel. You heard Ace. He said you have untapped power. That you are strong. You need to be stronger and fight harder. You can do it. Do it for Prisca. Free her and give her back her life and her choices."

Rachel hugged and squeezed him tightly. He felt so alive and assured. She never wanted to let him go. She closed her eyes, mentally preparing herself for the inevitable. If Gabe and Ace believed in her, then she wouldn't let them down.

"You can do this."

"I think we should separate," she said. "In case things go badly. I want to get as high as possible on rocky terrain, where no one is around for me to hurt or compromise."

"I need to be near you to keep an eye on things."

"You heard Ace," she said. "He said this was a battle. I had to go alone."

"We are a team," he said. "I won't let you go through this alone. I will stand by, but I will be close enough to help you if you need me. I was able to bring you out of it last time. I might have to do it again."

"Please, Gabe," she said, lifting her face. Tears

gathered in the corners of her eyes. "I need to know you are all right if I am to concentrate on Prisca. I need to have a clear head."

"Fine," he replied, sighing. His hand caressed her neck, then he kissed her, reluctantly releasing her. "I'll give you the necessary time, but I will remain close."

"Good enough," she said, relieved. It was some comfort to know he'd be nearby. "Thank you."

Rachel hugged him one last time and then walked away. The night called to her inner serpent. She couldn't help but be eager to be part of the forest, the mountains, and the night sky. She began to ascend the summit before the terrain was too hard to climb. Behind a dense thicket of trees, she discarded her clothing, neatly folding the items on a boulder, leaving her boots on top. She moved into a small clearing, closed her eyes, and allowed her serpent to break free into her golden form. Her serpent stretched out her neck, reveling in the scents of the night, eager to explore the fresh territory.

Rachel telepathically connected to Gabe in her mind, whispering that so far, she was fine. She had barely spoken the words before her serpent sped up, whipping by trees, which were only a blur as she traveled higher. She loved her fluidity, her grace, her speed. She moved into the mountainous range, startling birds and other wildlife. She traveled over rocks and instinctively knew where the underground caverns lay should she have need of them. Her senses stretched, seeking any danger.

When she came to a clearing high up on the mount, Rachel paused and coiled, head tilted toward the moon. She had never before attempted to go into the vortex in her serpent's form. Her gaze became mesmerized, eyes turning colorless. Rachel called out for the vortex to open. It appeared first as a small cloud over the tall pines, moving toward her. It then sloped until it hovered and then lowered just above her form. Her serpent relaxed, peaceful and serene. The beast held no uncertainty, allowing the renewal of her mind.

Rachel's serpent began swaying, trance-like. She absorbed the life given energy bestowed to her. In the vortex, orbs circled around her. She prayed for guidance, for strength, and for Prisca. Now radiating with energy, she sought out Prisca in her mind, calling out to the baby's serpent. Nothing happened at first. But a sense of spiritual direction filled her, leading toward a pathway. Her spirit separated from her body; her vision blurred in the blinding light. She began moving, seeking, floating above her serpent. Then she was traveling, everything moving in a blur.

She traveled over a beautiful canyon. Time ceased. Now there was illumination sweeping over the cliffs and hilly terrain. She willed herself to slow. Lower she moved, just gliding above the treetops. She felt nothing, but the sights were indeed beautiful. It was as if she were a ghost passing along in the breeze. Colors were brighter, vivid in clarity. There was no fear, only peace.

Prisca was close. She felt her now. The baby's soul force was that of a sparkling jewel. Rachel had no time to wonder why Prisca's spirit was in the vortex, but her form lowered onto a grassy field. Purple wildflowers filled every part of the rolling terrain. She recognized Lavandula and hyacinths. There were no borders, no trees, just an endless flow of vivid shades that appeared infinite. In the middle of the expanse, a baby girl sat.

The child's tiny body was bathed in light, dark curly hair framed her head, features indistinguishable. Protective orbs floated around her, appearing as other children to the girl. In Prisca's chubby palm, she held a crushed flower.

Something was amiss. Had the baby died? No, that wasn't right. She'd have known. Humans were body and spirit. Serpent guardians were human, spirit, and serpent—three in one—yet Prisca was separated from the others. This was the human soul of the child. Rachel cried for the baby, cried for her innocence, cried for her stolen grace. Though the child was lost, Prisca knew only peace. In time, the baby's spirit would grow in knowledge as she grew up in the vortex. It was unfair. Sadness fell over Rachel like a bucket of sand, cocooning her in sorrow. She shook free her emotions. No. She had to stay focused.

But what to do? She had found the baby's soul. Apparently, whoever held Prisca's body had no need for her soul, only her Mana, her serpent. But if she had found Prisca's life force then perhaps so could someone else. Her spirit could be captured or led astray. Prisca was an infant. She had no sense of evil. No defense. The corruption of the child would be complete. If she could find the infant, it was only a matter of time before something else did. Rachel couldn't take that chance. The spirits had led her to the baby for a reason.

"Prisca," Rachel said moving closer. The baby was beautiful and pure. She moved closer still, nudging the baby's toes with her snout, tickling them. "Hello, little one."

The baby smiled, bringing dimples to her cheeks.

Rachel paused, considering the situation. She drew

on the powers above, seeking guidance. At first, she denied the knowledge imparted to her. It seemed impossible. Yet...would it work? She trusted her guide's lead. She coiled, then opened her mouth, wider and yet wider still. The baby continued to stare. Gently, Rachel scooped the baby into her mouth and swallowed her whole.

Rachel felt everything at once. A newness of life. Innocence. Trust. Power. Then Prisca's memories, as few as they were. A woman's face came into view— Prisca's mother.

Rachel could only hope she wouldn't fail Prisca.

Chapter Twenty

The limited lighting inside the barn left Leah with nothing else to do but sit on the hay bale and wonder how she had gotten into such a precarious position. But being a prisoner wasn't as frightening as knowing her withdrawal and suffering would be worse. Already her back ached, her stomach nauseous. Panic began to settle.

"Would you happen to have a hit of something?" Leah asked Ernie. "I'm getting ill."

"No," he said. He puffed on a cigarette, paging through a magazine.

"Do you have any pain killers? I mean it, man. I'm getting sick. I need some help."

"Don't care," Ernie said. "Suck it up."

"Well, I at least need to go to the bathroom," Leah said. "I haven't gone yet."

"No." Ernie repositioned his large girth on the wooden chair. He barely acknowledged her requests, flipping to the next page.

"Do you really want me to use this cell?" Leah laughed. "For real? I won't be responsible for the smell."

"Think I'd fall for that one?" Ernie said, scratching his balding head. He kicked out his feet, stretching out his legs. The chair creaked in protest.

"I've been in here for hours," Leah said, rubbing

her arms. "I really have to go. I'll be quick about it." The cold had settled over her limbs. Her body trembled, and it hurt to move. Flu-like symptoms were beginning, and she'd be going through it cold turkey.

"Don't care," he replied. "Your problem, junkie."

Defeated, Leah slumped against the cage. Emotions filled her mind, emotions that were usually suppressed. Guilt ate at her. She supposed it was time she faced her sins, her past. She'd been a terrible mother to her girls. She'd abandoned them when life got too hard. She'd told herself at the time that they were better off without her, especially Rachel, who had the oddity of being a snake-like being.

What did the serpent women want with Rachel? She feared for her eldest child. She'd always known that Rachel was different, ever since her birth. The knowledge came without warning, thrust upon her. After she'd come home with her newborn baby, men arrived at her apartment, one claiming to be a doctor. He'd talked her into letting him examine Rachel and she, like a fool, had agreed. After that, she received a visit from Rachel's father. Cold and calculating, he spoke plainly that her time with the baby was limited. He had plans for their daughter and would return for Rachel when she turned five. It had been a terrifying revelation, almost as terrifying as the day she saw her lover turn into a beast—a frightening serpent.

After that, voices in her head began to whisper to her. Apparently, it was easy to track her movements through her mind. Stalking became common. Every time she went anywhere, she was followed. Watched. But it wasn't she they were interested in, only the young girl by her side.

Horrified, Leah had looked upon Rachel differently after that. She loved her daughter, but it was apparent that the girl shared the same lineage as her sire. Rachel also bore the odd birthmark on her wrist, which sometimes appeared like a half-moon and at other times a serpent. She tried to protect Rachel, searching for a way to rid her child of her curse. Help came in the form of a spiritualist, a man who claimed he could free Rachel from her bondage. He performed a cleansing, attempted to remove Rachel's snakelike birthmark with fire. It seemed to work for a while.

Leah moved from house to house. She changed jobs, ditched old friends, and yet her mind was still probed, haunted by her tormentors. To stop the tracking, she turned to opiates. The drugs affected her mind, confusing her tormentors. At first, she thought she could control it, but soon the drugs controlled her—and had been ever since.

It was the birth of her second daughter that revealed her addiction. Social services had gotten involved. Allegations were made, claims of neglect and abuse. Social workers took her daughters away, and with it came relief. Rachel was no longer her problem and became a ward of the state. Thankfully, Stacey, her younger daughter, had been adopted. But it didn't matter. Leah was lost to her addiction, to a disease she inflicted on herself. No one cared, especially herself.

"Look. I need to go to the bathroom," Leah said, more determined. "I mean it. My gut is hurting. It won't be pretty. Now, please take me."

"I will take you just to shut you up." Ernie stood and walked over to the locked door. "If I take you, you need to do as you're told."

"I swear it," Leah said, crossing her heart.

Ernie unlocked the door and motioned with his hand for her to walk in front of him. He moved behind her, standing close. He grabbed his flashlight and turned it on, lighting the way. They walked down the stone pathway to a small farmhouse. Inside the building, he flicked on an overhead light. A kitchen lit up, revealing outdated appliances, a linoleum floor, and worn cabinets. The room obviously hadn't been in use for a long time.

"Nice place you got here," Leah said.

"Back there," Ernie said, pointing to a short hallway. "There's the bathroom."

Leah moved by him and walked down the hallway. Sure enough, there was a small bathroom with a rusty toilet and sink. She turned on the light, closed the door, and locked it.

Quickly, she scanned the room for a way out. The window was small. She opened the closet door, which held only a few scraps of toilet paper. She pushed open the moldy shower curtain. An old bathtub was covered with silver fish and other dead bugs.

She went back to the window, prodding it with her hand. It was stuck fast. Great. Now what?

"Hurry up in there," Ernie said against the door. "You got one minute."

"Geez," she said. "Make a girl rush."

In defeat, she finally opened the door, his round face peering in. "What about dinner? How about getting me some?"

"Right," he said, grabbing her arm. He gave her a shove. "Get moving."

They walked back outside. Ernie turned on his

flashlight, leading the way.

"So, are you one of those serpents?" she asked.

"I don't know what you're talking about."

"You sure don't look like one," she said, looking him over. "You're too fat. The serpent men are usually pretty toned, muscular and buff. Sorry, man, but you just don't fit the mold. You just don't look like you have anything special in you."

"Shut up," Ernie said, pushing her shoulder. "You're one to talk. You're skin and bones. Not an ounce of flesh on you. And then there's your teeth. Ugh. You're probably have never seen a dentist."

"Whatever," she said. Her feet hurt from walking. Her withdrawal symptoms were getting worse. Soon, she would be balled up on the floor, sick. "Think what you want. I don't care." She paused. "You got a cigarette?"

"Don't smoke."

"Any booze or anything to help a girl out?"

"I don't drink, and I'm not a junkie either."

"I'm feeling pretty crappy." She offered him a hopeful smile. "I'd appreciate some help."

"Tough. Keep moving."

Leah gave up and went inside the barn. She was freezing, but it was warmer than being outside. Inside her cage doorway, she halted her strides, grasping the metal frame. "Hey, something is moving in my cage. What is that?"

"Where?" Ernie pointed his flashlight into the opening. "I don't see anything."

"It's in the corner." She pointed with her finger. "It's hiding."

"If you're lying…"

Ernie walked past Leah, shining his flashlight around the area. He grabbed her and dragged her inside, searching around the hay bales. Something moved.

"Hey, there really is something," he said, dropping Leah's arm and moving toward the corner.

As soon as Ernie was committed to finding what lurked in the cage, Leah darted out the doorway and slammed it shut, clamping on the lock. "Got you."

A cat came rushing out of the cell, squeezed through the bars, and ran out of the barn.

"Unlock this now!" Ernie said, furiously. "Now!"

"Sorry, can't do that. Be seeing you." Snidely, Leah grinned, enjoying her monumental moment but she stilled as Ernie's lips curled, eyes beady.

"Think you're clever?" Ernie laughed. "We'll see."

Ernie's eyes changed into round saucers, the orbs becoming dark and filling the white sections of his eyes. Leah froze as the man's features altered. His face contorted. He slumped to the ground, grunting and rolling his sizable bulk.

Stunned, Leah didn't wait around to see what was coming next. She'd been stupid. Of course, Ernie was a serpent. How could she be so wrong? Terrified, she fled the barn, running down the driveway toward the road.

Inside the barn, something shattered, a loud growl following.

Leah ran for her life.

Chapter Twenty-One

Gabe moved through the undergrowth, searching for Rachel's scent and seeking her telepathically, but their connection had been broken. Something blocked it. He'd also lost her physical form. She had simply disappeared. It was frustrating and scared him to death. She'd never been able to completely shut him out of her mind, even though she'd tried at times, but somehow this time she had. Was she doing it on purpose or was there something else?

He covered a lot of area, searching, listening intently. Other sounds reached him, mostly animals or birds. He sensed hikers miles away. Normally, he loved this rough terrain but tonight it was so vast and thick.

Lightning lit the inky sky. Rain was coming. Gabe's serpent sensed his panic, reacting and snapping at the slightest sounds. His tail thrashed, smashing saplings to bits. Finally, he ascended a huge pine tree and coiled at the top where he had an incredible view of the forest. He had always loved Maine, loved the elegant beauty of the land but tonight he hated his blinded vision, his insecurities. Without Rachel, he felt lost. In such a brief time, she had become a part of his life. But then Gabe sensed her nearby, allowing his instincts to guide him. Rachel was somewhere down the summit. Of course, she was returning to where she'd left her clothing. Hopefully, that meant good news and that she was not in a feral state.

Relieved, Gabe left the tree and slithered toward her destination.

Gabe sensed Rachel before he saw her. Branches, rocks, and undergrowth snapped beneath his form in his haste. He didn't know what he'd find and had to be prepared for anything.

And there in the clearing Rachel stood, human again, appearing incredibly beautiful with her striking features and soft shimmering hair, which hung almost to her waist. She appeared wild and free. She met his gaze across the short distance, and then motioned with her hand for him to come. Gabe's serpent moved toward her. His beast was just as enthralled as his master, dipping his head low, pushing his head into her waiting caress.

"Did I ever tell you how magnificent your serpent is?" She said the words quietly, rolling her palm along his smooth head.

"No," he said telepathically. Her touch was gently seeking but something was off.

"Well, I'm telling you now."

Gabe lifted his gaze, staring into her eyes. Stunned, he gawked at her transition. Her eyes were a blaze of color, a mix of purple and blue hues. They were brilliant and hard to behold.

"Your eyes," he said, awe in his tone. "They are translucent. How amazing."

Rachel slipped her hand under his throat, rolling her fingers along his skin. She buried her head against his solid form, hugging him as best she could. Her heat slipped over his senses, teasing his cooled form.

"I couldn't reach you," he said. "You blocked me

from your mind."

"I didn't mean to," she replied, lifting her head. She stood back, touching his face. "It wasn't me blocking you. It was Prisca. You are a stranger to her, and she gets afraid."

"But how…"

"Prisca's soul-force is inside of me," she said. "And I know where they're keeping her."

****

Rachel sat by the fire, next to Ace. Gabe came out of the woods, human and fully dressed in jeans and a sweatshirt. He quietly moved to them and sat down next to the open fire pit.

Rachel could sense Gabe's doubts. She couldn't blame him; she could barely trust herself. She felt different but in an empowering way. It was an odd state to be in, but she had to admit she felt better than she had the past few days. She considered Gabe, who returned her stare, puzzlement marking his brow.

"Is someone going to speak?" Ace asked. He rubbed his hands together, then spread out his fingers, seeking the fire's warmth. "Or leave me hanging. I'd like to get to bed sometime tonight."

"I will try to explain," Rachel said. Then she revealed what she'd told Gabe. Ace listened with rapt attention. Every now and then he would nod, as if agreeing with a point.

"So where is the human baby?" Ace said.

"She's in Pennsylvania, a place near Lebanon. She is being held inside an elite mansion. It has several hundred acres surrounding the fortress. Both humans and serpents are heavily guarding it. I can't tell exactly where Prisca is at the property, but I will be able to when we get closer."

"Closer?" Gabe frowned. "Rachel, we don't know much about this situation. It can be dangerous."

"I know," she said. She lifted her chin, stiffening her spine. "We are going to need some help. Plan it out. But at least we should have the element of surprise. I don't think they are aware that I now house the baby's soul."

"And when they do, they will seek to kill you," Gabe said pointedly. "You will be a target for any dark serpent."

"Exactly why we must leave," she said. "Tomorrow. We need to check out the perimeter and get a handle on things. "

"You're rushing it." Gabe stood, pacing in front of her. "I don't like any of this. We need time to see what we're up against. We just can't go whizzing in there unprepared. So after we have the baby, then what?"

"We have to protect her," Rachel replied. "Prisca needs to be in a place of sanctuary where she can grow up and make her own choices."

"Easier said than done," Gabe replied, shaking his head. He stopped pacing, gawking at Ace. "Well, what do you think?"

"I think Rachel is right," Ace said. He threw a few sticks into the fire. "We need to strike soon. There is no telling when they will discover the baby's soul is in Rachel. They will hunt her relentlessly and kill her to release Prisca's soul. Right now, Prisca is like a car without a battery. I see no other way."

"Fine!" Gabe looked over at Rachel, scowling. "But we are doing things my way, Rachel. No ifs, ands, or buts. I'm not just running in there to get us all killed.

We need to be prepared."

Rachel stood, glaring at Gabe. "Thank you for your faith in me. I really appreciate the attitude." She jerked around and walked away into the woods. "Leave me alone."

Gabe sighed, staring sightlessly into the fire. He ran his palm over his stubbled chin. "I'm just afraid for Rachel."

"I know you are," Ace said. "I can see how much you care about her."

"Things were different before Rachel came along," Gabe said. "I did what I needed to do to survive and tried to be effective. But now...I don't know if I can live without her. If something happens and I couldn't save her..." He swallowed hard. "She means everything to me."

"But she is a guardian," Ace said. "A chosen one. She must go where her spirit leads her. No one said that it would be a life of ease. There will always be tough battles ahead. We live in a cruel, indifferent world. Your human side is part of that. Death is your only escape. Don't be angry with Rachel for following her heart. This baby needs her. Think of what could happen if Prisca's soul is lost forever. When the girl physically matures, she will just be a vessel for evil."

"Why can't Rachel remain here with you?" Gabe began pacing again. "I can gather our warrior serpents. We can rescue the baby. Rachel will be safe and doesn't have to be a part of it. Afterward, I can bring Prisca to Rachel to release her soul."

"No!" Ace said. He pointed a stick toward Gabe's feet, causing him to stop. "Rachel was chosen for this quest, and she needs to be part of it. She wouldn't have been chosen for this challenge if she didn't have the capability of succeeding. You are the one who can't interfere with her destiny."

Gabe sighed, staring up at the stars. Minutes ticked away.

"Fine," Gabe said, shrugging. "But I don't have to like it."

Chapter Twenty-Two

Leah ran the length of the driveway toward the distant road. She could barely see in the dark, but the bright moon helped to guide her. She grew winded, breath labored, and her sides hurt. Her knee joints wanted to dissolve and give up. But she was in a life and death situation. And frankly, she didn't want to die, at least not yet. She needed to find Rachel. For what purpose, she wasn't sure, but she would do what she could to help her daughter against these dark beasts of prey.

The trees closed around Leah on both sides of the roadway. The wind shook the leaves, rustling branches. It was terrifying not knowing who or what was following her. Her heart thumped painfully against her ribs. She turned to the left, hoping it led toward a town. She had no idea where she was, but it appeared desolate. With each step, her hopes for a car diminished. Still, she plodded on.

Headlights came down the roadway. Leah moved to the middle of the asphalt, waving her hands at the auto. "Hey, stop!" she yelled.

The car slowed to a crawl and finally stopped, beams highlighting her form.

"Hey, lady. Get out of the road," a teenage boy yelled from the driver's side window.

Several more voices yelled at her from the

passenger side. Snickers, laughter, and music resonated in the quiet. Impatiently, the driver revved the engine.

"I need help!" Leah rushed to the driver's side door, grabbing onto the lip of the window. "Please, help me."

"Hands off," the teen said. He grabbed her prying hands and shoved them from the window. "You're going to scratch the paint."

"Open up!" Leah cried. She clawed at the door handle, which the driver quickly locked. "He's coming."

"Get lost!" the passenger said. He sucked on his cigarette, blowing the smoke toward Leah. More laughter and comments ensued from the two male teens in the rear seats.

"Got any money?" the driver said. "Gas ain't free. If you got some dough, I'll give you a ride."

"Money?" Leah's mouth dropped open. "No. But if you take me home, I'll pay you." Nervously, she looked over her shoulder. "Please. He's coming."

"Who's coming?"

"A…a serpent."

"A what?" The driver broke into hilarious laughter. "Lady, you're a nut job."

"She doesn't have money," one of the males in the back said. "Just leave her here, and let's go."

"No!" Leah reached over the driver's window, grabbing at the door lock. "You can't leave me. He's gonna kill me."

"Get off my ride!" The driver pried at her fingers, but she held on fast.

"Hey, Rick, you can't even get a crazy woman off of your car!" The front passenger laughed.

"Get off, you freak." Rick unlocked the door and opened it. The movement caught Leah off guard, sending her plunging to the ground. She rolled to her side, winded and stunned.

"Hey, see if she's got any money," the front passenger said. "Check her pockets."

"She ain't got anything," Rick said, climbing out. He stood over her and spat by her head. "She's a skinny nothing. Looks like a junkie. She'd probably rob us if she could."

"You got it all wrong!" Leah crawled to her knees. "We got to get out of here. He's coming."

A low raspy noise filled the air. The driver stilled, his face horrified. In the headlights, an enormous black snake-like being suddenly appeared. Its eyes were red, reflective, and deadly.

Leah's screams mingled with the teenager's, who'd quickly turned to flee. But then the serpent's tail whipped out, knocking him to the ground. The serpent slithered to the fallen youth, picked him up in its mouth, and threw the boy against a tree. The teen crumbled to the ground.

The passenger crawled over into the driver's seat, locked the door, and rolled up the window. The auto came to life, engine roaring. The driver put the car in reverse, backing up.

The car had only driven a few feet away when the serpent attacked. It rammed its head into the windshield, cracking the glass. Inside, the teenagers screamed. The serpent took its strong body and slammed into the driver's side of the car, creating large dents.

The serpent continued the assault, spun the car

around, and rammed its head into the quarter panel. With a mighty bellow, it shoved the car into a tree. The serpent approached the window, where frightened faces gaped in horror at the spectacle. The beast flicked out a forked tongue, leaving a trail of slime on the pane.

The serpent turned around, spying Leah stumbling into the woods. It gave chase.

Screaming, Leah dropped onto her belly and rolled into a ball, begging for her life.

Ernie's serpent reached down and grabbed Leah's leg, pulling her onto the road. Then he picked her up with his mouth, dragging the screaming woman down the asphalt toward the barn.

Chapter Twenty-Three

Hesitating, Gabe approached Rachel, who was sitting on the grassy bank, chin tucked to her knees. Her anxiety level rushed over his senses, as he picked up her moodiness. He moved behind her, laid his hands against her shoulders, and leaned down, kissing her soft cheek.

"Mind if I join you?"

"Suit yourself," she said, shrugging.

He sat next to her, picked up a loose rock, and rolled it around in his hands. "You know, the first time I saw you, Rachel, I knew we'd be friends."

"That so," she said, glancing at him. "Only friends?"

"Friends. Companions. Together in our causes." He stared at her, mesmerized by her eye color. She was so beautiful, strong, and vulnerable. He never expected to feel the way he did about her. "What did you think the first time you saw me?"

"I'm not sure," she said. "I wasn't sure what it was." She glanced away, hiding her pained expression. "I was attracted to you."

"And now…"

"I like being with you," she said. "I miss you when we're apart."

Gabe slid closer to her, putting his arm around her shoulder. "I'm sorry if you think I'm being a jerk. It's just that I haven't seen you in months and when I do, I find you in a dangerous situation that is only getting worse. It would be nice to have some time for ourselves. Be normal."

"I miss camp," she confessed. "I thought we would be hanging out all summer, and yet here we are in Maine in this terrible situation."

"That's how this life goes," Gabe said. "It's part of our cause, our purpose. I miss camp too. The kids. It was a crazy summer last year and now a crazier one this year. But it was fascinating meeting you and watching your development into your serpent and being a witness to it. At the time, it was hard knowing what you were going through and not being able to help. You had choices to make and that was your right, and yours alone."

"I remember it like it was only yesterday," Rachel replied. "Figured I'd be in Ariel's cabin that summer. She'd been an awful team leader to me and hated that I was there. But the first time I ever laid eyes on you, I felt your energy touch me, even though we'd never met, a connection. I knew you were special and so cute." She reached over and tucked a strand of his dark hair behind his ear. "I thought Michael was too, but I liked you. I was jealous of the other leaders and kept wondering if any of them was your girlfriend."

"I was too busy to have a girlfriend," he said. "I flirted a lot but at the time, I wasn't looking for one either."

"What about Ariel?" Suspicious, she peered at him. "She loves you."

"She thinks she loves me," he replied. "She is more like a sister to me. A friend. There was never anything romantically going on between us."

"But she wanted there to be something," she said. "I could feel her hurt. She hated me because she was jealous of my relationship with you. She wanted me to choose another path, become a dark serpent and fail."

Gabe didn't say anything, her words ringing partially true, pausing in thought. "Your decision wasn't her choice. She assumed the worst. But you're right. She was jealous of you. But I thought it was because you could possibly breed a pure serpent, and she couldn't. She will never be a mother to one of our kind."

"But how does anyone really know that I can?" she replied. "There is an assumption there."

"Because I am a male serpent," he replied. "I can sense it in you."

Heat stained her face as she glanced away. "I didn't know that."

Gabe leaned his head on her shoulder, rubbing his hand along her bare arm. "You could still have just a human child. But you also could have a child like Prisca."

"Then a child of mine would be in constant danger," she replied. "It wouldn't be worth it to have a baby. If I had a daughter like Prisca, she'd be a target for evil. No thanks."

"Perhaps," he replied. "You have time to think about it. But you're right—there would be risks involved. You would have to be prepared and find a way around the issues."

"Why are we even talking about this?" she asked, shrugging. "I'm not planning to have a baby. And even if I were, it wouldn't be for a very, very long time." She reached out and trailed her hand over his firm jaw. "I have to concentrate on helping Prisca. I have a job to do."

"We have a job to do," Gabe said, reminding her. He nuzzled her cheek with his mouth. She turned toward him, lips inviting. He kissed her, sliding her into his arms. Rachel laid her head on his chest, content to be in his arms.

"It's dawn," she whispered, listening to his strong heartbeat. Sunlight tinged the skyline as night fell away. The horizon brightened as the sun's rays made their first golden peaks.

Gabe tilted his head, smiling down at her. "It is morning, and we haven't even slept."

"I know," she replied. "I am tired." She stretched out her arms and fell against the grass. She kicked out her bare feet.

"Rachel." Gabe grabbed her hand, pulling it onto his lap. "Look at your scar."

She sat up, puzzled, and flipped over her wrist. "I don't understand. What do you think it means?"

"It's healed," he replied. "You were healed while in the vortex."

"It looks like a crescent moon," she said, touching it in awe. Her burnt scar was now housed in its original shape. She lifted her eyes to his. A smile curved her lips. "It must be a sign."

But Gabe only frowned, more concerned than ever.

****

After breaking camp, Gabe, Rachel, and Ace left Maine and headed toward Pennsylvania. Ace joined them, not for the battle to come but for the planning part of their invasion. Because Ace could manage a manual transmission, he was able to drive so Gabe and Rachel could get a few hours of sleep, cuddled up along the rear seat.

After stopping for dinner, the trio made light banter, each in their own thoughts. Gabe then sat in the passenger seat, allowing Rachel to stretch out in the rear. Eventually, she fell asleep, content with the normality of the drive. When she woke, she remained quiet and listened to Gabe and Ace's conversation, enjoying the natural banter between the men. It was more like a father and son relationship. She envied Gabe for having such a strong mentor and friend—something she'd been missing her entire life.

Later in the evening, they stopped for snacks and continued the trip. Violent thunderstorms crossed their path, pelting the car with heavy rain while sharp lightning cracked overhead. The closer they got to their destination, the darker Rachel's mood grew. The added weather delays only heightened her unease. Each crack of thunder twisted into her soul, denouncing her ability to save Prisca, causing her to second guess her mission.

It was past midnight when they crossed the border into Pennsylvania. The storms had ceased, and the moonlight eased from the clouds. Rachel wished she could change into her serpent. Traveling would be quicker. They would've arrived hours earlier, but it wouldn't do them any good to rush things. Besides, Gabe wouldn't abandon his car. So, she quieted her restless serpent, resisting her urges. The baby's soul force remained quiet in her as if she were sleeping. Hopefully, the baby dreamed of the flowered field and only felt the warmth of the sun and embracing arms.

They kept driving through the night. Eventually,

they entered Lebanon in Berks County. They traveled past rolling pastures and huge farms. Finally, Gabe pulled the car into a motel. Exhausted, they rented a couple of rooms to get some needed rest.

Just outside her room, Rachel spoke with Gabe. "We're close. I can feel it in my blood. I can try to connect telepathically to Prisca's serpent and get a better tracking."

"Not yet, Rachel," Gabe said, touching her shoulder. "You need to be patient. Prisca's serpent is unpredictable and still feral. I will meet with the other guardians and gather warriors in this region to see if they know these Ophites. Research is key. We need to get a game plan to proceed. We must take precautions to protect everyone involved with this mission and not go blind. I don't want to lose anyone."

"I know," she replied. Irritated, she stepped away from him, shrugging off his hand. "I'm not stupid. I don't want anyone to get hurt either. I'm just anxious to save Prisca. It's hard to allow her one more single moment with those beasts. What they have done to this little girl is unforgivable. I don't think I can relax, let alone sleep."

"You need to try, so you'll be fresh. You also need your energy." He moved closer, running his hand over her cheek, and briefly kissed her. "I'm right next door if you need me. You need only call out, and I'll come."

Rachel slid her arms around his neck, hugging him tightly. Part of her wanted to ask him to stay the night with her, but fear of his rejection kept her silent. Reluctantly, she broke free, opened the door, and went inside her room.

Sighing, Rachel put the small bag of her things on

the bed. Simple in design, her accommodation was the bare minimum. Although it was small, the room smelled fresh, and the linens appeared clean. She couldn't wait for a hot shower. Sighing, she entered the bathroom and turned on the faucet, stepping into the water. The water felt great, but her spirit was restless. Something stirred into her mind—Prisca.

"It's okay, baby girl." She pressed her palm against her heart. "I am coming."

Chapter Twenty-Four

Lustra rolled over in the huge bed, groaning. The sleeping medication she'd been forced to take was wearing off. Ever since she'd seen what they had done to precious Prisca, she couldn't stop crying or shaking. It had been too much, her beautiful little girl turned into that thing.

A sob escaped her. She'd proven herself to be weak and pathetic. Blake had won and had gotten his way. Guilt ate at her. Oh, why hadn't she tried harder to protect Prisca? To hide her baby? She'd had nine months to prepare and had miserably failed. Now it was hopeless.

A soft knock sounded on the door and then it opened. She didn't bother to look to see who was there nor did she care. They could kill her, and she would help them hold the gun to her head. She was already dead.

"Lustra," Ariel said. She walked over to the bed, shaking her shoulder. "Wake up."

"Leave me alone." Lustra shrugged off her hand, feigning sleep.

"You have to eat," Ariel said. "Blake will force a feeding tube if you don't."

"I don't care what he wants," she replied. She turned her face into her pillow, shoving her hands beneath it. "What does he care if I starve to death? He'll get rid of me that way, and that's less messy. That should make him happy."

"You are still Prisca's mother," Ariel said. "Someday, Blake might have to answer to her about his ill treatment of you."

"Good. Perhaps when she's grown, she can eat him." Hysterical laughter escaped Lustra. She rolled over, dragging the blanket with her. "What a putrid meal he'd make. He has a black heart and an even blacker soul."

"Get control of yourself!" Ariel shoved her shoulders. "You are making a complete fool out of yourself. You are mother to a wondrous being. You should be proud, for Prisca is magnificent."

"Was magnificent when she was just an innocent baby," Lustra said. "Now, she lives in what looks like an aquarium, and she is nothing more than a snake that you could buy at the pet store. What is magnificent about that? Her humanity has been stolen, and you people should all be rotting in jail."

"She is still your child," Ariel said, eyes narrowing. "Despite everything, Prisca isn't happy. She isn't thriving the way she needs to. She won't eat without being forced."

"I can't blame her," Lustra said. "You people have destroyed her childhood. She is just an innocent baby." She bit back a sob. "Or was…"

"You're wrong," Ariel said. "She is still Prisca. She might not be in her human state, but she is still your daughter. She's lonely…afraid, and she needs to see you. She might recognize your voice, and it might give her some comfort. She might even eat on her own."

"I can't," Lustra said, wiping at her tears. "I can't take seeing her like that. It's too awful."

Ariel sat on the edge of the bed. She placed her hand on Lustra's shoulder, rubbing it slowly as if consoling a little girl. "It's time for you to stop acting this way, Lustra. Whether you like it or not, Prisca is your child."

"No, she's not," Lustra said. Anger marked her features. "She has been stolen from me. I wasn't given a choice. Prisca belongs to Blake now. It's over. I am nothing."

"Do you want Prisca to die?" Ariel leaned closer, eyes beseeching. "Prisca feels lost right now. Abandoned. She is searching for security. She longs for her mother. You need to spend some time with her."

"Maybe it's better off she's dead," Lustra said, shoving Ariel's hand from her shoulder. She began to cry and rolled over in the bed, tucking her face into another pillow. "I can't believe I just said that."

"Get a grip." Ariel grabbed Lustra's arm, yanking her over to face her. "Prisca needs to know you're near. Don't you fail her. Nothing is set in stone with Prisca, nor do you know the future. Now will you at least see her?"

Lustra glanced away, wiping her eyes on her sleeve. After a long moment, she nodded.

"Good," Ariel said, clearly relieved. She stood and moved to the foot of the bed, waiting. "Then let's go."

Lustra slid her legs to the side of the bed, heart thumping painfully in her chest. Dread filled her mind. Perhaps she should just kill Prisca when she had a chance. That would keep Blake from ever using their daughter for evil. She'd pay with her own life, but frankly, it was perhaps the better option. She'd have to think about it. The thought brought a fresh wave of tears. She stood, grabbed her robe from the bottom bed post, and slid it on.

Quietly, she followed Ariel out the doorway and into the hallway. She kept her eyes focused on the blonde woman in front of her, hating the young woman's indifference to her daughter. They moved into Prisca's bedroom, passing a nurse, who then left the room.

Once again, Lustra had to force herself to walk up to the enclosure. Ariel moved to one side to allow her access. The heating lamp shed a reddish beam on the pale golden serpent. The animal lay coiled, staring sightlessly at nothing. It didn't move, appearing almost dead.

"We tried music to soothe her, but nothing works," Ariel said. "There is little response. Prisca has withdrawn from life. It's as if she is in a trance."

Lustra didn't reply, staring at what was left of her daughter.

"Talk to her," Ariel said. "Let her hear your voice."

"Make her a baby again," Lustra said. She glanced sideways at Ariel. "Can you?"

"Prisca's own serpent is protecting her." Ariel sighed, shaking her head. "You don't understand. Prisca is physically here, but her serpent is in control. The serpent will not yield Prisca to her human side. She feels safer that way."

"Then Prisca is gone forever." A huge tear rolled down Lustra's cheek. "It's as if she is dead."

"No," Ariel replied. "Prisca is in a dormant state. In protection mode."

Lustra studied the tiny snake. A bit of solace slid over her, a bit of gratitude and admiration toward the tiny serpent that dared defy Blake Howard. Prisca was a fighter. Perhaps she should fight with her, for her, and let Prisca know she wasn't alone. New resolve found a footing in her soul. Perhaps in time, she could find a way out of this mess...

"But she could be made a child again?" Lustra pressed. She needed to know if there was a chance.

"It could happen," Ariel said. "But not right now. But if her serpent dies, there is no chance for her recovery."

Hope filled Lustra. Her baby could be made whole. A human being. They could be together, and maybe she could learn to live with her daughter's affliction. They could stop Blake's evil schemes, one way or another. "Tell me what Blake wants from her?"

"He wants to control her," Ariel said simply. "He wants to use her Mana and the power she will possess in the future."

"But she is just an infant," Lustra said. "She hasn't even begun to grow up. How does he know what power she will hold?"

"She is putty to mold," Ariel said. She looked over her shoulder as the nurse entered the room. "I have already said too much. But know this; she will never grow up unless we help her. She is crying for her mother. Talk to her."

"Prisca," Lustra called. She leaned her head over the bed. "Prisca."

The serpent never moved.

"She's just a beast," Lustra said, disappointed. "She doesn't understand me."

"Try again," Ariel said. "Have patience."

"Prisca." Lustra reached a trembling hand down to the tiny serpent, touching her golden head with her fingertip.

The serpent swung its head and clamped her tiny fangs into Lustra's finger.

Lustra screamed, pulling free her bloody finger. "She bit me."

The nurse laughed behind her. "I should've warned you. That serpent is a nasty little thing."

"Make her a human again," Lustra said to Ariel. "Please. I want to hold her again. I'll do anything you ask. Just please give me back my baby."

Ariel just stared at her, and then glanced at the nurse.

"I'll see what Blake says about it," she replied. "He might know a way."

****

Blake stood with the shaman, studying the serpent. The shaman picked up the snake, which tried to wiggle free. When that failed, the tiny serpent snapped its head around, trying to bite his hand. He quickly subdued the tiny beast, cupping her neck with his hand. Ancient words slipped from the shaman's lips. His eyes closed in trance. Minutes ticked away as he tried to connect to the serpent's will but then his eyes opened, confused.

"I cannot feel her life force," the shaman said. "Her soul has left her body."

"How can that be?" Blake said. "It's impossible."

"Prisca's serpent sent the baby's soul somewhere to protect her," the shaman said. "It's hiding Prisca, and it is possible because it's happening right before our eyes."

"But where is Prisca's soul?"

"She could be anywhere," the shaman said. He closed his eyes, meditating. "Prisca's soul is somewhere in the vortex. The baby's spirit drifts freely."

"Can we recapture it?"

"I'm not sure," the shaman said. "Prisca's serpent is very cunning. I've never seen anything quite like this beast. This serpent defies the norm. I cannot detect her spirit, I might add. It's like smoke and mirrors. Time and space. This serpent knows how to deceive. She has knowledge of what we seek and has blocked our every move. It's amazing." He paused, eyes glistening. "Without Prisca's soul force, the child cannot change into her human form. Simply put, the serpent won't allow it."

"Outwitted by a baby snake?" Blake cursed. All his plans were being destroyed. "But how could this serpent know all of this? She is just a baby."

"Prisca comes from ancient blood, ancient wisdom," the shaman replied. "It's instinctive in her to be free from bondage to anyone or anything. Somehow, the serpent has effectively stopped our plans."

"Now you tell me this?" Blake paced in front of the shaman. "Now? After I worked so hard to make this happen?"

"I told you we needed to take care and proceed with caution," the shaman said. "I underestimated the power of Prisca's Mana."

"You're right, you did." Blake glared at him. "You said we, as descendants of the Ophites, would have the power to control the baby. Why would Prisca's serpent be upset? Prisca would be blessed, empowered, and worshiped. What is the problem?"

"You have to remember that Prisca could have all of that without us or you, if she so chooses," the shaman said. "She doesn't need us. We need her. You could return the baby to her mother and set them free, take the chances that Prisca will choose in time to be part of our sect. If you control the baby's mother, you could control Prisca for a time."

Blake growled and flung up his hands. His eyes turned black. "No..."

"Control yourself," the shaman said. "If you want to lead, then you need self-control."

"I already lost a daughter doing just that," Blake said. "I will not lose another." He glared at the tiny serpent, who stared back unflinchingly. "You think you won, you little brat. You will bring back Prisca's life force, or I will slay your mother in front of you."

The serpent continued to stare. Unafraid. Unyielding.

Blake grabbed the serpent, holding it up in a meaty fist. "I should smash you, you little beast."

"Blake," the Shaman said. He put his hand on Blake's arm. "Enough of this folly. Put her back into her crib. There is also another way, but it could be dangerous, and you could lose Prisca for good. The time is drawing near. Lord Talco is coming. We must prepare for the sacrifice. Prisca could die in the process."

"That's a chance I'll take," Blake said. "Let's get on with it."

Chapter Twenty-Five

Sunlight streamed through the cracks in the blinds. Rachel woke to the sounds of people conversing as they passed by her motel door. She groaned and rolled over in the bed. She was so tired. Her body felt as if she'd had a vigorous workout, but then her stomach growled. She was starving.

Rachel entered the bathroom, flipped on the light, and stood before the mirror. Purple-flecked blue eyes met her reflection, compliments of Prisca. It was weird having Prisca's soul force inside of her. She could discern the baby's aura, but it was hard to pinpoint just how she was able to do it. The baby was quiet again, sleeping or perhaps in a dream state.

A knock came on her motel room's door. She shut off the bathroom light and padded barefoot in her T-shirt and shorts to the entrance. She opened it a crack, peeking out. "Who is it?"

"Who else would it be?" Gabe said.

"Room service," she murmured. "I was hoping someone was bringing me a nice breakfast."

"Sounds good to me," Gabe said. "But that's not happening right now."

"What time is it?" she asked, taking off the chain. She swung open the door.

"It's close to ten," Gabe replied, walking into the room. "Get ready. We're going to be leaving soon.

We'll get food somewhere along the way."

"My, you're in a hurry. You could've at least told me good morning." She started walking away, but his arms slid around her waist. He nuzzled her cheek. She sighed, leaning into him.

"Good morning," Gabe said against her ear. "You look beautiful today."

"No, I don't," she replied. His warm breath tickled her ear sending delicious chills along her spine. "But thank you anyway."

"I'll give you a few minutes to get your things together. Just come out when you're ready. I'm making some phone calls."

After he left, Rachel brushed her teeth and then her long hair. She then put on a fresh blue shirt and a pair of jeans, using a belt to yank in the material to fit her slight frame.

She packed her few items and went outside to greet the new day. Gabe and three other men were standing near the car talking. She didn't recognize the strangers, but instinctively knew they were Guardians. They all glanced at her as she approached. Feelings of curiosity swept over her as she picked up their vibes.

"Rachel," Gabe said as she neared the group. "This is Ken, Ryan, and Eric. They will be going with us tonight."

"Hi," she said, noting they were all physically strong and fit. Warrior serpents at their finest. They nodded at her. "It's nice meeting you."

They acknowledged the same, each shaking her hand. But then awkward silence fell.

"We just finished our meeting," Gabe said, clearing his throat. "I can fill you in later."

A meeting without her, Rachel surmised. Gabe had said as much last night, or at least that he was contacting other guardians. Maybe she had been too tired to care then but now it bothered her that she wasn't kept in the loop.

"We'll see you later," Gabe said, dismissing the guardians. Without a word, the men turned and walked away, disappearing around the motel.

"Where did they come from?" she asked Gabe, who opened the passenger side door and grabbed her bag, placing it into the rear of the car.

"They are helping us," he said, glancing at her. "They live locally around here. There are more coming."

"They are going to help us free Prisca?" She leaned against the car, uncertain of the direction they were taking.

"Yes," he said. "The compound is about five miles from here. We are close."

"Maybe we should go it alone," she said. She tucked a stray piece of hair behind her ear. "We could sneak in and snatch Prisca. We'd have the element of surprise. They wouldn't expect that."

"I thought of that, but it's too dangerous. There are a lot of Ophite serpents in this area, all loyal to Blake Howard and his causes. We need backup, and I have to be certain of everyone's commitment to this mission."

"Morning," Ace said as he came out of the motel, joining them. He moved past them and stood by the car, expectantly.

"Good morning," Rachel responded. The mission was seeming more difficult by the minute. Uneasiness filtered over her.

"Ready?" Gabe opened the passenger side door, waiting for Rachel to enter the car.

Rachel frowned and climbed into the back seat. Anger began to simmer inside her. She was perturbed that Gabe had fully taken over the mission—her mission. This was not the way she wanted it.

Gabe climbed into the driver's seat, Ace beside him. He started the engine, backing out of the lot.

"Let's get a bite to eat, and then I'll lay out the plans so far," Gabe said to Rachel.

"Looks like you got it all covered," Rachel said. Her eyes narrowed reflectively in the rearview mirror. "You didn't even consult me or include me in your little meeting."

"Look, Rachel, you needed your sleep," Gabe said, meeting her piercing accusation. "Your body has been through a lot these past few days. I couldn't sleep last night so I did a bit of research and made a few calls. I reached out for help. We need help. Surely, you see that. I won't apologize for getting prepared for this mission. What's the big deal?"

"I thought we were in this together. A team?"

"We are a team," he said. "Why are you getting angry?"

"Because I am the one carrying Prisca's life force inside of me," she said. "I have been chosen for this task…a task I am being left out of."

"I'm not letting anything happen to you," Gabe said. "So, lay off."

"You are not my guardian!" she retorted. "I can protect myself."

"I can't believe you are arguing with me over this," Gabe said, gripping the wheel. "If you ask me, you are the one lacking trust. We are a team and, on this assignment, together, I am the team leader. Your team leader. That means I am in charge."

"Says who?" She crossed her arms, glaring at him.

"Me."

She rolled her eyes, and then stared out the window. "You can be such a jerk sometimes."

"Then I'm a jerk," he replied. "But I'm still in charge of this mission."

"Stop arguing," Ace said from the passenger seat. He leaned between the seats, looking meaningfully at Rachel, then toward Gabe. "I know everyone is being testy right now. We have a reason to be. But arguing over moot points isn't the answer. There is no reason not to have backup, Rachel. It doesn't hurt to be overly prepared. We don't know what exactly we're up against. You can't hold that against Gabe."

"Whatever," she murmured, watching the passing landscape. Ace was right. She knew he was right, and still Gabe could've kept her informed. She shook off her thoughts, studying Gabe's dark hair curled just past the nape of his neck. Gabe avoided her, his attention now on the roadway. He was angry. His thoughts were closed off to her, but the yank of the gear shift spoke volumes as the car sped up. Perhaps Ace was right. She was stressed. Maybe being too sensitive. She trusted Gabe's decisions, more than her own. Still, warrior or not, she was not without her own reprisals.

The car pulled into a small restaurant. Without speaking to one another, Rachel and Gabe followed Ace in through the front door. The couple sat across from Ace, and they all ordered coffee, omelets, bacon, and ham.

An awkward silence fell over the group. Ace shoved down most of his food, then paused, staring at the couple. He cleared his throat, considering them. Then he addressed Rachel, fork pointed in the air. "Did I ever tell you some of the antics Gabe pulled as a kid?"

"No," she replied, knowing Ace knew he hadn't. But she appreciated his efforts to lighten the mood. Ace became a chatterbox telling tales of Gabe's childhood in Maine. Ignoring the vibrant stories, Gabe continued to eat, not adding any input.

Rachel listened to the tales of whopper fish being caught and the time Gabe got stuck in a tree. Ace was overly dramatic. The tales were indeed tall. She found herself relaxing. And after a few minutes, she realized Ace had disarmed her emotions. She was enjoying his stories. Gabe, however, seemed determined to devour his meal and not make conversation.

"Of course, if Gabe had his serpent at the time, he could have just changed like that." Ace snapped his fingers. "Now, he practically lives in the trees."

Rachel smiled, slipping a sideway peek toward Gabe. He was pensive, moody. She regretted yelling at him. Maybe Ace was right, and they were all stressed out. The Lord knew she certainly was. She nudged Gabe with her boot tip. He paused over his meal, meeting her regard.

"Do you want the rest of my ham?" She pushed her plate toward Gabe. "I know how much you like it."

"Sure." Gabe picked up her remaining two slices and put them on his plate. "Thanks."

After they were done eating, they walked outside. Rachel stalled near the door, grabbed Gabe's hand, stopping him. Ace noticed and proceeded ahead to the car.

"I'm sorry," Rachel said softly. "I didn't mean to snap at you earlier."

Gabe studied her and nodded. "Okay."

"Is that all you're going to say?" She waited for his reply, drowning in his blue eyes.

"What do you want me to say?"

"I guess nothing," she replied. She dropped his hand, turning away but he caught it again, pulling her into his arms.

"I won't be sorry for trying to protect you, Rachel. I am a warrior serpent. It's my destiny." He kissed her lips, then lifted his head. "You're my destiny."

They left the diner and drove a short distance, pulling into a long driveway. Gabe parked the Camaro in the rear of a small ranch house. Other cars were present.

The three of them walked to the back door. Gabe knocked. A curtain moved, and then Eric opened the door.

"Let's go into the dining room," Eric said, ushering them inside. "More room."

Ken and Ryan were already in the dining room, heads bent over a large map. They nodded to the newcomers, continuing to study the map.

"How are you making out?" Gabe asked, standing next to Ryan. His gaze also swept over the drawing.

"This is the map of Paradise Farm," Ken said. He slid his finger around the perimeters. "As you can see, we have a large area to cover."

Rachel and Ace leaned over the table to look. Rachel tried to make out the various symbols. The mansion area was highlighted in yellow. There were several other buildings. Red X's were marked sporadically throughout the print.

"For the most part we are dealing with forest," Ken said. "Most areas are fenced in and then there are security cameras everywhere. There are two roads coming into the property. One leads to the mansion, the other passes the house and leads to some outer buildings. I think getting onto the property won't be a problem. It's what is beneath the mansion we must worry about. The mansion was built around a cavern. The entrance or mouth of a cave is somewhere beneath the building. There are miles of tunnels traveling in and out of this portal. It runs deep—deeper than I could ever estimate. There is no telling just how exactly far the passageways go. But from what I have learned, the cave is a conduit to the ancient realms and, more importantly, to Lord Talco. It is also deceptive. There are many pitfalls and traps. From what I gather from others, the cave is only accessible every three years. How it gets opened is a mystery. It's a supernatural occurrence linked between the Ophites sect and Lord Talco."

"Who is that?" Rachel asked, heart lurching at the name.

"Blake Howard rules these parts, "Ken said. "But he serves Lord Talco, who is an old serpent who rules the underworld. He is partly human, but he denies himself ever altering into one. As you know, in our serpent form, we don't age; only our human side does. So Talco is incredibly old and incredibly wise. He only comes to the mouth of the cave when called upon during this time period. He is greatly feared and has a temper when roused. But he is very generous to his followers, thus Blake Howard's source of wealth."

"So, the mansion was built over the cavern," Rachel said. "It's just a front."

"Yes," Ben said. "Talco demands loyalty from his followers. Worship. He fancies himself a god. An altar is set up in front of the cave's mouth where gifts are left for Talco. If Talco likes the offering, he will leave gold or silver. But if he doesn't then he might demand retribution in the form of a sacrifice."

"A sacrifice," Rachel said. "Like what kind of sacrifice?"

"Usually a young woman hybrid, preferably a pure serpent with utmost beauty."

"What…what does he do with them?" She hated the images that crept over her.

"No one is sure," Ken said. "The woman is never seen or heard from again. One can only wonder. It is said amongst the Ophites that it's an honor to be taken by him."

"That sounds barbaric," she said, disgust in her features. Prisca filled her mind. The baby was truly being held by dangerous people—dark serpents with little regard for life.

"The truth isn't always pretty," Ken said. "But it is the way of things. Ever since the fall of mankind, a battle has raged between both worlds. We serpents are cursed and yet blessed, but we have been given a choice in our destiny."

"Why do the dark serpents hate humans so much?"

"Because mankind had been put above all beasts," Ken said. "Including serpents. Humans are weak, pitiful, and predictable. As a punishment for our part in man's fall from grace, we were yoked together in their fate, living on both sides of the same coin. We see the human flaws, and yet we, as hybrids, have been charged to interfere in their lives at times and put them above ourselves. Ophites refuse this commission, preferring darkness and living in their hatred. They've stamped out their human side and seek the day when they can rule over the earth without fear of divine intervention."

"You mean the creator?" She stared at him.

"He is the most powerful being of all."

"I admit, I am still learning."

"It's not our job to understand it or judge."

Rachel shivered, glancing away. She felt small in the scheme of things.

"But why doesn't he just end this all?" she finally said, hands spread imploringly. "Why doesn't he intervene?"

"He does intervene," Ken said. "What do you think we are?"

****

The afternoon wore on as other Guardians arrived at the modest home. Rachel was introduced to several other warrior serpents. Everyone studied the map of Paradise Farms, the locations, exits, and danger points. The mansion was owned by Blake Howard, a formidable attorney, who had political connections and powerful friends.

When Michael and Tina arrived from Second Chance Camp, Rachel hugged them, happy to see familiar faces.

"I really missed you both," she said. She hadn't seen Michael since the night when he and Gabe had come to her aid against the dark serpents.

"I missed you too," Michael said, kissing her

cheek. "Hey, bro." He thumped Gabe on the back. "How's it going?"

"Same old, same old." Gabe jokingly shoved him. "You been keeping out of trouble?"

"Yeah. It's been really quiet." Michael glanced at Tina, who shrugged.

"Quiet," Gabe repeated, laughing. "I wouldn't know what that is like."

"Cool eye color," Tina said, staring into Rachel's eyes. "That's one crazy trick you pulled with Prisca's life force. How did you know what to do to protect her?"

"It just came to me," Rachel said, shrugging. "Being in the vortex helped. I only hope I can help her."

"We're all here for you," Tina said. "I won't be coming on the mission, but I wanted to be here for moral support. As you know, my gift is healing. I'm not much of a fighter and would only get in the way. I promised Michael I'd head out of the area and return to Second Chance Camp, but I will be in constant contact with him and Gabe. If anyone needs me, just call out to me and I'll come."

"I appreciate it." Rachel hugged her tightly. "Thank you for being a wonderful friend. I really appreciate it."

The doorbell rang, and Ryan went to answer it. Rachel sensed Ariel before she actually saw the woman enter. Instantly, she bristled. A dark void surrounded Ariel; something was off. Prisca stirred in her mind.

Ariel strolled into the room, scanning all the Guardians. Wearing jeans and a sweatshirt, she appeared relaxed and formidable with her hair tied up in a knot. The blonde woman smiled at everyone, but her cool blue eyes remained steadfast. "So, you thought you would have a party without me?"

"Ariel," Tina cried. She rushed over to the guardian and hugged her. "Where have you been, girl? We've been missing you."

Ariel hugged her and then hugged Michael, who also gave a cozy welcome. When Ariel saw Gabe, her eyes clouded for a moment, but then she went to him and threw her arms around his neck, squeezing tightly.

"Thanks for coming on such short notice," Gabe said, kissing her cheek.

"Well, that's me," Ariel replied, grinning. "I like getting myself into trouble with this gang." After a moment, she turned and critically skimmed her gaze over Rachel, arching her slender brow. "Well, hello, Rachel."

"Hello," Rachel replied. The moment was awkward. Already Ariel had judged her and found her lacking. She stuck out her hand before she'd be forced into an awkward hug. "It's nice to see you again.'

Ariel stared at the offered hand, then smiled. "Looks like you're in trouble again, Rachel. Seems like we are always getting you out of it."

Rachel stiffened at the cold words, dropping her hand. "I didn't ask for your help; Gabe did. This was my assignment, and I didn't have a choice."

"We always have a choice," Ariel said, her words blunt. "My question to you is are you going to stand your ground when things get crazy?"

Before Rachel could even blink, Ariel walked away, leaving the room.

Furious, Rachel resisted the urge to follow Ariel

and tell her to leave. The woman had nerve, and she was sick of her attitude. It filled her with doubts and new fears. Once again, Prisca stirred in her mind. The child's spirit was uncomfortable around Ariel. She had to wonder why, or perhaps she was imagining it. After all, she didn't like being around Ariel either and maybe the baby could sense it.

After a while, Ariel joined the group again, participating in the discussions with the attendees and tossing sly glances at Gabe. Jealousy pricked Rachel's heart. She tried to shrug it off, glad that Gabe appeared not to care that Ariel was throwing out hints. Miserably, she waited out the hours as the afternoon changed into evening.

All of the attending guardians, twelve in all, went outside into the clear night. It was time to energize with the moon and be in the vortex. They moved into the rear yard, into an accessible area. They took hands and formed a circle. Gabe called for the vortex to open.

Slowly, the vortex hovered over them, appearing as a misty cloud. It opened revealing a blazing light. The group stood inside of it as it lowered over their forms. Electricity snapped the air as the circuit was complete. Raw energy ran through their fingertips, circling around them in heated friction.

Rachel stared up into the vortex, wondering what vision she would behold. She opened her mind to receive insight into her plight with Prisca.

Silence greeted Rachel. No voices spoke to her. It was as if she were deaf in the vortex. She felt abandoned and lost. Was she alone in her mission after all? She needed help to keep focused, to preserve her mind and thoughts. Even the love and acceptance were lost. She felt utterly alone.

When the ritual was complete, Rachel stood confused beneath the moon. Suddenly, she was very insecure. Gabe came over to her.

"What's the matter?"

"I don't know," she murmured. "Something is wrong. What about you? Were you given a message?"

"To continue," he said. "We are doing what needs to be done."

Relief filled her. Well, at least Gabe was certain. That was good because she needed his guidance after all. Without his assertion, she had her doubts.

She glanced over at Ariel, who stood near a tree observing them, realizing the woman hadn't joined them in the ritual. Hatred from Ariel filtered over Rachel. It was powerful, twisting inside her soul. Whatever she had done to deserve such hatred, she hadn't a clue. Gabe, on the other hand—Ariel was loving him with her eyes from afar. With discernment, Rachel realized she could read Ariel's emotions, something she'd had trouble within the past. Her telepathic abilities were indeed improving.

The guardians returned into the house. The plan was set to begin at midnight. They sat and talked for a while, eating a few snacks. Rachel sat with Tina, who was informative and talked about the camp at present. Ariel, however, said little, sat apart from everyone, and seemed preoccupied in her thoughts.

Ace grabbed a pack of cards. "Who wants to play Gin?"

Everyone appeared disinterested, but then Tina announced, "I'll play."

Michael stood and moved to the table, seating

himself. "I guess I can."

At quarter of twelve, Gabe pushed back his chair, breaking up the vigorous card game. "I think we should get going. Thanks, everyone, for coming. It means a lot to me and Rachel."

"I will be leaving as well," Tina said. She hugged various members of the group. Michael followed Tina out to her car to say goodbye in private.

"I also want to tell you all how grateful I am." Rachel faced the remaining guardians. She stood next to Gabe and took his hand. Her gaze encompassed the group. "I just wanted to say thank you all for helping us with this mission. Prisca is worth our efforts. She is a special little girl."

Murmurs of approval and kind response followed, but Ariel just stared at Rachel, a frown upon her mouth.

Prisca stirred within Rachel.

****

The moon was bright, illuminating the sky. The group in the house dispersed into the deepening night. The plan was to surround the mansion compound, taking out security as they went. They were teamed into pairs.

Rachel met Gabe in the clearing behind the house, both now in serpent form. She followed Gabe as he led the way. They traveled very quickly, the landscape rural and mostly trees and open fields. It would be five miles till they reached the outer limits of the property.

"Whatever you do, Rachel," Gabe said telepathically, "Do not block me from your mind. I am linked with all the others, and we must work together to achieve our goals. If we go down, we all go down together."

"I understand," she said. She didn't like that she wouldn't be communicating with the other Guardians, and he had efficiently kept her out of that discussion.

"Good." He reached out and nudged her face with his. "You should see your eyes right now. They are crazy beautiful."

She paused as his simple words comforted her, then realized how easily he'd charmed her from her sour mood.

"I feel your roiling emotions," he said. "But you are strong. Stronger than you could ever imagine. If I could, I'd keep you from having to come along."

"I know that." She wanted to argue her points but held quiet. They were headed into danger, and now was not the time.

"Now I want you to go be with Michael and let me clear the way. He is up ahead of us waiting for you."

"What do you mean be with Michael?" she said, pausing. She snapped her tail at him, halting his process. "I'm sticking with you."

"No," he said, staring her down. He pressed his snout against hers. "You're not. You have to do what I say, or this mission is off."

"So once again, you kept me out of your plans!"

"You are getting angry over nothing," he said. "And we're not discussing this right now. I am the leader, and this is how it's going to be. For once, just do as I say without arguing. We're wasting time."

"Fine!" she said. "But we will be talking about this later."

Gabe moved ahead of her, ignoring her questioning stare.

With no choice but to follow him, Rachel pushed

away her feelings. She needed to be levelheaded, but didn't he realize she wanted to protect him as much as he wanted to protect her?

Michael was waiting for them, his strong form coiled and sleek in the dew, but she was unprepared to see Ariel with Michael. The big blonde was in human form. She stood, feet braced, and shoulders squared for the coming storm.

"Why is Ariel here?" she asked Gabe telepathically.

"She will be with me," Gabe said. "She is a good tracker, and she can fight."

Rachel sensed the other female's pleasure in her anger. Gabe drew closer to Michael. She tried to read his thoughts, hear their private words but he effectively shut her out of his mind.

"I will keep Gabe safe," Ariel said, moving closer to Rachel. She tilted her head, staring into Rachel's eyes. "I have always watched over him and will continue to do so. You need not worry. I won't let him down."

Rachel stiffened at Ariel's words. There was definitely an insult somewhere in the mix. Gabe noticed them, pausing across the way, sending her reassurance. Abruptly, Ariel turned and walked toward him. They disappeared into the night.

Rachel watched the couple leave, torn between following them and screaming in rage. Jealousy ate at her heart. She'd been effectively shut out of the loop.

"We will wait here until Gabe contacts me," Michael said. He moved next to her, reassurance in his tone. "I know what you're thinking, Rachel, and we aren't going to follow them. I gave Gabe my word."

"Well, I didn't," she replied. She lifted her chin, glaring at him.

"Rachel, let Gabe do his job," Michael said, his words calm. "He is good at tracking and he's a strong warrior. This is what he's good at. He has the experience that you are lacking."

"And I suppose Ariel does too?"

"Yes," he said. "I know you don't like to hear that. There is no need for your jealousy. You hold Gabe's heart. This is a work in progress. Ariel works well with Gabe. The two have been in many battles together. You should be happy she is with him."

Rachel didn't like hearing she was lacking where Ariel excelled. Perhaps she really was jealous of Ariel, the admission brutal. The beauty had many talents. In some ways, she admired Ariel. She had even tried to befriend her, but Ariel held her with cold regard, not remotely interested.

"In time, you will be everything you want to be," Michael said. "You must have patience. Please, Rachel. You could bring more danger to Gabe if he thinks you aren't following orders. He will stop everything he's doing to protect you. You can't give the enemy any leverage. Keep your feelings out of this battle for everyone's sake."

She paused, considering him.

"Okay," she said. His words had sliced into her heart. "You're right. But you tell me the second Gabe calls out to you if there is a problem because Lord knows he won't call out to me first. Being left in the dark can also be dangerous. I need to know what's going on as well. Please. Don't try to protect me. I need to have my wits about myself."

"Of course," Michael said. "We're all in this to win."

****

The night was quiet as the Guardian serpents moved onto Paradise Farms, setting up their perimeters. Now all were in serpent form as they moved into the thicker brush to avoid the security cameras, seeking any hidden underground passageways. The property was patrolled by several serpent guards, cloaked in their human forms. The unsuspecting Ophites were quickly taken out by the efficient Guardians, who worked together in progress.

Gabe and Ariel arrived at the small guard shack, where three guards were stationed. Ariel slithered around the booth, peeking through the glass panes. With a slash of her tail, she smashed the overhead camera. It fell and hit the corner of the building before crashing to the ground.

Inside, an elderly guard jumped up from his chair, staring at the fuzzy image on the computer screen, while the other guards left the building, moving into the night.

"There's no one out here," the first guard said. He flicked on his flashlight, shining it along the driveway.

"They're here," the second guard said. He rapped on the glass with his fist, giving a thumbs up sign to the older guard, who quickly picked up his phone.

From the trees, Gabe dropped down on the first guard, knocking the man flat to the ground. He slammed his massive head into the man's head, knocking him out cold before he could change into a serpent. He turned to find himself looking into the eyes of a serpent, as the other guard had altered in the meantime. The serpent's lightning bolt between his eyes blazed with color. Gabe met him head on, while Ariel tried to get into the guard post.

Ariel rammed her head into the front glass window. It barely moved, let alone cracked. She slithered around the building, looking for a way in. The roof had a sky window, which was partially open to let in the night air. Quickly, she slithered up the building and shoved her head inside the narrow opening, forcing the metal frame to break. She lowered into the room.

The older guard had changed into a dark serpent. He was older and heavier than the other guards, taking up a lot of the room. He was waiting for her, snapping at her face as she dropped down. She hissed, baring her fangs, enjoying his fear.

In fury, he smashed his body around the small enclosure, his awkward movements giving her leverage. She quickly weaved her body around his, sinking her death bite into his heart. She burst out of the side door just in time to see three more serpents coming toward them.

Instinctively, Gabe and Ariel worked together as a team. Gabe took on the larger of the serpents, while keeping an eye on the weaker snake that was looking for an opportunity. Ariel headed off into the forest, a dark serpent following.

With a snarl, Gabe pinned the first beast and delivered the death bite into his heart. The other serpent tried to flee, but he chased him, making quick work of destroying him. He followed Ariel, who came back toward him, now alone.

"Ready," he said telepathically.

She nodded and turned around, heading toward the

mansion in the distance.

****

When Gabe telepathically messaged her that he was fine and making headway, Rachael was relieved. She followed Michael deeper into the tree line as they slowly made progress. They moved their forms upward and into the limbs of a large oak. Branches snapped and leaves rustled as they traveled, continuing to use the trees for coverage. When they came to a clearing, they paused, Michael assessing the area around them.

"Wait here for a minute." Michael dropped to the ground below, studying it with his keen instincts.

Rachel watched him, ever alert to the tiniest sound. She could feel Prisca inside her mind, tense, fearful. The baby's anxiety was adding to her own.

"Shush, little one," she whispered in her thoughts. "I won't let any harm befall you."

Michael was off and moving onto hillier ground. She slid down and followed him. They passed several outbuildings. Horses neighed from one of the barns, restlessly sensing the guardians. Somewhere off in the distance, a dog barked. They reached a long, twisted driveway. As they moved closer, a courtyard of sorts emerged. They passed the damaged guard shack, which appeared as if a small tornado had recently descended.

The mansion was bigger than she had ever imagined, surrounded by ornamental statues, benches, and stately gardens. A black iron fence surrounded the mansion. Light posts glowed in a welcoming ambiance, a stark contrast to her danger-filled senses.

A commotion came from beyond the mansion, thumps and groans. Michael nudged her with his head. She followed him around the building and into the shadows.

"Where's Gabe?" she asked Michael.

"He's already on the mansion's roof," Michael said in return. "Clearing a path for us to follow."

"Gabe," she said into his mind, wanting to connect with him, but no reply. He was the most frustrating man. Though she appreciated his protection over her, it was also maddening.

Michael was off again, this time headed for the right side of the mansion. In the swimming pool area, a graceful gazebo stood with whimsical engravings. Within seconds, Michael slid up onto its roof and then continued onto the porch overhang. Rachel followed him. At the adjoining mansion roof, Rachel saw Gabe, who was watching her progress.

Michael's powerful body slid up the wall, until he joined Gabe and Ariel. Rachel followed, frustrated that Gabe continued along the rooftop without waiting or speaking with her. The mansion held many valleys with alcoves and recesses. Gabe dropped down onto a lower rooftop.

"I was able to open a window," Gabe told Michael and Rachel telepathically. "It's a bit narrow, but you can wedge through, though do so as quietly as possible. I will go inside first, then Ariel. Wait several minutes and then follow us. I will instruct you as we go. Do not question my actions. Just do as I say. When I say."

Rachel cringed, knowing his words were directed toward her. She wondered where the other guardian warriors were at but trusted Gabe's discretion.

Into a large window, Gabe disappeared with Ariel following him. Rachel held back from trailing them, knowing Michael would stop her should she try. The minutes ticked away as the moon slid out from behind the clouds, beaming down on them. She pulled the light source of energy into her soul, sensing Prisca's love of warmth and security.

"Let's go," Michael said to her. "You are first. I will follow."

Within seconds, Rachel slipped through the window's opening and dropped down into a large room. The lavish bedroom appeared as if used for a magazine cover. Her senses told her the room was just for show and hadn't been used in months.

Inwardly, Prisca panicked.

****

The mansion was huge inside, boasting many intricate hallways. Gabe passed several empty bedrooms. In the hallway, he encountered a man, who was also a dark serpent. The man barely cried out as Gabe grabbed him, dragging him into one of the bedrooms. Quickly, he silenced him, leaving his crumpled body in one of the adjoining bathrooms.

Ariel had entered from another direction, informing Gabe of her whereabouts and surroundings. She also encountered a staff member and took him out. After they cleared the south section of the building, Gabe gave the go ahead for Rachel and Michael to follow. His instinct was at its highest level, guiding him accordingly. He telepathically connected with the four other male guardians entering the mansion, their points of entry on the first floor. The remaining serpents were outside, guarding the entrances and exits.

Danger lurked everywhere, but he sensed it came from beneath the mansion. He needed to get lower. From his study of the mansion's plans, he recalled where all four staircases were housed. He opted for the staff staircase, which led down to the service kitchens.

Ariel joined him as they slithered down the steps and then entered a huge stainless-steel kitchen. Everything was pristine, polished to a shine. No one was around.

He didn't like it. There should be more opposition. They couldn't be this lucky. It was too quiet.

"What do you think?" he said into Ariel's thoughts, who was scanning the room.

"Below the mansion," she said. "They are all down there."

"And the baby?"

"She is too."

Gabe sent Michael the signal to follow them. When Rachel and Michael came into the kitchen, he ignored the beseeching panic from Rachel. She didn't like taking orders from him. Resented it, in fact. But it was something she would have to live with for now. She didn't understand how it was for him. That he needed to protect her. It was his job.

"Stay here," Gabe said telepathically to Rachel and Michael. "Ariel has confirmed the path is clear to get to the basement. I will keep moving forward. There are other guardians coming in from the other side. We will meet up when the time is right."

"Gabe," Rachel said into his thoughts. "Please be careful."

"You do the same," he said. "Listen to Michael."

Off the kitchen, two entrances led to the basement, one for staff and one for maintenance. He waited for confirmation from Eric, who had taken the main route from the west side. Finally, Eric spoke telepathically to him.

"Twenty serpents are underground."

"That many," Gabe said. "We might need more backup."

"I'm here if you need me," Ace abruptly interjected into Gabe's mind. "I'm not that far off."

"No," Gabe said. "Stay where you are. After we get the baby, I will need you to get Rachel and Prisca far away from here while we wrap up things."

"Eric and I are coming to the north side of the mansion," Ken said telepathically. "I found one of the tunnels leading to the basement. We're heading in now."

"Be careful," Gabe said. "Ariel and I will be coming down the south staircase. Michael?"

"I'm listening."

"I'm counting on you to see to Rachael's safety," Gabe instructed. "I am blocking her from my mind for now, so she has to get her information from you. I don't need to be arguing with her and need to stay focused. So please manage her. You're good at that. Stay somewhere safe until I contact you. Make sure you have a way out. Keep Rachel in tow. When we have the baby, we'll be moving fast and bringing her up to you. You will need to get outside and get to Ace. Get Rachel and Prisca as far away as possible. You know where the safehouse is. That's where to go. We'll meet up with you later."

"Copy that," Michael replied.

"Ready?" Gabe asked Ariel.

"Yes," she replied.

Gabe opened the doorway leading to the basement. Warning bells shattered his thoughts. This all had been too easy. Too easy taking out the guards. Too easy getting in the mansion. Maybe it would be too easy to die.

The night waited expectantly.

Chapter Twenty-Six

Rachel hated the waiting. It felt like hours when it had only been minutes. Every sense in her body was alert to the tiniest sounds. Inside her, Prisca remained restless. She hummed to the baby, soothing her. It seemed to work. The anxiousness faded and then disappeared. If only she could pacify herself so easily.

"That's nice." Michael broke into her thoughts. "Even subconsciously your voice is beautiful."

"Thank you," she replied. "I didn't know you were listening. I don't consider my singing voice beautiful."

"Well, perhaps you weren't hearing it as I had," he replied. "It was nice and sounded like an Irish ditty."

"It's something my mother used to sing to me." She turned her gaze on Michael, who coiled protectively by the kitchen doorway. Even though he was speaking telepathically, he was ever alert to danger. "Don't shut me out, Michael, or shield me from what's going on. I am tired of Gabe treating me like some fragile little girl."

"He's not, Rachel. You are too sensitive. It's his way—the way of a warrior."

"Warrior." She cocked her head. "I do understand his way. Lord knows, he saved me how many times? But I can fight too. I have my own strengths and abilities. I might be new to all of this, but I am always learning and getting stronger. I've been discovering something new about myself every day. I want to be treated as an equal. I am a Guardian."

"I hear you on that," he replied. "Gabe is how he is. There's no changing him. But knowing this, anyone he cares about is subject to the same treatment. Male or female. Got it? Gabe would rather die than let anyone he cares about be harmed or suffer."

Michael's words hit home, and she shook her doubts. Michael was right. She needed to put her stubborn pride away. Perhaps she was acting more like Prisca instead of herself. They were a team of Guardians fighting for the same cause. Gabe was a warrior serpent, his gift in the art of warfare. One of her gifts was the gift of knowing, discernment, usually involving humans and their flaws.

The minutes ticked away. Still nothing.

"Michael. What is happening? Has Gabe connected with you?"

Michael paused, turning his great head toward her. "I'm having trouble connecting with him and to the others. There is interference. I don't like this."

"What should we do?"

"I want you to stay here," he said. "I want to move closer, perhaps a bit underground to see if it helps."

"No. I am coming with you. We need to stay together."

"Rachel," Michael said. "No. I've been given charge over you. You will stay here. I'm not planning to go far but if for some reason I don't return, you are to retreat and go straight to Ace. That's an order."

Without her agreement, Michael exited the kitchen, his great gilded form disappearing from view. Frustrated, she watched him leave.

"Michael…"

"Stay!"

Rachel recoiled at his words. He could be just as dictatorial as Gabe. Why was she always the last one to know what was happening?

Once again, she was stuck waiting. Not knowing.

"Hush, Prisca," she said. "I'm worried too."

****

At the foot of the staircase, Gabe paused, instincts strained. Ariel followed him. A corridor led to the right or left. At the foot of the stairs, the ground was concrete, but it was cracked with missing portions. It was dark and a bit cold. Wind traveled through the opposing hallways, spreading loose dirt across the pathway.

"Which way?" Ariel asked, pausing her sleek form.

"I'll take the right."

"Then I'll go left," she replied, slinking off into the dark.

Gabe's eyes quickly adjusted to the lighting. He slithered down the corridor, which dipped down on a slow incline. It was as if the ground had been victim to a previous earthquake, destabilizing the concrete floors. The generous walls were limestone, glistening in the dark. The portal opened wider. He came upon the first room, which was empty. Scents of multiple serpents lingered in the area and infused the dampened earth.

Water dripped somewhere off in the distance. Every nerve in his body was strained. It was hard knowing direction, his senses muddled. There was activity nearby, yet all remained still. He hated his warped senses; it was becoming more dangerous by the second.

"Michael," Gabe called out to him. But the other serpent didn't respond, nor did any of the others. Their connections had been cut off. Somehow, the atmosphere of the building had effectively ceased their ability to communicate. He called for Ariel. Also no reply. If he couldn't contact the others, he was on his own and blinded to danger. To succeed in the battle, they needed to work together. It was time to retreat, recoup, and strategize from another angle. He had been too hasty in this mission. But he had feared Rachel would take it upon herself to try and free Prisca from the dark serpents' hold. He couldn't risk her life. But now it could be his undoing.

He began backtracking to find Ariel to team up with. When he neared the staircase, she appeared out of the dark.

"I found something," she said telepathically. "Come with me."

"I couldn't communicate with anyone or you. Why now?"

"I'm not sure," she replied. "Somewhere along the way, there is a barrier inside these walls. Here by the staircase is the only reception."

For a moment, he studied her. Mixed signals resounded in his form. "I think we should leave and regroup."

"That's fine," she replied. "But I wanted you to know that I have found a room with a tunnel. It leads somewhere beneath the mansion and most likely runs to a meeting chamber. It's where they are located. Prisca too. I can sense them."

"I don't like this."

"I think we should continue," she replied.

"What about the other Guardians?"

"They are on task," she replied. "Why do you doubt yourself?"

Her simple replies baffled him. For the first time, he doubted her wisdom.

"We are near the cave's entrance to Lord Talco's realm," she said. "None of us have ever been this close to this part of the underground world. It's been cleverly concealed with unique safeguards both physically and spiritually. Blake Howard and the Ophites are known for their ingenuity."

"Michael?" Gabe tried again to seek out his comrade. No response. He had no idea where Rachel was and if she was safe. He could only hope his trust in Michael was well placed and they would all survive this night of hell.

"Let's go," he said to Ariel. "But be ready to flee at any moment."

"Follow me." Pivoting, Ariel was off and sliding along the inky hallway with Gabe trailing. The way became a tunnel, all signs of normal construction fading. The walls and floor were now solid limestone, glistening in dampness.

Ariel led him to the entrance of a room. The doorway was rounded, off centered. She paused. "In the back of this space, there is an entrance to a cavern followed by another tunnel. I believe we can find what we are looking for. Hopefully, the others will join us."

"You're sure of this?"

"Yes."

"Follow me." Gabe ducked into the room, which was small and damp. He found the entrance in the rear and tucked his head inside, allowing his senses to readjust. He entered the next cavern, which became another tunnel. The way curved and narrowed in spots. It was hard to imagine a baby in the environment but then again, Prisca was part human and serpent.

Another doorway appeared, and he dropped several feet into another room. It was so dark his eyes readjusted to allow him to see as he regained his senses. He turned to Ariel, hoping she still followed but she was nowhere in sight. Suddenly, a loud metallic crash filled the room. Above the doorway, a gate came slamming down, cutting off the entrance to the room. Hissing in rage, he threw his body up the slight incline, slamming his head into the metal. It was impenetrable, the impact forcing his body to drop to the floor below. High above him, a light flickered and then illuminated the room. He glanced around at what he perceived to be his prison cell. Around him was a solid stone floor and walls. Above him a raspy screech broke the quiet as a metal grate opened. A man peered down at him, his eyes razor sharp and inquisitive. His features were strong, clean cut, and an aura of authority surrounded him.

"You made this too easy, Gabe," the man said. "I thought I'd get more action from a Warrior Guardian. I'm disappointed."

"Who are you?" Gabe already surmised who it was, yet he waited for confirmation.

"Why, I'm Blake Howard, at your service. Welcome to my home."

Ignoring the introduction, Gabe moved around the room, seeking a way out. He was painfully aware of Blake's pleasure at his capture. With no other recourse, he rammed his head into the celled doorway, which wouldn't budge. He tried again, his head aching from his abuse.

"You cannot escape," Blake said. "This room was built to hold someone such as yourself. I hope your accommodations are to your liking."

Gabe ignored the taunt, continuing to move around his cell, looking for cracks or flaws in the impenetrable stone. He could only hope that Ariel had escaped and had already assessed the situation, hopefully getting help.

"We'll talk again real soon," Blake said. "I've got plans for you."

"Wait..."

The metal lid closed with a click and the lights went out, throwing the room into darkness. But then another noise began, a low sputter. The room began to fill up with a gray substance. Gabe lowered his head to the floor to avoid the obnoxious smells, but already the toxic effects were taking their toll.

He had no idea what was in the fog, but his eyesight diminished, thoughts fuzzy. Dizzily, he slumped over, falling into blackness. His last thought was of Rachel.

****

Rachel was sick of waiting. There was something terribly wrong. Michael should've been back a while ago and he wasn't responding. She moved to the doorway, which led to a vacant hallway with a polished marble floor and elegant furnishings. She returned to the kitchen and coiled by the stove, deciding her next move. She'd been told to leave and find Ace. She couldn't just go if there was trouble, despite orders.

Suddenly, Ariel entered the kitchen, in her human

form, fully dressed in dark attire. The blonde woman's hair had been pulled into a tight bun on top of her head, appearing very disciplined as well as beautiful. Her large blue eyes narrowed in on Rachel.

Rachel lifted her golden head, glaring at the other woman. Every instinct screamed betrayal. "What are you doing here?" She telepathically spoke to Ariel, who ignored the question, running her palm down the sleek steel countertop as if deciding if she'd even bother to answer. Rachel tried to discern Ariel, but her readings were cloudy and mystical, all smoke and mirrors.

Ariel leaned against the counter, crossing her ankles, appearing to be very bored. A moment, she said, "They've gotten Gabe. They also have Michael as well. I'm not sure about the others. It was an ambush, a trap."

"And yet you are here." Rage ran through Rachel. She'd never trusted the other woman, but she never thought Ariel would betray Gabe. Telepathically, she said, "What have you done? Where did you get the clothes?"

"I found them, of course," Ariel responded, glancing at her attire. "You need to leave and go to Ace. I will manage the situation."

Rachel resisted the urge to bite her, but she played out the game of lies. "Not without Gabe and Michael."

"You won't find them, Rachel. They are being held beneath this mansion. You lack the skills and the discipline to succeed. I will take you to Ace, and then I'll figure out our next move."

"No!" Rachel replied. "I am not leaving."

"You're not a warrior." Ariel said, laughing. "What do you think you can do?"

"I might not be a warrior, but I can fight." Rachel

flung her head around, her anger peaking. "I am strong. I might be new to all this, but my instincts are true. Do not doubt my abilities."

Critically, Ariel's gaze slid over Rachel's form, mouth tightening. A wicked gleam entered her eyes, alarming her rival. "Very well, we will see. Perhaps you might be of some use. I think you should change your form. We can hide easier as humans and move around undetected."

"I don't have clothes to wear."

"So, we'll find some."

"Fine," Rachel ignored the obvious warning bells. "Let's get moving."

Chapter Twenty-Seven

With a pounding headache, Gabe opened his eyes, realizing he was now human. Blearily, he scanned the unusual room. Wearing hooded robes and also in their human forms, most of the Ophite's cult members were situated in a circle with the centerpiece, an archaic altar. Against the rear wall, a huge gate hung open, revealing the mouth of a cave. A gray mist funneled out of the open portal, rolling along the ground in an eerie mystical pattern. On both sides of the cave, torches blazed in heated ardor toward the ceiling. A huge marble serpent stood at the helm of the altar, red eyes glittering in the flickering lights. Feathers adorned its body. The statue played tricks on the eyes, appearing alive against the shimmering candlelight.

Gabe hurt all over. His arms and feet were bound in heavy chains. A steel noose hung around his neck, attached to a metal ring in the wall. His chest and feet were bare. Someone had put a pair of dark shorts on him, and he was cold, shivering in the dampness.

No one appeared to notice him. They were congregated in small groups, talking. If he didn't know any better, he would swear it was a party of sorts, a ludicrous celebration. Blake Howard entered the room, and the voices hushed, attention drawn only to him, awe on their countenances. Anticipation filled the air, an expectancy. Also arriving with Blake, several serpents entered, an odd mixture of colors—some solid browns, oranges, or blacks, while others in various diamond or circular patterns.

"Welcome, my brothers and sisters," Blake greeted. He adjusted his red flowing robe. "Tonight is a special night indeed. Please make yourselves comfortable. As you know, we have been waiting for this night for many years. I wasn't sure if it was ever going to come about, but my faith has not failed me. Oh, no. I have been enlightened. I've seen a vision of the future." He threw his head back, a wicked smile cresting his wide mouth. He lowered his eyes to the observers, touching them. "I've seen a vision of perfect harmony and tonight, tonight, my family, we will see a new dawn." He put his hands together, raising them up triumphantly. "A new coming of age."

The ground beneath them trembled as the candlelight wavered, casting shadows against the glistening walls.

A darkly cloaked woman approached with a concealed basket. She set it on the altar and lifted the clasp. She slipped her hands into its debts and brought forth a small, wrapped bundle. Carefully, she sat it in the middle of the altar. The blanket moved and then the head of a small snake emerged. The tiny tongue flickered as it turned its head toward the subdued crowd, then protectively drew back into its covering.

"Prisca," Gabe said beneath his breath. He had never seen one of their kind in an infant form. It was mind blowing. Everything he knew, everything he believed in was being questioned. This child was innocent. She had been stripped of her humanity and her future. Rage surged through him.

Blake walked over to the altar, his eyes riveted on the snake. "She has been a naughty girl. A naughty girl, indeed." His index finger slid over the tiny head. The snake recoiled in response.

"But soon she will know how special she is. I wonder what marvels await her?" He moved away, standing near the cave's entrance. He held out his arms wide and closed his eyes, inhaling deeply. After a pause, he slowly opened his eyelids, revealing murky polished orbs. "Lord Talco comes and so does our sacrifice. She comes."

Another rumble shook the room. The temperature dipped in response. Anomalous crimson radiance filled the mouth of the cave.

Sacrifice? Panic seized Gabe. Who was the sacrifice? And then he knew. It came in a rush. Oh, how could he have been so stupid. He had led them all into a trap.

****

The fact that Ariel knew her way around the mansion did not escape Rachel's notice. The woman was preoccupied, rushing into one of the bedrooms, flicking on a light switch.

"Here, put this on," Ariel said, after rummaging through the closet. She dropped an item on the bed. "It should fit."

"What's this?" Rachel nuzzled the material puddled on the bedspread.

"The best I can do," Ariel said. "There is nothing else in the closet. Now change into your human form and hurry up about it. Time is of the essence."

"Fine," Rachel said. Hatred burned in her heart toward the other woman. It was hard to control her bitterness toward Ariel. There had never been much love between them, but she had tried in the past to put their differences aside. Now she understood just how much Ariel hated her. But did she hate her enough to betray Gabe?

Rachel picked up the snow-colored dress, pivoted around, and moved to the corner of the room. She willed herself into her human form. Chilly air hit her skin as she gathered the dress and slipped it over her head. It fell over her form, sleeveless, silky and form fitting, ending at mid-thigh. It was hardly suitable for their cause. She appeared to be going out to a prom, not on a rescue mission.

Rachel walked to the dresser, opening a small drawer. A mix of scarves, handkerchiefs, and laces were inside. She ripped through the items, finding a pair of panties. She wrinkled her nose. Oh well, desperate is as desperate was. She quickly slid them on.

"I need something for my feet."

"Here." Ariel handed her a pair of pink sneakers. "These should fit."

Again, Rachel doubted Ariel's honesty. The woman was deceitful. But she'd allow the charade to continue if it gave her information as to where Gabe was located. After that, she'd figure out a way to help him and the others.

"Ok. Let's go." She turned to find Ariel watching her, a hint of envy in her gaze. She brushed by her, heading toward the door.

"I will lead," Ariel said, thrusting her way past Rachel. "Follow me."

They traveled back down the rear kitchen staircase. Ariel moved around a corner, hastening through a small hallway. A door stood ajar in the corner, steps visible.

"Another staircase?" Rachel paused. Both Michael and Gabe had overlooked this entranceway. The mansion was obviously a series of mazes and illusions. Anxiety gripped her. They were moving down into the Ophites' lair. She tried calling out to Gabe in her mind. Nothing. She tried Michael and then Ace. Again nothing. She was alone, except for Ariel. Not a reassuring thought.

Ariel entered the stairwell and began to descend.

"I don't like any of this," Rachel whispered, following her. "Something's not right."

"Shush," Ariel replied. "I gave you a choice, and you wouldn't leave. You are going to give us away. Be quiet and just follow me."

"Fine," Rachel replied, resisting the urge to shove the woman down the stairs. "Do you even know where we're going?"

"You babble too much," Ariel said. "You need to just follow orders. I know where I'm going."

Rachel bit back her retort. Ariel enjoyed the powerplay and she wasn't giving her anything more for leverage.

Darkness greeted them at the bottom of the staircase. The air held an electrical current. A cold breeze slid along the glistening limestone floor. It inched along Rachel's exposed skin, chilling her flesh.

Rachel took a second to gain her momentum. Nothing seemed real. Her sense of direction and purpose was off. In her mind, Prisca stirred. Fear. It filled the baby's soul, entering Rachel's consciousness. She grabbed her temples, squeezing her palms against her skin.

"What's wrong with you?" Ariel said. She pivoted around, facing Rachel.

"Something is really wrong," Rachel said. "There is danger all around us."

"What else did you expect?" Ariel said. Her brows dipped together, her mouth twisting into an ugly sneer. "The gifts bestowed on you are all a waste. You have no idea how to use them. You are utterly predictable and a coward."

"Thanks for the vote of confidence," Rachel responded. She shoved her hands to her side. Her anger drove Prisca's fears from her thoughts. "Which way?"

"Right."

They moved down the hallway. Boarded up windows were spaced out every ten feet. Rachel's inner serpent's eyes adjusted in the dark. The walls became glistening limestone, slick and wet with moisture.

"Are we almost there?"

Ariel just glanced over her shoulder, her eyes narrowing in on her nemesis.

Rachel stiffened. Her throat hurt. Chanting filled her thoughts. So odd to hear it only in her mind. It was a ceremony. She was hearing it through Prisca's soul force. The child was close, but something was wrong with the baby. Warning bells slammed her temples, the desire to flee. But it was too late for that now. They had come too far in to abort the mission, and she would see it through.

Ariel moved quicker, her long legs making for an easy stride. "We've got to hurry."

They rounded a corner. The corridor broke into three hallways. Ariel moved farther to the left. The floor began to dip in small increments. The way narrowed. Incense broke the air in a heady, sweet smell of something indiscernible.

Suddenly, Ariel stopped and sniffed the air. She then turned toward Rachel and grabbed her arm to pull her closer. "Come here," she said. "Listen."

Rachel moved close to Ariel, straining her ears for sounds. The ground beneath her trembled ever so slightly. The hallway before them appeared endless. They were deep in the mansion's underbelly. But Gabe was close. He was faintly in her senses.

"I don't like this," she said to Ariel. "None of it. You are blindly leading us into danger. What are you doing? This is wrong!"

"If we leave now, Gabe will die," Ariel said. "So will the child. Is that what you want?"

Ariel's words washed over her, the warning quite clear. She had no doubts now that Ariel had betrayed them, for what reason she had no clue. She kept her emotions in check. It was better that the woman believed she had succeeded with her deception.

"I'm trying to get my bearings," Ariel said, ignoring Rachel. "Just stay still while I concentrate."

Rachel's thoughts scattered. She was alone in this now. She had to quickly figure things out and find Gabe.

"Put your hands against the wall." Ariel grabbed Rachel's right hand, pressing it into the wall. "It's pulsating. Can you feel it?"

Rachel pressed both her palms against the wall. Beneath her skin, vibrations shook her hands. The wall almost seemed alive. Ariel moved in behind her, placing her hands beside Rachel's. Suddenly, Ariel grabbed Rachel's shoulders and shoved her into the wall. Abruptly, the hidden portal opened, sending Rachel spiraling forward. She lost her balance and fell into a heap onto the stone floor. Her long brown hair flung wildly around her face. The voices ceased their relentless chant. The rustling of heavy breath caught her unawares. Slowly, she lifted her face to the fearsome man who stood over her.

"Welcome home, Rachel."

****

When Rachel entered the chamber and fell, all sound ceased. The silence was deafening. She lay at the feet of a cloaked man. Finally, she lifted her head, horrified by his scented familiarity with her nightmares. She yanked her dress over her thighs, very aware of the curious and elated Ophites in the cavity.

Blake Howard smiled. It wasn't a nice smile, but one of a mocking quality.

Terror struck Rachel's heart as her memories traveled to the past. Suddenly, she remembered being a young girl again and the boogie man who had been real. She couldn't place the man's face or his name, but she remembered his scent. In that moment, she knew she'd forgotten this man on purpose, her only way of dealing with her fears.

Confused, Rachel slowly stood. All eyes beneath the many hoods focused on her in greedy anticipation. On the altar, she saw the tiny snake—Prisca—or what was left of the baby. The serpent sat coiled, void of movement. Deep within her, Prisca's life force stirred at the recognition of her physical form.

Sympathy for the small beast swelled inside her, but Rachel squashed it down. Now was not the time for getting emotional. Her eyes fell over the hushed crowd.

She sensed Gabe before she saw him, instinctively locating him at the rear of the room. Gabe's strong naked shoulders were pressed against the wall, held there by a neck chain. In his human form, he wore only shorts and appeared utterly defeated. His bleary eyes spoke volumes.

"Gabe." The name escaped her before she could catch it.

Gabe's gaze fused to hers, anger and fear interchanging within seconds. They were in deep trouble, and both knew it.

Rachel searched for Ariel in the room, furious at the guardian's obvious betrayal. She called out telepathically to the blonde guardian, but the woman was gone or at least in hiding, perhaps even cloaked. Unsuccessfully, she tried telepathically connecting to Gabe, Michael, and Ace.

If only she had listened to her inner sense of unease about Ariel. But she had been so caught up in her mission and Gabe, she had ignored her instincts.

Rachel jerked around, facing the man intently watching her. His dark eyes glowed feverishly in the lamplight.

"Who are you?"

"Don't you know me?" A smirk crested his full lips, deepening the grooves in the corners of his mouth.

"Should I?"

Yes, yes, yes, Rachel's mind screamed. She did know him. It was coming in glimpses. Fear rose steadily. She fought down her panic. Now was not the time to fall apart.

"My name is Blake Howard."

"And that means what to me?" He was the

mansion's owner and the one who stole Prisca. But hearing his voice pricked her mind so she remained impassive. Better to play along.

"Still nothing?"

"The fact that your name holds nothing significant to me speaks volumes."

Blake's smirk froze. His brows lowered as he considered her.

"And you've got a mouth on you," Blake replied. "I was hoping for more charm and grace. But knowing your mother, what else could I expect?"

"You knew my mother?"

"I know your mother," Blake replied, shrugging.

Blood pounded against Rachel's skull. Memories came rushing back as the dam that concealed them broke free. Fragments and pieces filled her thoughts, her mother frantically packing their bags one day. The woman had been terrified. She'd begged her mother not to move again. Blake Howard's face swam in her memories. He'd looked the same, hardly aging. As a small child she remembered him showing up, examining her as if she were an exotic insect, but her mother had never called him Blake. She called him Mr. Howard. After he'd left, her mother referred to him as "That Beast." After that they were always on the run, living in different motels, houses, and even shelters.

"I remember you," she said. The words were barely a whisper in the silent room. "What do you want from me?"

Blake laughed. It was a chilling sound, not a true cackle, but a snarl of sorts.

"My dear, dear Rachel. You surprise me with your bravery. You've become more than I expected and yet you could be so much more with a bit of guidance."

"From you?" Her brow lifted. She stilled her own mocking laughter.

"Perhaps."

"No thanks," she said, crossing her arms defiantly. "I can only fear what someone like you could teach me. You have stolen a baby and have torn her from her soul force. What type of man is capable of such a thing?" Her chin lifted a notch. "You need to give me Prisca. Now!"

His eyes darkened considerably, seemingly ember chips.

"I've reached my patience with you, Rachel," Blake said, moving closer to look into her eyes. "Your interference with Prisca has set my schedule back. But it also has had its rewards. My plans have changed, and I have you to thank for that, my girl."

Something rumbled beneath Rachel's feet. A gust of air stirred the torches. She turned to look at the mouth of the cave. Uncannily, it gave off a bizarre light. Somewhere off to her left, shadows moved against the walls—evil spirits, watching and waiting.

A shaman stepped across her field of vision. He began to chant softly beneath his breath. He held a gilded scepter of a coiled serpent, which was entwined with vines.

"Tonight, you have fulfilled your destiny, my daughter," Blake said.

"I am not your daughter." Rachel's heart thudded in her chest, the word daughter biting deep. Inwardly, she knew the truth and had always known it, but she had hidden it away in her memories, so far back that she had forgotten it ever existed.

"I have chosen my path," she said, defying him. "I have made my choices. I walk with the light. Leave me be. You have no hold over me."

"Ah, spoken like a true beast. You intrigue me, daughter. I have been watching you from afar, as I have all my children. And you have not failed to disappoint me. In fact, you have made me proud in many ways. You have only begun to tap into your powers. But sadly, you have chosen another path, thrown away your chance to become invincible. And all for what—to save a few humans not worth saving. They are like insects. They're born. They die. More come along. All born to folly. So, don't speak to me of this path you're on. It's an illusion to make yourself feel important. It's a lie. You will gain nothing for your troubles but grief." He paused, rubbing his hands together. "Think of this night as your intervention. As your father, I am stepping in and changing your course. Tonight, my daughter, tonight you will begin a new one."

Rachel froze at his remarks. Terror gripped her soul as his words slid like molten lava over her. Again, the walls trembled. Electricity snapped in the air.

"He comes." Blake closed his eyes, lifted his chin, and smiled. Inhaling, he opened his eyes, now blacker than ever.

"Who is coming?" Rachel hated the fear in her voice.

"Lord Talco," Blake said. "He comes not for Prisca as you have supposed, but for you, Rachel. He has chosen you, my precious daughter, to be his for all eternity. You have been given a great honor."

"No." Darkness pressed against her temples. Icy fingers held her in its grasp.

"Prisca was merely bait," Blake continued. "After all, she is your sister. It was only natural that you share a kinship with your own bloodline. I will continue with my plans for my newest daughter. You will release Prisca's soul force to rejoin her physical form. She will be carefully raised and guided as you should have been. But this time, it will be by me."

"No," Rachel said. "You have no right to interfere in my life or hers. You don't own me or choose my path. I do."

"Nevertheless, you will accept this gift. You have no choice."

Helplessly, Rachel glanced at Gabe. His eyes reflected her fear as he strained against his bindings. She tried to reach him in her mind but was met with a blank wall.

"He can't help you," Blake said, noting her regard. "No one can."

Rachel gazed around at the sea of faces. Glowing eyes reflected the lamplight. There was no help in the crowd. She couldn't fight them all, not alone. Even her serpent would lose.

She stared up at the ceiling. Where were the other Guardians? Why wouldn't they come?

"They have been defeated," Blake said, matter of fact.

"You can read my thoughts?"

"Of course, daughter. I have been inside your mind since you were a child. Perhaps you thought of me as the boogey man or that persistent chill you could never really shake. You and I are connected." Blake stroked her cheek. "Such a pretty girl."

Rachel jerked her head away. Blake began to chant

beneath his breath. Serpents and human hybrids began to chant with him. The words were foreign to her, but then they made sense as for some reason she could understand them. It was a welcoming ceremony. The ancient verses were chanted—praises and promises of devotion. Feeling sick, Rachel spun around, looking for an escape. The wall she originally entered was now blocked by several serpents.

Blake seized her arm, drawing her against him.

"I have made my choice," she said, struggling against his hold. "You cannot undo what I have committed. I am a guardian. My path is set. I have chosen light."

"So, you have," he agreed. "Now you will choose again."

"Never."

With a flip of his hand, Blake pulled her back against his chest, arm across her throat, facing her toward the crowd. A wall portal opened, and two cloaked figures entered the room, dragging a woman between them. One of the female's shoes were missing and her bloody foot was swollen and bruised. The woman's hair hung stringy down her narrow back.

"Let me go," the woman said, struggling against their hands. She snapped her head to one side, trying to bite her captor's finger.

"Mom," Rachel said weakly. Raw emotion held her rapt. She found her voice again, only louder. "Mom?"

At first her mother didn't respond, so intent was she on berating the pair. They ignored her antics, bringing her to stand before Blake. Finally, Leah's eyes fell upon Rachel.

"Rachel," her mother said. All life drained from the

woman's features. Instantly, she paled, her resistance at an end. "You are part of this?"

"Not exactly," Rachel said. Shock and bitter emotions swept over her. It had been years since she had seen her mother. Wild eyed, her mother was thin, sweaty, and shaky. Old hurt filled Rachel with intense pain. And yet, she had the urge to throw herself into her mother's arms for comfort and swear her undying love, beg for forgiveness for some unimaginable sin she'd committed that caused her mother to hate her so. She had learned long ago, there was nothing worse than a parent's abandonment. Her mother had failed her. Failed Stacey. She blinked away the tears that gathered.

"Hello, Leah," Blake said against Rachel's ear, facing his former conquest. "The years have not been kind to you."

"Well, I see you look the same," Leah spat. "Apparently, the years are overly kind to you. Why am I not surprised? You've sold your soul to the devil."

Blake laughed beneath his breath. "Just as mouthy and just as foolish. I don't know what I was thinking picking you to bear one of my children."

Anger lit Leah's eyes. She stared at Rachel, shaking her head. "Oh, Rachel. How could you have been so blind to have trusted this man?"

"Trusted him?" Rachel shook her head at the assumption. "Is he…really my father?"

"Yes."

Rachel knew the truth in her heart but had hoped for a miracle. She felt nothing for the beast behind her. No kinship. No bond.

"You should have told me," Rachel said. "You had no right to hold this information from me."

"How could I have told you that your daddy here wanted to raise you for his own vile purposes? I protected you as best as I could, never knowing if you were going to turn into one of those beasts. He followed us, chased us down on any whim. He could read my mind." Leah lifted her hands in defeat. "I took drugs to keep him out. Confuse him."

"Stupid woman," Blake said." Do you honestly think that it worked?"

"Yes. It worked, didn't it?" Leah's chin rose defiantly. "You couldn't find us."

"My charges had no trouble finding you in the streets, woman. Here you stand before me. Here is my daughter, coming home when I needed her most."

Leah's face paled.

Rachel jerked out of Blake's arms, facing both her parents. The two cloaked women grabbed Leah's arms again, steadying her.

"I don't care who you are," Rachel said to Blake. "You are nothing to me. Let us go."

"No, Rachel. I don't think so. See, you have been promised to Lord Talco. He comes for you, and he's got quite a temper if he doesn't get his way."

"I will not go with him."

Blake paused, considering her. He nodded to one of the cloaked women. With a jerk of her hand, the woman pulled out a knife, holding it against Leah's throat.

"No," Rachel said. The sight was chilling. As much as she detested her mother, her heart gave a painful thump. "Let her go."

"Your life for hers," Blake said. "Lord Talco will not be denied."

Panic pressed into her thoughts. Rachel stared at the dribble of blood that flowed from Leah's throat, whose eyes had filled with terror.

"How do I know you won't kill her anyway?" Rachel fought for precious minutes, hoping for a plan or a solution but nothing came to mind. The noose tightened around her neck.

The knife bit Leah's throat. "I will give you ten seconds, daughter, and she will be dead. You can either do it my way or yours."

Leah panted, catching her breath. "He will probably kill me anyway, Rachel. So do what you will."

Somewhere off, Gabe shouted, "No, don't do it."

"And Prisca?"

"She is my daughter. However, I will give her a reprieve for a time so she can have a childhood."

"You beast," Leah shouted. "How can you betray your own daughter?"

The chanting that eerily continued grew in pitch. Energy filled the room. More shadows drifted along the walls.

"Make your pact with me, Rachel," Blake ordered. "I want your vow. Five seconds. I don't have all night."

The cloaked woman grabbed Leah's hair, dragging her head back against her shoulder. Leah gasped, swallowing hard. More blood flowed.

"Don't do it, Rachel," her mother said. "He will kill me anyway. I've lived my life. I've been a terrible mother. I'm not afraid to die."

Her words drew bitter emotions inside Rachel.

"I don't want you to die," Rachel said. She turned toward Blake, shoulders slumped. "I...I will do as you ask."

"Your word, daughter." Blake said.

"You have my word," Rachel repeated.

"Take Leah away," Blake said to the cloaked women. "Back to the barn."

"No," Leah screamed as she was dragged away. "Don't do it, Rachel. Don't do it." Her cries mixed with Gabe's as they herded her from the room.

Blake grabbed Rachel's arm, pulling her toward the altar. Prisca was no longer on the slab. Blake turned Rachel around, pushing her down onto the stone. She sat down hard, stunned by how quickly she had lost this battle. She should have listened to Gabe, not rushed into this situation. Now she had lost Prisca, her mother, and Gabe. Who knew what would happen to them? And as for her? She swallowed painfully.

The shaman approached, eyes glowing in the lamplight. His painted face glistened with moisture. In his hands, he held a goblet. He slid it into Rachel's hands. "Drink this, child."

The icy metal cup burned Rachel's skin. The liquid inside was dark, cold. The scent was something foreign. Ancient.

"What is it?"

"Herbs, rare spices, and honey."

Rachel didn't believe him. She sought Gabe in her mind. Still nothing. But Blake looked at her, then at Gabe. How he could read her thoughts without her knowledge baffled her. He frowned, moving in front of her. "Stop your musings. You will forget all about him in time."

Would she? What a depressing thought.

"Drink it, Rachel," her father said. He grabbed her hand, putting the cup to her lips. "I will bring back your mother and kill her in front of you. Then you will free Prisca's soul force or I shall feed her to Lord Talco. And I will kill your love—Gabe. Now drink. Your fate comes for you."

Rachel doubted her father would kill Prisca, a potential victim to his schemes. But her mother? Yes. Gabe, yes. She closed her eyes and drank. The drink was both sweet and bitter. It swirled on her tongue like liquid fire, burning a path down her throat. She felt strange, dizzy. The torches began to dance, tiny faces beckoning from within. Brilliant light emanated from the cave, colors she couldn't recognize or describe. The room grew hazy as her mind disconnected.

Prisca's soul trembled as the shaman ordered Rachel to release her. She had little time to reason it out as her mind began to fade. Blindness overtook her. Everything appeared foggy. Her voice failed as she tried to speak. Was she babbling? Confused, she stopped resisting, slumping against the altar.

Somewhere came a commotion. Gabe's voice yelled at her but was cut off. Chanting filled the room. Rachel felt herself being lifted and moved onto the slab. Helplessly, she lay face up beneath the stone serpent. Its red eyes cut through her muddled vision, staring at her with unbridled eagerness. But then Rachel blinked. Did it move? But that was crazy.

Something cool touched upon her forehead as a finger created the symbol of the serpent upon her brow. Blake Howard stood over her, his eyes black and soulless.

Rumbling came from the cave's entrance. Dust from the ceiling sprayed down upon her. She tried again to speak, but her words were mute. The room grew colder. In a dormant state, she struggled to keep her thoughts focused.

A low guttural sound came from the mouth of the cave. The arriving beast spoke power. Fear held Rachel in its grasp. Lord Talco was coming.

The chanting reached its crescendo. Suddenly, it ceased. Silence gripped the room in a penetrating state and then a shift of movement. Her father's face disappeared. Her vision cleared though she was helpless to move.

Suddenly, a huge serpent's face appeared, but it was unlike any serpent she had ever encountered. An albino. The beast was completely white with red glowing eyes. His long fangs gleamed in the lamplight. A yellow crescent scar of a moon stood on the snake's forehead. He reeked of dirt, lime, and of ancient embers. His form was taut, muscled, and in some respects beautiful.

Then the beast spoke. "Mine." Its tongue flicked out, touching Rachel's cheek. She tried to scream, but her mouth fell open in muted terror. She barely felt the beast as it opened its huge mouth and picked her up like a rag doll. She hung from its mouth, the silent observers now upside down. For a moment, she saw Gabe crumpled on the floor in a heap. Inwardly, she cried out to him. No response.

The atmosphere changed as they entered the cave. The light hurt her eyes. She struggled to see against its brilliance. Then they began to move. Down. Down. Down. Darkness overcame her. Rachel drifted off to sleep.

Chapter Twenty-Eight

The horror of watching Rachel being carried off by the freakish beast would haunt him forever. Gabe struggled to his feet, fighting his bindings. He tried to shift into his serpent but failed. They had done something to him.

Rachel appeared so lifeless and helpless and then she was gone, disappearing into the mouth of the cave. The cavern's entrance grew obscured as the fog receded. It changed into stone, becoming just a part of the walls. The only sign that a cave had ever existed was the large iron gate that still hung open.

Gabe cursed himself as a fool for not being more careful. What a protector he'd turned out to be. Rachel was gone, and it was his fault. He'd failed in his mission to rescue Prisca and in the process lost Rachel, maybe forever. It was hard to wrap his mind around what'd happened.

Voices began conversing in the room. Blake began shaking hands with the people in attendance, who then exited into the corridor. Apparently, congratulations were in order and a huge celebration was to follow. Two Ophites closed the gates across where the cave once stood, locking it with a huge padlock. One of the men handed the key to Blake.

After a few minutes, six hooded figures were the only ones in attendance. Blake approached Gabe. It was hard to fathom the now unassuming man had such an evil heart.

"You've witnessed quite a feat tonight, my boy," Blake said, rubbing his hands together. "I suppose I have you and your friends to thank for my successful mission. You've brought Rachel right to my doorstep, and I can't thank you enough."

"You're going to rot in hell one day," Gabe replied. Blake's eyes were now blue, and he appeared smug. "Where is Rachel? What's that thing going to do with her?"

"Rachel will serve Lord Talco all the days of her life. If she pleases him, he might allow her to live. If not…" Blake paused, then shrugged. "I have never been to Lord Talco's mystical realm. I heard it's magnificent. Perhaps you should envy Rachel for making such a wise choice. She might charm him."

"Choice!" Gabe repeated. "She had no choice. You gave her none." He struggled against his bindings, willing his serpent to come forth, but he didn't have the ability. "She was your daughter!"

"I have had many daughters," Blake said. "Though most disappoint me. But have no fear; I will father more." He paused, studying Gabe. "I can see why Rachel was attracted to one such as you and the love she holds in her heart. I do believe she might've joined our cause if not for her pining away for your absent love. In time, you will become a distant memory to her, a dream of sorts, but alas, you've fulfilled your purpose. I have no further use for you." Blake nodded to his cloaked comrades. "Take him away."

Surrounded by the six guards, Gabe was then released from his bonds. Strong hands gripped his biceps as the Ophites surrounded him, ensuring his compliance. For now, he'd play along. Desperately, he sought out Rachel telepathically, but she was lost, seemingly as far away as another galaxy. The pain in his heart stabbed as fiercely as any blade ever could.

The guards forced Gabe down the long stone corridor. The way then opened, walls and floor now concrete. Moving in front of a doorway, one of the guards opened the gated entry with a key. Gabe was thrust inside a small chamber. The room held a narrow cot with a blanket at the foot. The cell fell into darkness as the door was secured.

For several minutes, Gabe assessed the gate's strength. His shoulder grew sore from his efforts. Once again, he called to his inner serpent. No response. What drug had Blake given him to force his serpent into seclusion? He couldn't reach Michael or any of the guardians. Were any of them even alive? He had no way of knowing.

Gabe tried to reach Ariel but once again he'd been blocked. On purpose? He could only wonder. How good his hands would feel around her throat. How dare she abandon them all? Why hadn't he sensed the evil intentions within her? He had to admit, he had been preoccupied with Rachel and her plight. He had allowed his emotions to control him instead of his common sense. Now he was alone, unsure of his warriors' whereabouts. And Rachel…he swallowed hard. Who knew what she was facing now? He lifted his gaze toward the ceiling. They needed divine help but even that seemed impossible from the bowels of the mansion. His lack of faith shook him to his core.

Throwing himself down onto the cot, Gabe ran his

hands through his hair. *Think, Gabe. Think.* He had to find a way to escape and somehow save Rachel. But how?

Chapter Twenty-Nine

Time ceased. There was no way to know just how long she had been in Lord Talco's realm. They were deep inside the earth, somewhere far below the surface. Although there was no light source, the walls gleamed in a bright rose-colored sheen. It was incredibly beautiful. Magical. But Rachel found little joy in her surroundings.

She had been left alone in a large chamber. A hot spring bubbled in the middle of the room, surrounded by marble statues of fairies and snakes. Marble benches faced the pool in a three-tier pattern. Everything in the room had been carved in exotic patterns of animals, flowers, and vines. A doorway led to a bedroom of sorts. But the bed had also been carved from marble, glistening against the vibrant colors of the walls. A soft fleece was draped over the bottom of the bed.

Rachel struggled with her memory and any sense of time. Her brain was foggy and listless, unassuming. There was only one doorway leading from the chamber. It remained open for now, although it was guarded. When she regained her panicked bid for freedom, she had tried to leave the portal but had come face to face with a huge serpent, who spied on her every movement with malevolent eyes. Like Lord Talco, this serpent was also white but held flecks of gray along its spine. Just being near the creature, she trembled.

She was lost, spiritually, mentally, and physically. Rachel had no sense of direction. Her inner serpent was in a dormant state, and she felt oddly alone and helpless. The cold and desolation became her only friend. She would need her serpent if she ever had a chance to escape. Without her alter ego, she was powerless.

She both feared and yet anticipated Lord Talco's visit. He never spoke to her and for the most part just observed her. If it was a mind game of control, to break her down, he was surely winning for she was losing herself—her sense of being, her free will. Her thoughts were scattered and then would abruptly focus, blindsiding her. It was like a nightmare, repeating over and over again, never to wake up.

When Lord Talco entered in human form, Rachel recoiled in shock. And what a form it was. His skin was translucent and pale, so pale that the veins beneath his skin were branchlike and vividly blue. His hair was snowy white, flowing and curled over his bared shoulders. The tips of his whimsical ears were barely noticeable, but still caught her regard. His eyebrows were just as colorless. His eyes were the most shocking of all, crimson with chips of black in their midst. His being spoke of power and esteem. Neither fat nor thin, Lord Talco was lean with skin smooth as glass. He wore black leggings and boots. It was hard not to look at him for he was stunning. There was something that drew her to him.

His presence evoked her fears of the unknown. She hated her vulnerability, her desire to run and hide or just to beg for mercy. How pathetic she'd become, so weak and frail. But without her inner serpent's assurances, she indeed felt extremely human.

"Rachel," Lord Talco greeted. "I see you're awake." His eyes slid possessively over her form.

Rachel trembled beneath his examination. Something about his predatory eyes chilled her to the bone. She gazed down at the golden gown she wore. Someone had dressed her in the finery from what appeared another era, although she couldn't be sure. The material was silk, soft to her skin. It hung to the floor, hiding her bare feet.

"What do you want from me?"

Talco didn't answer, still studying her. He drew his head back and inhaled the air around her. "Like honey."

Rachel swallowed hard.

He returned to staring at her, expression void of any emotion. Finally, he reached out and grabbed her around the throat, dragging her toward him. Slowly, he turned her head from side to side, fingers digging into her jawbone. His eyes gleamed with pleasure.

"Interesting, child. You intrigue me."

"Please, let me go."

He ignored her plea. Again, he smelled the air around her face. One finger bit deep into her neck, finding her pulse.

"There you are, my naughty, girl." He grinned. "Your serpent is angry with me."

His words came as a shock. She feared her serpent had deserted her.

"So, you are wondering where your serpent has gone?"

She froze, barely moving. He had read her thoughts. Read her fears.

"She's partially asleep," he said. "Drugged and

dreaming. She will eventually return to you, hungry and wanting her freedom. I will be extremely happy to assist her in her efforts."

"What do you mean?"

He released her. Her throat ached from his hold.

"I want your serpent's powers, Rachel. And you are going to give them to me."

"What do you mean?"

"You have rich Mana in your veins, child. Your gifts have barely been tapped. You have no use for them anymore." He reached out, trailing a long finger down her cheek. "You will give your powers over to me. You can do it willingly, or I will simply take them."

"I don't understand."

"When your serpent is allowed to awaken, she will seek the moonlight and want revenge but as soon as she breaks free, I will possess her powers. Think of it as food for my soul and you are going to feed me. I will have your serpent's essence, and she and I will become one."

"No!" she said. "You can't have her. You can't have us." Although her words were spoken in defiance, Rachel was terrified by his assertions. He planned to steal her serpent, and she was powerless to stop him.

"If you survive the process, perhaps you will live for a time. It matters not. You can only survive here for a short while. The climate is not kind to humans. Without your serpent, you can never return to the surface world. The elements..." He shook his head, clucking his tongue. "The cold alone will hasten your demise. But in your death, know that your serpent's power will live onward and a part of you will live on through me, enjoying the power and the beauty that you've never found for yourself. Your supremacy will at least be able to reach its fullest potential."

"You can't have her," she said, stepping away from him. "My serpent and I are one and part of one another. We will not separate or give you anything. This I can attest."

He laughed, showing the first bit of emotion she'd witnessed.

"You can't stop me," Lord Talco said. "But you can cause yourself needless pain in the process." He moved toward the doorway, then glanced over his shoulder. "You need not tell me when your serpent awakens. I will already know when she stirs. You can't keep hiding her inside for much longer. It won't be hard to provoke your alter ego. I am eager to see her in all her glory and then take what's rightfully mine."

"You have no rights to her!" Rachel cried, but he was already exiting the room. Numb, she walked over to one of the benches and slumped down. Her head fell easily into her hands as her tears flowed. What was she going to do? All was quiet within her. But it was only a matter of time when she merged with her serpent.

And there was nothing she could do to stop it.

Chapter Thirty

Inside his bedroom, Blake undressed and pulled on his blue satin robe. It was almost dawn, but he wasn't tired. He'd never felt more alive. Exhilaration raced in his veins. What a rush. Never had a ritual progressed so smoothly. The ancient ways of the Ophites had not failed him. He had spent years studying a way to break the guardians' protective hold over hybrid serpent children, shattering the boundaries of their free will. Past spells had failed, miserably so. Most teenagers who'd chosen the path of the guardian never returned to the way of the shadowy world. Except for Rachel. She was now a defector. Her Mana ran deeper than any of his prior children, her connection to the ancient queen as bright as a candle in the darkest of nights. She was priceless. He almost regretted handing her over to Lord Talco, but he had made a vow, a promise. To betray the powerful lord would've meant war, which would only have led to the demise of his way of life. Besides, he'd been rewarded accordingly, and all was not lost—he still had Prisca.

How was the little brat faring?

Leaving his bedroom, Blake walked down the hallway to the nursery. All was quiet except the clock ticking in the foyer. He entered Prisca's bedroom, attention drawn to the glass enclosed bassinet. The warm lighting lit the room in soft hues.

Mary, his daughter's current nursemaid, was asleep in the rocker, hands folded across her abundant abdomen. A slight wheeze escaped her gaping mouth.

Blake ignored her, glancing into the baby's enclosure. A frown marred his features. The baby was still in her serpent form. Why hadn't she changed back into a human? The shaman had performed the ritual and had said it would happen.

"Wake up, woman," he said, tapping Mary on the shoulder. The nanny was mortal, loyal and efficient in the care of children. Or so he had thought. She leaped in the chair, almost upsetting it.

"I'm sorry, sir," Mary said, features fearful. "I must have fallen asleep."

"You think?" He shook his head. "Why is there no heating lamp over my child? She is still in her serpent form. She needs warmth. Perhaps that's why she hasn't changed."

"I was told she would probably return to her human form by dawn." She looked at her watch. "I thought she'd cry and that would wake me. It's five thirty and still nothing. She's been rather quiet, much like before."

"Indeed. I will seek counsel," Blake said. "Let me know the moment anything changes. And for God sakes, put the heating lamp on her. She must be kept warm." He touched the serpent's head. It snapped its tiny jaw, hissing.

"You little brat," he said, jerking his hand away. "We will see who is hissing at whom."

With that, he stormed out of the room to seek out the shaman to demand answers.

Chapter Thirty-One

For what seemed like eternity, Gabe waited in his cell. He was given food and water but wouldn't trust the fare. They could be poisoning him or even giving him the same toxin which was preventing him from altering into his serpent's form. Now he was weak and sickly. His belly had ceased its rumblings and constantly ached.

His jailors came into his room in pairs, mostly nonchalant hybrids. He sensed their serpents within and their eagerness to provoke a battle with him, often through taunts. They left disappointed as he remained impassive.

Twice a day, Gabe was escorted down the hallway to a latrine. He took the opportunity to seek out telepathically the other guardians, hoping it was only the impenetrable walls that prevented him from doing so but so far, no luck. He had no idea how anyone had fared or if they were even alive. Hopefully, a few had escaped. And Ariel...he frowned, anger burning deep. He had no idea what was to be done with her—he had so many decisions to make.

One of his captors, a man with a shaggy beard provoked him the most. Deliberately, the burly guard would shove the tray of food into the room, so it'd spill out onto the floor, not that it mattered anyway, because Gabe refused to eat. But now he was growing weaker and losing weight. He couldn't keep this up for much longer.

Perhaps that was what Blake Howard intended, a mind game. Gabe had to wonder why the leader hadn't just killed him outright. What was Blake waiting for? Surely, he hadn't intended on allowing him to ever leave or to uphold any promises to Rachel.

In the middle of the fourth night, Gabe woke up drenched in sweat. He'd been dreaming and floating beneath the stars. It'd been peaceful, the moon bright above him. He longed for Rachel, missing her more by the hour. Where was she and what terror did she endure?

Then the first wave of pain hit him like a piercing blade. It shocked him as he gasped for breath. He doubled over, falling to his knees. After a few seconds, it struck again. His gut wrenched, knotting his insides. His skin was on fire, slowly burning along his limbs. Then he understood—his serpent was awakening and now restless. It demanded release, and he felt the powerful beast beneath his flesh. The pain along his spine was terrible, his bones throbbing. Bile filled his throat and incredible thirst. His vision was off, blurry, and then became sharp.

Gabe lay on the floor, curled into a ball. The agony was excruciating. His thoughts dimmed as his serpent's temper simmered, finding no release.

"I'm sick," Gabe called out to the guards. His voice was weak. "I am dying, and I need help."

"Think anyone cares?" one of the guards barked through the bars.

Gabe groaned, rolling onto his side. He began to throw up bile. Then a strangle cry roared from his throat. The noise was enough to reach his jailors. The door opened as two guards entered. One of the guards nudged Gabe with his foot, evoking a moan from the younger man.

"Come on, get to your feet," the larger guard said. He reached down, grabbing Gabe by the armpits, lifted and shoved him against the wall.

The jarring thud of his body connecting with the stone wall was the last straw. Gabe's serpent roared to life, angry, hungry and in a terrible state. It wanted to survive. Within seconds, his clothing ripped to shreds as he altered. A low guttural sound escaped his throat. His serpent thundered to life with only one goal—freedom. The starving beast's thirst for the night sky was boundless. Before either guard could react, Gabe's serpent grabbed the larger of the two by his head, smashing him into the cot. His tail whipped around, knocking the shorter guard off his feet. With a twist, he grabbed the shorter guard by the leg and hurled him onto the other fallen jailor. Both men began to change into serpents, but before they could succeed, Gabe exited the enclosure, closing the gate. The guards were now locked in the cell.

In a flash, Gabe moved down the hallway. Around a corner, a narrow staircase led upward. He moved up the stairs and found the door ajar. It was dark and quiet. He slithered into what appeared to be a library. Moonlight created a crisscross pattern on the plush carpet. He moved beneath the beams, feeling his energy renewing within. He tucked his head against the large bay window. In the courtyard below, Ariel's serpent met his regard, a bundled cloth inside her mouth.

"The rear kitchen door is open," Ariel said

telepathically. "Hurry."

He didn't stop to think about Ariel's betrayal. So many questions filtered in his brain. This too could be a trap, but he had little choice. He'd have to trust her in the moment.

Gabe exited the library. With his size, it was almost impossible not to make any noise. He moved through the hallways and found the kitchen. The rear door was unlocked and slightly open. Once again, he hesitated. If Ariel were betraying him, he'd make her pay; that much he knew for certain. And in the mood he was in, he'd welcome the fight.

Across the lawn, Ariel waited in the shadows. He followed her into the darkness.

****

When Gabe caught up to Ariel, they were miles away from the mansion. They stopped in an area which was secluded, overgrown, and held rocky terrain.

"What have you done, Ariel?" Gabe coiled before her, his temper at its peak. "You have betrayed all of us. You've betrayed Rachel and the other guardians."

Her serpent's eyes glowed feverishly. She dropped the mesh bag before him. "Have I? You see I have Prisca."

"At the cost of Rachel's life," he said. "You left all of us. I should kill you for what you have done."

Ariel hissed at him, stretching out her gilded neck, staring him down. "You know nothing, Gabe. I have betrayed no one. Your precious Rachel is alive."

He stiffened at her words. "How do you know that?"

"Let's get to a safer place," she replied. "They have just discovered Prisca is missing. They will be trying to find her."

"What about Michael and the others?"

"They are being held captive in an underground location just north of the mansion, but for the most part, they remain unharmed. Several escaped but were injured and are now in healing. Follow me."

Ariel picked up the sack and fled up a rocky slope. He had no choice but to follow for now. But he had his doubts. With little recourse, he fought the flicker of hope that burned within his soul. Dare he hope Rachel was still alive?

They traveled through Berks County, heading north toward Allentown. Ariel led him to an old abandon hospital. Although it was overgrown and held a few broken windows, the brick foundation was strong.

Ariel lifted off a grate that covered a basement window and dropped inside, her form scraping the window's edge. Gabe followed her, plunging onto the concrete floor. There were many rooms in the basement and a few remnants of hospital equipment. They traveled through the basement, reaching the morgue.

Once inside the area, Ariel shut the metal door. She placed the sack down on an old gurney. "I have supplies here," she said. "Clothes and food. Prisca will be reunited with her mother."

"Her mother?"

"Yes. I brought Lustra here. Prisca's serpent is dying, and we need to move her to a secure location. She's near death, and without Prisca you will never see your precious Rachel again."

"Why should I believe anything you say? You've yet to explain yourself." Gabe moved toward the table, grabbed the sack with his mouth, and opened it. Inside the tiny golden snake lay limp. Gently, he nudged her with his snout. So cold. So lifeless. He lifted his head, angry and demanding. "Start talking. I'm not going anywhere with you without answers."

"Very well." She moved away from him, securing the room. "Rachel is alive. Your fear of her demise is unfounded."

"How can you say that? You saw that thing that took her. She gave up her freedom to save us all."

"Rachel gave up nothing," Ariel hissed into his mind. "Her mission was to save Prisca, and she did. She fulfilled her vow."

Gabe's teeth gnashed together, tail whipping in anger. "Prisca is still a serpent. Her human side is gone, and her serpent is dying. So tell me Ariel, how exactly did Rachel benefit in forfeiting her life and her freedom? A life in hell with that beast?"

"No," she said, lifting her head. "I also had a mission and have fulfilled it. I was sent to join the Ophites' cause. Although my feelings about Rachel are well known, I found little to rejoice in my betrayal. Mine is not to question but to do a guardian's bidding. Rachel's sacrifice saved Prisca's life."

"Bah! I can't believe a word you are saying."

"You have lost your faith. There is always a reason for what occurs. You have been blindsided and have forgotten who you are."

"Perhaps," he said. "But now I am questioning things."

"I know that." Ariel hissed, shaking her tail. "We all have doubts at times."

"I heard you come in," a soft voice spoke, breaking into their conversation. Lustra stood in the entranceway, eyes on the tiny serpent. She rushed to the tiny beast, gently picking up the limp form. She cuddled Prisca close to her chest, holding her against her skin. She turned toward Ariel, "Is she alive?"

Ignoring her, Ariel slithered out of the room. "Your clothing is in the other room," she said into Gabe's mind. "Mine is upstairs. I will dress and return in my human form."

Frustrated, Gabe left Lustra and Prisca, moving into another room. On an old cot sat a duffel bag. Inside he found jeans, a dark cotton shirt, boxers, and a jacket. A pair of socks and boots completed the assembly. He changed into his human form, dressing.

When he returned to the morgue, Ariel was also human, dressed in similar clothing. He could barely stand the sight of their betrayer. He paused, watching the woman interact with Prisca and Lustra.

"You are the only one Prisca responds to," Ariel said to Lustra. "You are her only hope. You must reach through the barrier she has created within and bring her back to you. Keep her close to your heart. She also needs your warmth."

"Please, baby girl..." Lustra's eyes filled with tears. "Don't die on Mama."

"Let her hear your voice," Ariel said. "Do whatever is necessary to make her feel safe. When she is stronger, she needs to be taken into the vortex. Only then will she have a chance to recover."

"You need to give me better answers," Gabe said, assessing Ariel. "You've much to answer for."

"I will answer your questions, Gabe, after we get Prisca in a better state." Ariel grabbed a chair, sliding it closer to Lustra. "Here, sit with her."

"She is so cold," Lustra said. "Please come back to me, Prisca. I love you. Whatever your future holds, I will be here for you. I swear it." She slid her finger over the serpent's head, humming softly.

"See," Ariel said. "She is already responding to her mother's touch." A pleased smile touched her lips. It disappeared upon seeing Gabe's frown.

****

Outside of the abandoned hospital, Gabe kept watch over the entranceway, leading to where Prisca and Lustra were snuggled together. Next to him was a bag of food, the only good thing he could thank Ariel for remembering. He was weak and had lost weight. He needed his strength for whatever lay ahead. He drank three bottles of juice, devoured two cheese sandwiches, and ate a bag of potato chips. He polished off the meal with several brownies. It was frustrating not knowing where Michael or the other guardians were or if they were even alive. Ace was also not responding when he reached out. Now he had to gather a new group of warriors and plan a new rescue mission.

Gabe glanced up, frowning. Ariel stood hesitating by the corner of the building. In her eyes, he saw hurt and longing. Her feelings were easily revealed, and yet her proclaimed love for him was severed as she had betrayed him and their kind. Despite her words of loyalty, his trust had been shattered and he'd never forget it or let his guard down around Ariel ever again.

"Are you ready to talk?" Ariel asked, moving closer. She stood over him, uncertainty on her pretty features.

"Go for it." He balled up his trash and tucked it into the bag.

"I'm sorry, Gabe, that you're so angry with me. My mission was to ensure Rachel would be at the mansion during the ceremony. It was important that she unite with Prisca and save her. I merely did as I was ordered. I didn't know what the outcome would be or that Lord Talco would take her."

"And who gave you such an order?"

"I was messaged in the vortex and told to ensure Rachel would follow through with her mission and use any means necessary."

"So, you joined Blake Howard?" He shook his head. "Your story stinks. He already had Prisca in his possession. We were there to save her, including Rachel. There was no need for Rachel to be sacrificed."

"Your mission would've failed with or without me," she said. "I had a vision. Blake would have ambushed you and had you all killed. Instead, I saved your life. I talked Blake into using you to help Rachel submit to his demands. It worked extremely well. I know you don't believe me. But Rachel is right where she is supposed to be. She had a purpose, and she is now serving it."

"You don't know that. You are making excuses and hoping you're right. I guess we will never know the truth. How convenient for you."

Hurt funneled into her features before she masked it.

"I would never deliberately hurt you, Gabe," she said. "I know how you feel about Rachel. It's true I have little regard for her. I have never hidden that fact. But I am still a guardian, and I made an oath to my kind. I obey orders when directed. And whether you believe me or not, I followed through. I will now be marked by Blake Howard for betraying him. My life is now on the line as well."

"At this point, I really don't care." He paused, clenching his fist. He leaned against the door, shaking his head. "That thing that took Rachel, he will have no pity, no remorse. I have no way of finding her. Rescuing her. I have to start all over, and I don't even know where to begin. I know nothing of this Lord Talco, nothing at all."

"There is something you should know," Ariel said, hunching down beside him. "Rachel has to still be alive because Prisca is still alive. The baby's soul did not separate from Rachel when Lord Talco overtook her. Prisca's soul is still merged with Rachel's. The shaman's ritual failed, and the thing is Blake is oblivious to it. He thought Prisca would return to her human form. I took her before he finds out the truth."

"So what does that mean?"

"I don't know. I just know that Prisca is only partially here. I don't know if that's anything that can help us."

Us. Gabe shook off his anger, stifling the words he wanted to hurl at her. There was no us. He doubted Ariel wanted to help save Rachel. In fact, he would even go as far as to think she'd hope she'd die. He never felt so helpless.

"I need to find a way into Talco's realm to free Rachel."

"You cannot," Ariel replied. "It is sealed up from this world. The portal only opens every three years."

"Are you telling me Rachel will be gone for three years? That there's no way to reach her before then?"

"The portal is opened only from the inside," Ariel

said. "Lord Talco only comes to the surface to obtain a sacrifice, a victim. I don't know what he does thereafter. He then rewards the Ophites with financial security. There is nothing you can do to change this."

"I will find a way," Gabe said. "I will not give up."

"That's fine," Ariel said. "But I have spent time with the Ophites. I know this as a fact. You cannot save Rachel."

Frustrated, Gabe stood and began to pace, heart thumping painfully. He had to find a way into Talco's cave by then, not to mention battle the Ophites. Lord Talco was a foreign beast, whom he knew little about. If he even managed to get through the portal, he wouldn't even know where to begin to look for Rachel or what he'd find. And by the time he had it all figured out, she could be dead, if she was not already."

"She's not dead," Ariel said. "You must believe me. Prisca would already be dead if she were. Rachel is not without her own gifts."

"What good are her gifts when she's probably living in a hell-like state?" Gabe said. "She lacks any experience. Her life as a guardian had barely begun."

"I understand your fears, "Ariel said. "But Rachel must walk this path alone."

"Says who?" Gabe snared her with his gaze. He pointed his finger into her face. "You? What do you know? You know nothing…nothing at all. I can't imagine her fear."

"Stop assuming the worst," Ariel said. "Fear makes us stronger. Fight or flight. We all get lost. We make mistakes. You must remain committed to our cause. Seek respite in the vortex."

"Bah," Gabe said. "I'm pissed off. I can barely

stand being in this world right now let alone in the vortex."

"Through failure we learn," Ariel said. "We wallow in our pity, but then we reenergize and come out stronger."

Gabe considered her. Her version of things reminded him of Ace. The two serpents barely knew each other, yet they had a common thread, preaching their sermons.

"I will find a way to save Rachel or die trying," Gabe said. He squared his shoulders, face determined. "But right now, Michael is in danger and so are the others. The least we can do is rescue them."

"We don't know if they're still there," she said. "They could've been moved by now."

"I can't telepathically reach anyone," Gabe said. "That tells me they are still beneath the mansion."

"There is another possibility," Ariel said. "Blake was using a drug to subdue their serpents, keeping them in human form, which you know all too well. He has several ways he administers it, either by ingestion or airborne, such as what he used with you. It does wear off over several hours. The ingestion can last for several days. Without the power of their serpent, they cannot communicate telepathically."

Ariel's words slid over Gabe, confirming his assumptions. They needed to be in serpent form to make an escape. He hadn't eaten Blake's tainted food, so his serpent woke up, but Michael and the others might've partaken in the fare. Lord knows it was a battle not to indulge.

"If I hadn't escaped, what would you have done?" Gabe studied Ariel as she pondered the question, searching for her hidden treachery.

"I've been watching you, knowing you weren't eating the food. And the fools that were guarding you weren't paying attention or making a record of it. If Blake knew, he'd have force fed you or perhaps used the gas again."

"Why didn't he just kill me?"

"Because it doesn't serve him one way or another if you live or die. He is always on the lookout for pawns in his newest game. And then there is the hope that you will join him. Change sides. He needs warrior serpents such as you and Michael. He might've offered you something in return for your service. After you'd agreed, he'd tie you in so close to him that you could never escape. He'd own you and use you for his own devices."

"Okay," Gabe said. "What about you? How did you get close to him?"

"It wasn't easy," she said, lowering her eyes. "Blake sent out dark serpents to search for Rachel. I went to Second Chance Camp and basically hung around undetected for a couple of weeks. When the serpents made a showing, I confronted them. Told them I would help them find Rachel. They took me to see Blake. I was very convincing, and he genuinely believed in my interest in joining him and being part of their sect. I proved myself to him, locating Rachel's mother. I also partook in some of the rituals and battles."

"Well, you convinced me as well," Gabe said, bitterly glaring at her. "I'm still not convinced you're telling me the complete truth. You're happy to be rid of Rachel."

Ariel crossed her arms as a flash of resentment filled her features. "If it were up to me, Rachel could live with Lord Talco the rest of her life. I wouldn't care or give her another thought. But it's not up to me. Rachel has a purpose. She is a guardian. Apparently, she is needed. Wanted. And so, it doesn't matter how I feel or what I want. Rachel has been chosen for this task with Prisca. If she survives this journey into Lord Talco's lair, her rescue will not be by my hand but by another. Maybe even her own."

Gabe inhaled as the weight of what Rachel was up against came crashing over him.

"Gabe," someone called from across the yard.

"Ace." Relief rushed through Gabe's soul at the site of his childhood mentor. "You made it out?"

"Yes," Ace said, moving toward him. They grabbed one another in a bear hug.

"Michael?" Gabe said, breaking apart.

"Still there with the others. But I know where they are and how we can get them out."

Chapter Thirty-Two

Rachel lay on her bed, numb to all feelings. She tried to sleep but every time she did so, the nightmares returned. She was always lost and in darkness, so utterly alone. If only she could dream again, something happy, a memory perhaps.

But her memories of her human existence were fading. She was having trouble remembering faces, names, and places. Even Gabe's face was lost to her. When she concentrated on his features, they were blurred, indistinguishable. She cried. Not for anything in particular, but because it was the only emotion she could muster. Feeling sorry for herself came naturally and yet she did not really have a reason for the sentiment. She supposed it was because she was losing her grip on reality.

Strange looking half breeds would appear in her room. Albinos with red eyes, like Lord Talco. She supposed lack of sunlight created the illusion. If a human saw one of the underworld beings, she had no doubt they'd think they had found an extraterrestrial. They never spoke to her, just watched with eyes that never blinked.

And then there was her food source. She was never given a meal, only a large goblet of a murky substance. She wondered what was in the liquid. It had no scent. No true color. At first, she'd refused to drink the staple but under threat of forcing it down her throat, she complied.

Time eluded her. She had no idea how long she had been kept in Lord Talco's lair. She was having trouble remembering numbers, letters.

Soon she would just exist, she realized when her mind cleared for a brief moment. In some ways, perhaps her predicament was like that of a brain-damaged victim—how horrible it was to forget oneself and your loved ones.

Rachel fell asleep. The darkness returned, surrounding her, penetrating her soul. This had to be hell, a place of loneliness, she decided. No flames. No pitchfork poking her. Only the separation from life—a sad state of being. In her dream state, she found herself in a long corridor, walking, never getting anywhere. She moved faster, but to no avail. It was like that of a hamster on its wheel, running and running, round and round. Doors were on both sides of the corridor. She tried opening a few but to no avail. She moved along to the next grouping. The knobs would disappear just as her hand made contact. Panicking, she began running, passing a lengthy line of endless doors. After a time, she slowed, walking down the corridor.

"Rachel." Her name washed over her.

"Who's there?" She jumped, trembling all over. A warm rush of air swept over her skin. She woke up.

"I see you're awake," Lord Talco said. He sat down on the edge of the bed, stroking her arm. "The dreams can be the worst. They will disappear in time."

"And so will I," she murmured. She studied him, finding him oddly attractive. He continued to stroke her flesh. She didn't resist. It was the only interaction with another being, and she was starved for the tiniest crumb of companionship. She reached out and stilled his fingers. "It's a shame I will have to kill you."

Lord Talco's face revealed his astonishment at her words. Then he smiled, a rare phenomenon indeed. It was an ugly smile. "The sooner you give yourself over to me, then the sooner you can find forever peace."

Rachel grinned, suddenly giddy. She pushed away his hand and rolled into her fleece, her only source of comfort.

"Did you ever walk on the earth?" She peeked out from beneath the blanket.

"A long time ago," he admitted.

"What was it like?"

"Sorrowful and cruel once man grew in numbers. I have paradise right here. What more do I need?"

Rachel giggled, pulling the blanket over her head. She slid it down, smiling at him.

"You're mean," she said in a childish voice.

"What's the matter with you?"

"Nothing." She giggled again, dragging the blanket over her head, and then peeked out from beneath its covering. "Boo. I see you."

Alarmed, he stood, glaring at her. "You are losing your mind, woman, and sooner than I've expected. I will leave you to it."

"Bye, bye." She stretched out her arms, waving her hands and then rolled into a ball, plopping her thumb into her mouth.

Chapter Thirty-Three

With Prisca's ultimate security at risk, Gabe and Ace moved both mother and serpent to a hidden safe house. The country estate was located eighty-five miles northeast of Paradise Farms. The home was nondescript but held extra security measures to ensure not only seclusion, but an immediate response in an emergency. Warrior serpents maintained the hideaway and had sworn to protect Prisca and Lustra.

Lustra was quite comfortable with the arrangement and for the first time, Gabe noticed her interacting with the tiny serpent. Prisca's altered state was weak but still clinging to life. Gabe was hopeful for the baby's recovery, noting signs of activity within the tiny form. He found himself drawn to the tiny snake. After all, Prisca was connected to Rachel. They were sisters in more ways than one.

When Gabe returned to the abandoned hospital, ten news warriors greeted him, having heeded his request for help. Ace had already informed the group about the Ophites and the captured guardians. When Ariel stepped from the shadows, Gabe broke off from the pack to greet her. The guardian had betrayed him once. It was hard to put any trust in his onetime comrade.

"I will not betray you," Ariel said, standing before him. "I sense your bitterness, and I can hope in time that you can forgive me. I want to go on this mission. I will not fail you."

Gabe ignored her hopeful expression. He wondered if Ace had warned the newly arrived warriors of her possible betrayal. If not, maybe he should. They didn't need another trap should he use her services. At that point in time, Ariel could still be a threat to their mission.

"You doubt me," Ariel said, lifting her gaze to his. She squared her shoulders, feet braced. "I understand your concern, but you need the group focused on the true enemy, not me."

"Easier said than done," he replied, blocking her from his inner thoughts.

Color faded from Ariel's face at his implication. Wounded, she turned around and retreated into the building, leaving Gabe alone.

Gabe wasn't affected by Ariel's distress as it was nothing compared to what Rachel had faced and was most likely still facing, abandoned by the ones who were supposed to protect her. It was time to finalize their plans. They would strike that evening, just after midnight. It promised to be stormy weather, and they sorely needed the cloud cover. Surely, Blake Howard would be expecting them.

"I know where our guardians are being held," Ace said. He stood before the warriors in a blue denim jacket and jeans, hair tightly knotted on the top of his head, emphasizing his proud brow and weathered features. "Before I managed to flee from the building, I saw the guards leading Michael and at least four other guardians into one of the lower chambers. They were injured and remained in their human forms due to Blake's ability to keep them that way. "

"And the pathway in?"

"There is a tunnel we can use," Ace said. "It runs beneath the barn to the mansion. They were using it to bring in Rachel's mother. Blake Howard might be aware that we know of this entrance, but it does lead almost directly to Michael's location. If we're quick enough, we could use the same route to escape."

"It would help if we knew how many serpents were inside," Gabe said. "There were about thirty or more Ophites in attendance during Blake's ceremony. I don't know how many more were outside of the domain. But to secure a kill, make sure to strike completely through their heart chambers."

"On my way out of there, I had killed five serpents," Ace said.

"Good," Gabe replied. "So, it would be a reasonable assumption that we are dealing with at least twenty-five to thirty serpents."

"I agree," Ace said. "Blake might have added additional security to his force."

Gabe exhaled, considering his words. "There are twelve of us."

"Thirteen if you include Ariel," Ace said, shrugging, face impassive.

"Still undecided on that accord," Gabe said, glancing toward the building. Ariel stood in the deepening shadows, watching them.

"That choice is yours to make," Ace said. "It might take a few days to round up more warriors. If not, that's two to three Ophites to every one of us."

"We are out of time," Gabe said. "There is no telling what Blake Howard will do with the men. He already might have killed them. He's got nothing to lose since we've got Prisca and Rachel is no longer involved."

"He could trade Prisca for the guardians," Ace said.

"I've thought of that, and it's not happening."

"I agree." Ace rubbed his square jaw. "But I'm thinking of a replica, something to throw them off."

"Blake isn't a fool."

"I know that, but it might at least give us some leverage, even if it's for only a moment. It doesn't hurt to have a strategy."

"I'm sure I can locate a similar golden snake," one of the male guardians spoke up. "Something near her size."

"I suppose it wouldn't hurt," Gabe said, body taut with tension. "Go find a replacement, and be back here by eight." He turned to the other two guardians. "I would suggest everyone just rest up before tonight. Make peace with your inner serpent. Pray for guidance and protection. We will not have time for the vortex, especially with a storm on the way."

The group dispersed, each seeking their own comforts. Gabe walked into the hospital, noting Ariel had disappeared. Inside the structure, the crumbling block walls and depressing atmosphere matched his sobering mood. He needed to spend time resting and prepare himself mentally for the challenge at hand. Just as he was moving toward a vacant room, he felt Ariel before he saw her.

"Have you decided if I can join you?" She stepped from the shadows, her features somber. Her blue eyes revealed her dismal hope.

"You move as stealthily as a cat," Gabe said,

considering her. She was a beautiful woman, strong and cunning, but she would always be a sister to him, despite her best efforts to change his stance. "You have enhanced that skill."

"I have learned to use blockers on my enemies and even illusions."

"And am I your enemy?" He studied her reaction to his words, probing her thoughts.

"Go ahead and search my mind," Ariel said. "You will find nothing amiss. I have been truthful. I will not regret what I was commissioned to do."

"And do you have any more such orders of betrayal?"

The question caught her off guard. She lifted her chin, features flashing her resentment.

"If I had, you would be the last to know." She crossed her arms, leaning against the wall. "Make up your mind. Am I in or out?"

Her snarling assertion washed over him, reeking of honesty. "Fine. You can come, but know I will be watching you and will not hesitate to act if you betray any of our warriors."

Chapter Thirty-Four

Lustra sat on a wooden rocker, holding Prisca in her arms. The snake's tiny head wavered upright, staring up at her with dark eyes. A tiny tongue slid out of Prisca's mouth. She moved closer to her mother's warmth.

"My sweet girl," Lustra said. She rolled her thumb along Prisca's smooth head. "I wish I could see you in your human form. How I miss your sweet little face. Your beautiful eyes. Not that I don't love you in your serpent state. If only you could be whole again."

The serpent loosened its coiled form, tilting its head to one side.

"Can you understand me, Prisca? I feel in my heart that you might. What can I do to help you?"

The snake began to move, wiggling. It slithered down Lustra's arm. She caught the serpent before she could fall. "My, you are feeling better, aren't you? I've never seen you so restless."

Again, the serpent tried to slide off her mother's lap. Lustra stood with Prisca, moving around the small bedroom, unsure of how to manage her daughter.

"I suppose you could roam around the room," Lustra said. "There is no way out. Or perhaps I should put you back into your crate. You are feeling cool to the touch."

She walked over to the serpent's makeshift bed. In

the middle of the aquarium, a heating lamp illuminated a flat rock in the center. Woodchips lined the bottom. In one corner sat a pretty doll. Two dead pinkie mice lay near it, untouched, and yet the snake seemed stronger.

"When are you going to eat?" Lustra asked. "It's been three days, and you haven't touched a thing."

Lustra lowered Prisca inside the enclosure and tried to slide the serpent off of her palms, but the tiny beast wouldn't have it. Using her mouth, the serpent clamped onto her mother's finger, holding tight.

"I see you don't want to go into your cage," Lustra said, returning to the rocker. "I don't know what you want."

Prisca lay compliant on her mother's lap, then slid up against her breast. Lustra sighed, humming a lullaby. The baby snuggled closer to her mother's throat and then slid along her shoulder, hiding beneath her thick hair.

"You are going to get tangled," Lustra said, trying to pull her daughter out of her long strands, but the snake was quick. Suddenly, the serpent slithered over her shoulder, moved through the wooden chair slats, and dropped onto the floor. Quick as a wink, Prisca slid beneath the bed.

"Prisca!" Quickly, Lustra knelt on the carpeted floor, ducking her head beneath the bedframe. Prisca wasn't there. Panicking, she scrambled along the floor on her knees, skirting around the front of the bed. "Prisca. Where are you? Come back to Mommy."

Lustra crawled around the bed, still on all fours. She reached the side dresser, peeking beneath. Not a sign of Prisca. Panicking, she spun around. She had to be somewhere. She stood and moved into the opposite corner. Another bureau with a lamp was her next objective but before she could reach it, something moved beneath the drapery.

Kneeling, Lustra moved the curtain away from the wall. Coiled, Prisca's golden form was pressed close to the wooden trim. The serpent turned her head toward her mother, snout lifting.

"What are you doing?"

Lustra peered closer, ready to scoop Prisca up. That's when she saw it. Tiny black legs were sticking out of the sides of the serpent's mouth.

"Ugh," Lustra said, realizing what she was looking at. "Are you eating a spider?"

The snake moved its head, mouth twisting. One of the spider's legs moved as it tried to escape its confines. But then Prisca's mouth moved again and then clamped shut. The spider was now disposed of.

Stunned, Lustra put out her hand. Prisca slid onto her palms. She picked up the baby and returned to the rocker. Now Prisca was content, crawling up under her mother's neck, secure and protected.

Lustra could only wonder at it all.

Chapter Thirty-Five

Just after midnight, the guardians climbed into a large van and left in the dismal rain. Staying in their human forms, the warriors, along with a replica of Prisca, were quiet and thoughtful. Ace drove for just over two hours and then parked the auto near a reservoir. Together, the warriors traveled the remaining miles on foot. They trekked through an open field until they reached the outskirts of Blake's property line.

Along a riverbed, they dispersed, altering into their serpents, all with the exception of Gabe, who chose to remain human for now. Quietly, they regrouped. Gabe carried the sack holding Prisca's replica, hoping not to have to use it as leverage.

"Ace will lead us to the barn," Gabe said, reminding everyone through telepathy. He sensed Ariel's irritation at his words. The female serpent knew the property better than any of them, yet he couldn't trust her not to take them into a trap. Time would tell if she would betray him again. "We will travel together. No one is to be alone, only in pairs. We fight and will give all for our missing brothers. The spirits above are with us. We have that on our side."

Each acknowledged Gabe's words, agreeing to the terms.

"If any one of us falls, I want to thank you in advance for your sacrifice." Gabe paused a moment, then added, "But we dedicated our lives for these challenges. I believe we can win this battle. Let's go."

With Ace leading the way, they filed in behind him, each alerted for any signs of danger. It wasn't long before the lights from the mansion stood out in the dampened gloom.

"Our target location is at the horse barn," Ace said. "They were holding Rachel's mother there."

"She's the last of my concerns," Gabe replied. Although he protected human life, he had little regard for Rachel's mother. As a parent, the woman had failed miserably, and his sympathy was dismal at best.

Just before the barn, the guardians spread out, moving around the building, each using their keen instincts to alarm the others if trouble approached. Ace moved to one side, keeping watch as Gabe opened the barn door and entered. Inside he was met with a dimly lit environment and unnerving quiet. In the dark, he sensed someone watching him. He closed his eyes, using his senses to detect any dark serpents. Two of them were detectable but beneath the building.

Gabe passed several empty stalls before coming upon an accessible area. Three huge kennels stood side by side. Inside one structure, a woman watched him, fear in her eyes.

"Who are you?" Leah rose to her feet, grabbing onto the bars. "Hey, you?"

Gabe lifted his finger to his lips to shush her.

"Are you here to rescue me?" Leah whispered, pressing her face against the metal. Her large eyes bored into him.

Angry at her noise, Gabe shook his head.

"Then why should I be quiet?"

Ace and the other guardians slithered into the building, moving toward the middle expanse. Ace entered an empty stall, lifting his snout in Gabe's direction. "The entrance is in here."

"I will be back," Gabe said to Leah, who appeared shocked after viewing the group of serpents. "We are guardians and friends of Rachel's. For now, be quiet, or we won't return."

Leah clamped shut her mouth, visibly shaken, plopping herself down upon the cot.

Gabe moved to where Ace waited. He grabbed a rake and removed the straw-covered lid, which hid the underground tunnel. Without a word, Gabe jumped into the hole, landing with a thud on the hard floor. He moved to one side of the corridor while the guardian warriors slid down behind him with their huge forms. Ace stayed behind, ensuring the portal remained open.

The concrete corridor was lit by emergency lights. A junction broke off in a different direction, but Gabe continued moving forward toward the mansion. A flurry of activity came from the right and left of the adjacent tunnels. Gabe moved against the wall, allowing his guardians to pass. Ariel moved behind them, waiting in the dark for any trouble.

They all advanced forward. For the most part Gabe ignored Ariel, focusing on the objective. The tunnel divided again, and Gabe paused, uncertain.

"This way," Ariel said telepathically, nudging him with her snout. "It will bring us to the closest entrance to Michael's locked chamber."

Gabe frowned, staring into Ariel's eyes. She expected him to just blindly follow her lead. Last time it was a trap. If she failed him again, all would be lost.

"Trust me," Ariel said. "Please."

Gabe paused, considering her plea. He closed his eyes, seeking the truth in her mind. Although Ariel had the ability to deny him entrance into her thoughts, she willingly allowed him. Finding nothing amiss, he abruptly turned to the right, following the corridor.

Two hidden portals abruptly opened. From within, four serpents came crashing out, moving into the tunnel with them. Their bulky forms sent Gabe flying into the wall. Within seconds, Ariel was engaged in battle. The other serpents moved to aid her. Gabe ducked from the blows and rushed through the opening.

Inside was a huge conference room. Tables and chairs were set up for meetings, or so it appeared. Gabe ran through the room, moving toward the opposite doorway. Ducking his head outside the portal, another hallway was spread out in both directions. The doorways were on both sides. He sensed dark serpents coming from both directions, and he opted to make a dash. He made it past the first doorway, ducking into the next. Inside was another office. He went behind the desk, crouching down. When movement passed the doorway, he scrambled to exit the room, continuing onward.

"Michael," he called out telepathically, seeking his friend. Although he did not reply, Gabe sensed the other guardian nearby. He moved through the next doorway. An elderly man, wearing wire spectacles, sat at a desk. Before the man could react, Gabe grabbed him around the throat and rendered him unconscious.

"Ariel, what's happening?" Gabe called out to her.

"Just keep moving," she replied. "We're busy now."

Relieved, Gabe continued onward. He came to an alcove with a metal door and shoved on the handle. Above the door, an alarm lit up. As soon as he entered the new corridor, two serpents were waiting for him. Before he could change into his serpent, they were upon him. The first serpent smashed into him with its snout, knocking him into the wall. He collapsed, rolling over as the beast came again. But before the Ophite warrior could strike, Gabe found his footing, throwing himself out of the way. He jumped to his feet, running. Abruptly, the second serpent's tail slammed into his legs, sending him spiraling along the polished floor.

On his belly, Gabe closed his eyes, allowing his beast to emerge. A jolt of adrenaline hit him as his serpent woke, furious and hungry for battle. Just as the first serpent reached for him, Gabe pivoted around, eyes gleaming, sinking his teeth into the beast's jaw, shaking him like a rag doll. He dropped the serpent's head and sank his fangs into the serpent's heart, stilling it with a death blow. The second beast attacked from the rear, sinking its fangs into Gabe's tail. Gabe turned and attacked. The other serpent had a powerful bite, but Gabe was agile and swift, coiling around his nemesis, squeezing and then killing the other serpent.

With the taste of blood in its mouth, Gabe's serpent sounded his battle cry, warning all who opposed him. The other guardian serpents fell in behind him.

Gabe could sense Michael through an adjacent wall. Swiftly, he turned left down a corridor, crashing through a double door. A huge cage sat in the middle of a room. Michael and the other guardians were eagerly waiting for them. Gabe slithered over to the cage's door, grabbed the lock, crushing it with his jaw.

Overhead, a portal opened, and Blake Howard glared down at them. The man was furious and shook his fist.

"Hurry," Gabe said into Michael's mind. No response. Most likely, Michael's abilities were being suppressed but it mattered not. All of the men filtered out of the structure, rushing to escape. Gabe, Ariel, and the others followed, protecting them as more dark serpents arrived in the hallway. Battles ensued. Gabe raced ahead of the group, barreling his way down the corridor, protecting the men who tried to keep up. Just as he moved into the corridor, he once again had to engage in fighting.

Three serpents attacked Gabe all at once. He opted to take out the largest of the trio. It was difficult to keep moving, watch his back, and deliver a death bite. Exhausted, he yelled as once again, he was bitten, blood flowing. Now he was being dragged the opposite way. Michael lunged onto the beast's back, trying to slow the progression. The other men fought as well, but one of the serpents ran into them, sending them crashing into the wall.

Gabe fended off one of his attackers as another was ready to strike his throat. Abruptly, that beast fell short of its mission. He turned to see Ariel dropping the serpent's head upon the floor, now dead and yielding.

"Thank you," Gabe said telepathically as he delivered the death blow to the remaining serpent.

Ariel didn't reply. She raced past him, already lunging at two new emerging serpents. Gabe followed her, and they swiftly took down their rivals.

The guardians regrouped, fighting their way out while protecting the men, rushing down the tunnel toward the barn. Ariel emerged inside the barn first, the rest of the group following.

Their success came to a standstill. Ace was lying in the middle of the floor, blood oozing from his neck. Next to him, two dark Ophites kept watch. In his human form, Blake Howard stood with Rachel's mother pressed against his chest, one arm clamped around her neck. In his other hand, he held a knife, pointing the tip at her throat.

"Why didn't you call me?" Gabe said telepathically to Ace.

"You needed to finish your mission," Ace said. "Now take these demons out."

"You are very cunning, Gabe." Blake spoke to the guardians. "Now you will surrender, or this woman will die."

"Do you think she matters to me?" Gabe telepathically answered Blake.

"She matters because she is human," Blake said aloud. "You are sworn to protect them."

"I am sworn to protect the innocent," Gabe replied. "This woman is far from it. Do you think I care what you do to her?"

"You're not a good liar," Blake said. "This is Rachel's mother. You would never cause her death. I know you care too much for my daughter."

"Rachel is gone. She won't even know."

"Can you take that chance?" Blake asked. "We don't know if Rachel will return someday. She might not be happy if you allowed her mother to be killed, but I do have a proposition for you."

"Go on."

"I want Prisca. I'm her father, and I have a right to have her with me. A simple swap, and you can all be on your way."

"She isn't far," Gabe said, pausing to consider the situation. He carefully blocked his true thoughts from Blake's prying mind.

Uncertainty crossed Blakes features yet hope lit his eyes. "Where? Where is she?"

"I need only get her."

"Very well," Blake said. "We will all wait right here for your return."

"Gabe, don't…" Ace said in warning.

"If Prisca must be sacrificed, then so be it," Gabe said, following the charade. He slithered through the double doors of the barn, exiting into the misty night. He moved past the barn and into the woods. He slid up the top of a tree and grabbed the bundle tied to a branch. He returned to the barn, holding his parcel.

"Everyone leaves first," Gabe said telepathically to Blake. "Then you can have her."

"How do I know you have Prisca in that bag?"

Gabe untied the bag's bindings. He shook it out, spilling the golden serpent onto the floor. Before Blake could further inspect the small beast, he scooped her into his mouth, hiding her from view. Expectantly, all stood at an impasse.

Blake squared his solid shoulders, speaking to his Ophites. "Let them go."

Gabe nodded toward the guardians and his men. "Carry Ace out," he said telepathically to Michael, who then nodded. The drug must have been wearing off. Together, the men lifted Ace's large form, carrying him outside.

"Now, the woman," Gabe said, as Blake was still holding Rachel's mother hostage.

"Set Prisca on the floor," Blake said. "And I will release her."

Gabe opened his mouth, dipped his head forward, and dropped the golden snake onto the ground. Dazed, the serpent sat coiled, tongue flickering. Shoving Leah out of the way, Blake moved toward the snake.

Rachel's mother scampered to her feet and raced toward the barn's doorway as Gabe retreated.

"Prisca." Blake reached down, scooped up the pseudo-Prisca, and lifted her. His brow dipped into an angry line. He threw the snake across the room, where it landed in a pile of hay. He screamed, "Get him!"

The Ophite warriors came to life, rushing at Gabe. A loud roar cracked the air as Blake Howard turned into his serpent, large and ready to engage in battle.

"You will die," Blake said telepathically to Gabe.

"Not by your hand."

Already weakened by his earlier battle, Gabe struggled against his attackers as Blake came forward, but then an energy emanated into the room as Michael and two other serpents returned.

"Need help?" Michael said. "My serpent is hungry for blood."

Ariel and three more serpents appeared. Outnumbered, Blake recoiled, slithered into the rear stall, and dropped into the hole in the ground.

"Should we give chase?" Michael said to Gabe.

"No," Gabe said, noting the two dead serpents. "We'll save it for another day. Let's get everyone out of here."

The guardians left, traveling through the underbrush and disappearing from view.

"We need the van to transport Ace," Gabe said to

Ariel and Michael. "We need to get him somewhere quiet so he can begin to heal."

"You did good, kid," Ace said into Gabe's thoughts. "I will turn so you can transport me easier, but you need to stop with all the fuss. It's getting on my last nerve."

"Well, you'd better not die on me," Gabe replied. "So, hang in there."

****

Battle weary, Gabe continued to monitor Ace as he spent time healing in his serpent's form. In the alternate state, Ace's healing was rapid and supernatural, unlike his human body, which would take weeks to recover.

Temporarily, they returned to the safe house, which held Prisca and her mother, monitoring Paradise Farms from afar. Gabe sought information on the Ophites and their origins. He especially sought insight into Lord Talco's world, his devotees, and underground lair. Not much was known about the lord except that he lived inside a deep earthly cavern, one inaccessible for ordinary serpents. The Ophites worshipped the dark lord, and in return he rewarded his followers with prosperity.

Gabe searched online, learning all he could about Rachel's bloodline, finding she had Indian lineage connected to Queen Meru. Rachel's ancestors were known as gifted healers with insight into the spiritual world. He supposed that's what drew the Ophites to her in the first place.

Ariel had disappeared again. The blonde guardian had simply left, not revealing her intended destination. He was still angry with her, even though she had battled by his side. He didn't bother to search for her. If she wanted to talk, she knew where to find him.

Gabe descended into the basement of the house. Limited light filtered in through the windows. Ace lay upon a set of mats, curled up with his great dark head facing the stairway. The older serpent stared as Gabe approached and grabbed a nearby chair, sitting down by his mentor.

"I have failed Rachel." Gabe didn't bother using telepathy. He leaned his head into his hands, tired and defeated. "She's lost to this world. I want to return to Paradise Farm and find a way into the cave's entrance. Ariel claims it's impossible and that the entrance is sealed, only opening with sorcery."

"You need a seeker," Ace said telepathically. "A serpent with the ability to see beyond rock, dirt, and water. Someone who can provide a roadmap to follow."

"How can I find such a serpent?"

"I'm already working on it. I know of a man who travels in many circles and has journeyed into many distant territories. He is of ancient blood and has endured centuries of unrest in the serpent world. He has agreed to send someone to aid our quest. If there is a way to locate Rachel, he will tell us."

Hope flickered inside Gabe. He closed his eyes, swallowing the lump in his throat. After composing himself, he said, "Thank you, Ace. Know that my purpose in this life is my servitude, but I need her by my side…"

"I understand," Ace replied. "Love is strong. It's what binds us together and might be the very thing that brings her back to you."

"I hope so," Gabe said. "My existence will be bleak indeed if she is lost forever."

****

At the end of the week, a visitor arrived. The elderly man was quickly ushered in by Michael, who shook his hand, welcoming him.

"My name is Dominic Bungalow," the man said. "I was looking for Gabe?"

Gabe, having heard the voices, moved into the foyer. Dominic was nothing like he'd pictured. The man was tall and appeared gaunt, with wiry wisps of gray hair. His eyes were sunken into his angular face. He wore dark dress pants and a green collared shirt. But the most noticeable attribute was the man's incredibly long arms, which hung well past his knees. His hands were also peculiar, overly large with pointed fingernails. Gabe intuitively knew this man was of a strange serpent variety, but the hybrid also had another unique quality that he couldn't decipher. It was indeed perplexing.

"Welcome," Gabe said, pumping Dominic's hand, which dwarfed his own. "It's a pleasure to meet you. Ace said you would be arriving today."

"Where is Ace?" Dominic asked, his melodic voice as peculiar as his appearance.

"He is down in the basement, resting."

"I would like to see him."

"Certainly," Gabe replied. He ignored Michael's questioning brow and led the way from the room. Inside the basement, Ace lifted his serpent's head, intently watching their visitor.

"Leave us," Dominic said to Gabe. "I'll call for you when you're needed."

"Ace?" Gabe waited for Ace's response. He knew nothing of this visitor, and his confidence was indecisive. Ace had been healing in his serpent's form, though he needed a bit more time to be completely healed.

"It's fine." Ace moved his head, repositioning himself.

Gabe nodded and returned upstairs to find Michael waiting for him in the living room, sprawled out on the coach.

"Well?"

"They wanted to be alone." Gabe sat on a wing chair, facing him.

"We need to talk." Michael sat up, his demeanor solemn. "I want to move Prisca to another location. We are too close to Blake and his followers. It's only a matter of time before the Ophites come searching for her, and we will be in another battle. Prisca needs to be in a place where she can grow up in peace—even if it's only in her serpent form. We have to make plans for her."

"I know," Gabe said, rubbing his hand over his jaw. "But Prisca is still tied spiritually to Rachel. She is her sister, and perhaps we can use that to our advantage."

"I don't agree," Michael said, eyes narrowing. "This innocent baby has been through so much, and she is still in limbo. We don't know how damaged she is. I say enough is enough. We don't risk innocents to get what we want."

"I understand what you are saying," Gabe said, stomach tensing. In his heart, he admitted Michael was right. He had been keeping Prisca close to him in the hope of some kind of resolution, but in truth he never considered the infant's danger. Not only was she in danger from Blake and his followers, but her physical life was on the line. After a moment, he said, "I can't believe we did all of this for nothing. I need guidance on how to proceed."

"I know it's frustrating," Michael said. "But you need to come to terms with the fact that perhaps Rachel has another purpose, one taking her on another path. You might not be part of it. You need to prepare for answers that you might not like."

"No." Gabe stood, pacing in front of Michael. "I am questioning everything right now. I am really pissed off. I can't sleep. My imagination is on crazy overdrive. My faith is weak, and I am so lost in this...I am lost without Rachel."

"Gabe," Ace called telepathically to him. "Come down to me."

"I know you are trying to help." Gabe paused, facing Michael. "And you're right. Prisca is innocent, and I've been selfish thinking of myself. Go ahead and make plans to move her to another location. I've been summoned by Ace."

Not waiting for Michael's reply, Gabe walked down the staircase and into the basement, wondering if Ace had overheard his outburst. Ace had been his mentor for many years, and the man would not approve of his comments but at that point in time, he'd couldn't care less.

"Ace?" The injured serpent wasn't on his mat.

"I'm right here," Ace replied.

Gabe pivoted around. Ace was in human form, sitting on a chair, fully dressed, and looking radiant. "I'm healed."

Gabe's mouth dropped open at the implication.

Ace's peculiar visitor had magically vanished, but how? The basement wasn't that large. The man would've had to come upstairs.

"Dominic is gone," Ace said, answering his questioning brow.

"But I never saw him leave. Heard him."

"Dominic has his ways," Ace said. "He is a healer. You can see the results." He lifted his arms, dropping them to his side. "I've never felt any better."

"Amazing." Gabe walked around the chair. "Care to explain?"

"Nope," Ace said, getting to his feet. "I'm hungry. I want a plate of pasta and a glass of milk." He walked to the stairs, jerking his head around to look at Gabe. "Coming?"

"Sure."

****

"I see Prisca is progressing," Ace said, standing in the modest bedroom.

Instinctively, Lustra, who was sitting in the rocker, wrapped her arms around the serpent, holding her closer. Gabe took note of the infant's health. Sure enough, Prisca was alert. Her tongue flickered out of her mouth as she turned her head toward them, cocking it to one side.

"She's caught two spiders all by herself," Lustra said, pride holding her features. "And then today, she finally ate a pinky mouse."

"Is that so?" Ace reached down, touching Prisca's head. The tiny serpent lifted her head, studying him. "I am no threat, little one."

Gabe moved closer. He slid one finger over Prisca's head. She moved toward his hand, arching her neck. There was something special about the baby's perception.

"I think she likes you," Lustra said, a pleased smile cresting.

"May I hold her?" Gabe asked. Before Lustra could answer, the snake slid against his hands. Cupping his palms, he loosely held her. Prisca coiled and stared at him with black eyes. He lifted her toward his face, meeting her steady gaze.

"It's good she trusts you," Ace said. "She's connected to Rachel in many ways. It will make things easier when we take her into the vortex."

"No." Lustra glared at Ace, arms crossing. "My daughter has been through enough. I was told when Prisca feels safe again, she might change back into her human form. I am working on that goal. I want to hold my human baby."

"Prisca is broken," Ace said. "An important part of her is missing—her soul force. She needs to reunite both her serpent and her humanity. Without her soul's aura, she cannot bind the two or communicate telepathically. In time, she has to make decisions that will affect her future path. Her enlightenment has been dimmed, almost nonexistent. She won't be able to join the guardians, connect to the vortex, or open the portal. She needs these things to be complete to survive."

"Why can't she just be a normal child with a normal mother? I want my baby back."

"You cannot change what she is," Ace said, shaking his head. "And you can't keep her in this limbo. She must return to her true self. Help her. You forget that she is a target for darker forces. And without her soul force, her future will be bleak should they find her. She must have her freedoms returned to her so she can attain her future gifts and protect herself."

Lustra lowered her head, her anger becoming sorrowful as she wept.

Ace reached down and touched her hand. "I know you don't understand, but we are on your side. On Prisca's side. Prisca has a purpose and a journey to take. She can only reunite with her soul force in the vortex. The spirits will guide and protect her. There are no guarantees, but we have to try. You could get your daughter back—whole. Her serpent will return into its earlier state of hibernation until she matures and Prisca the child will have no memory of this event."

Hope lit Lustra's features. "She will be like a normal girl for a time?"

"Yes, until she is mature, usually around eighteen."

"When will you take her to the vortex?"

"Tonight," Ace said. "There is a new moon. It's a perfect opportunity to try to reunite Prisca with her soul force."

"As long as she's safe," Lustra whispered. "I couldn't bear to have her under duress again."

"We will keep her safe," Ace said. "It is our duty."

"Okay." She clasped her hands together, nodding her head.

Gabe placed Prisca into her eager arms. The inner connection he'd felt momentarily with the snake dissipated. It was hard to walk away, almost as if he were walking away from Rachel, but with Ace's direction, he followed his mentor out of the room.

Chapter Thirty-Six

Rachel woke from her stupor, confused. The world around her was incredibly beautiful. Brilliant, crystalized walls held etchings of various symbols. A waterfall flowed from a crevice in the rock, bubbling over fissures and landing into a pool of water. The sound was soothing to her senses.

She slid to a sitting position. Beneath her, a woven mat had protected her from the cool rocky terrain. The room was bigger than her earlier placement. It held no furnishings, only the artwork on the sleek walls.

Tentatively, she moved her bare feet along the edge of the mat and stood. An icy blast stung the bottom of her feet, but she barely registered the pain as she moved toward the pool, collapsing by its side. She dragged herself to the short ledge, staring at her reflection in the sparkling water. Her eyes appeared very dark, reflecting liquid amber. Her long auburn hair hung wildly along her shoulders as she moved closer. She placed her index finger into the middle of her watery image, stirring it, which scattered her image into tiny ripples.

She cupped the warm water in her palms and brought it to her mouth, sipping at it, finding her throat parched. A long shadow cast over her reflection, blending with her own. Startled, she turned her head to see who'd approached.

Above her, a young blue-eyed man stood. His dark

hair hung loosely along his solid shoulders in a pleasing display. He was dressed in a one-piece body suit, which glittered in silver, emphasizing his strong toned form. When he smiled at her, a slight dimple appeared in one cheek.

"Don't you recognize me, Rachel?" The man held his hand toward her. "Have you forgotten me so quickly? Let me help you up."

His face created havoc with Rachel's memories, yet still she struggled to identify him. Puzzled, she felt a stirring of mistrust but then familiarity. She placed her hand into his palm as she stood on shaky legs.

"My name is Gabe," he said, steadying her. "See. That wasn't so bad."

Rachel held onto his arm as the room spun but then he took her hands, placing them around his neck, pulling her flush against him.

"I missed you." Gabe pressed her head against his chest.

Instinctively, Rachel clung to him, seeking comfort but then she listened for his heartbeat, finding none. Frowning, she tilted her head to stare at him. Words failed her. She parted her mouth to speak but as she did so, Gabe kissed her. She instantly weakened, her senses confused. She clung to his shoulders to keep from falling. Still the kiss continued, searching, tasting. Something slithered against her tongue. She gagged, shoving it away with her own.

A moan escaped Gabe's throat, or was that a growl.

Warmth spread over Rachel, her body like lava. She met Gabe's passionate kiss, her senses awakening to something once lost. She only knew that his arms felt strong and protective. She closed her eyes, drawing him in even as her eyesight dimmed. A tickle began in her throat as the never-ending kiss devoured her. She stared into his open gaze, drowning in his beautiful pale blue orbs. They were so incredible, just as incredible as the bluest of skies on a clear summer's morn. She blinked as memories came trickling through, the beach and waves against the sandy shoreline, boats sailing against the horizon, shells, and sea life.

Something nagged her thoughts, but she couldn't care, she was drowning in sensation, blissful and helpless to stop it. His unflinching stare consumed her. Her throat was now numb, scratchy. Her body further weakened, her legs as heavy as lead. Still, Gabe suspended her, propping her upright in his strong arms, all the while still kissing her.

"Yield to me," he said against her lips. "You are mine."

A word formed in her mind but was instantly lost. If she could just say the word, she could remember what it'd been. It was on the tip of her thoughts. She tried to find the right word, any word, forcefully concentrating in her haze. Surely, she knew a word. She struggled to speak, breaking free in a panicked moment. She tried to release his arms.

"No," Rachel said, her voice barely a whisper.

"Yield your all to me, Rachel," Gabe said, recapturing her mouth with his own. It was as if she hadn't spoken, and she wondered if she had. He cuddled her, his hands gliding down her spine, clasping her around the waist. Now, he spoke telepathically. "Free yourself, Rachel. Your serpent wants to be free. Change, darling. Bring her forth. I promise you will then have all you could ever wish for, your forevermore with Gabe and everlasting peace."

His words were meant to entice, offering her paradise. Danger closed around her thoughts, pressing against her temples. Weakly, she shoved at his chest, squirming. If only she could have a moment to think or to reason.

Gabe drew her back to him, his lips closing over hers. Something pulsated in her mouth, long and rubbery, intruding into her throat as it probed. She panicked, the danger clearer and unrelenting. Terrified, she bit down on the object of vulgarity, which instantly collapsed, filling her mouth with a vile liquid.

Anger erupted in Gabe's chest as he shoved her away, causing her to fall to his feet. Grayish matter clung to the corners of his lips, dribbling down his chin. The blue of Gabe's eyes had faded into a black abyss. He stood, glaring down at her, his features an ugly sneer, raising his fists.

"You think you're clever, girl?"

Rachel couldn't speak, but openly stared at his abrupt change.

"I will have you, Rachel. One way or another." Lord Talco grabbed her by the shoulders, throwing her against the wall. She crumbled into a heap. But then she pulled herself into a sitting position, her fear dissipated. Grimly, she smiled, tucking herself into a ball, wrapping her arms protectively around her knees.

"We will see," she said, finding her voice.

Lord Talco cursed her name. Cursed the earth. And cursed all of humanity.

Chapter Thirty-Seven

The moonlight spilled across the yard, bringing a distinctive glow to the objects encompassed by the light. Michael, Ace, and Gabe met in the middle of the expanse. Two other guardians joined them, keeping watch nearby. By Gabe's feet, a basket sat, lid securely closed.

Energized, Gabe gave himself up to the light, seeking and absorbing its essence. He grabbed Michael's hand, who in turned grabbed Ace's, who grabbed Gabe's other hand. The circle was formed. Energy snapped the air. A current ran through their fingertips. Round and round it traveled through the men, growing in tempo. A haze of light rose around their heads, drawing them into the welcoming vortex.

In the golden peaceful domain, blinding illumination drew them ever closer until they were no longer just humans but part of the ethereal atmosphere. Indiscernible mists and shapes swirled in the background.

Warmth and a welcoming embrace slid over Gabe's soul, analytical in design. Speech came in the form of another language, a predawn ancient dialect. He waited for its direction, conveying his request without speaking the words.

He concentrated on Rachel, seeking counsel. He pleaded for help, for enlightenment, and for protection over her soul and then did the same for Prisca.

While still in the vortex, one of the guardians watching over them slid Prisca into his waiting hands, her serpent's form wrapped in a silk scarf. Without releasing his grip on Michael's hand, he lifted the bundle with his fingertips, elevating her into the abyss.

"I offer you Prisca the infant," Gabe said. "To rejoin that which had been forcibly removed so that one day this child may choose the path of enlightenment. To remove the sting of the evil curse placed upon her head and to reunite her to her former state, to entrust Prisca to our cause as we may then continue in the battle that we were ordained to partake."

Energy crackled around them in a heated frenzy. Minutes ticked away though there was no sense of urgency. Gabe's arms grew tired, but he ignored the sensation, standing firm. He lost awareness of a time or place. Prisca grew buoyant and weightless as a feather. The serpent raised her head, tilted toward the light. Her golden profile radiated with inner beauty. A beacon of lavender hues hovered around her, swirling gently around her form.

Abruptly, the vortex closed, and darkness fell over the group. Gabe lowered his arms, uncertainty in his features. Quickly, he adjusted the silk scarf and rewrapped it more securely around Prisca, returning her to the basket. No one spoke as the other guardians walked away. Michael shrugged his shoulders and followed after them, leaving him alone with Ace.

"Well?" Gabe picked up the basket, facing his mentor.

"We shall wait and see," Ace said. "Let's get Prisca back into the house and under the heating lamp.

We don't want her to take a chill." He pivoted and moved toward the house, Gabe following.

Chapter Thirty-Eight

Furious, Blake Howard paced in front of his roaring fireplace as the wood crackled in the hearth. He hated to lose. It peeved him that he'd been tricked by a bunch of guardians. He should've killed them while he had the chance. He'd held onto his prisoners for leverage should there be a future need, and with Prisca missing, his need was great. He pivoted around toward the three burly men, who fearfully considered him.

"I can't believe you can't find Prisca," Blake said, his voice razor sharp. "She couldn't have just vanished into thin air."

"The guardians have hidden her effectively," Zethro said. "Using blockers so we can't track her."

"What about Lustra? Find the baby through her mother."

"From what we learned, Prisca is with her mother, but the guardians are protecting them."

Blake stood in front of his main henchman, poking the man's chest. "I pay you a lot of money to do what I order. Your incompetence knows no bounds. Must I do everything myself?"

"We have a lead," Zethro said, lifting his jaw. "We discovered Ariel is currently in Philadelphia although Prisca isn't with her, but she has separated herself from the other guardians. There appears to be a source of discord amongst them."

"Ariel? That traitor!" Blake scoffed at the news. "She betrayed the guardians. She betrayed me. The woman has her own mindset. What good is knowing where she is located if Prisca isn't with her?"

"No offense, Blake, but what good is the baby serpent without her soul? Seems to me like a waste of time locating her."

"Moron!" Blake backhanded Zethro, leaving a red welt against his cheek. The other two serpents stepped away, clearly afraid. "How dare you lecture me on something you know nothing about!"

"I apologize," Zethro said, bowing his head. "Please forgive me."

"Bring me the shaman," Blake ordered. "He can help me find what is lost."

"Yes, sir," Zethro said, nodding to the other Ophites, who then dispersed.

Shaking his knuckles toward the ceiling, Blake struggled with his rage. Even with Rachel gone, she'd still interfered with his hold over Prisca. Somehow, she had kept the ritual from being fully completed and now had cost him another daughter. He moved toward the fireplace, staring into the fiery pit as the flames licked eagerly at the timber. The shaman had a lot to answer for and one way or another, he'd get his answers or there would be hell to pay.

Chapter Thirty-Nine

Ace and Gabe entered Lustra's bedroom, bringing with them Prisca's basket. The petite mother sat on the rocker, clearly distressed. Upon seeing them, her hand flew to her mouth, eyes fearful.

"How is my daughter?" Lustra's voice was barely audible.

"We shall see." Gabe set the basket on the bed, glancing at Ace, who nodded approvingly. Gabe removed the wooden lid. Inside the scarf, Prisca was still coiled and unusually still.

"Let me hold her," Lustra said. Before any man could react, she shoved her hand into the carrier and picked up the serpent. She pulled the tiny beast to her chest, all the while murmuring soothing words of comfort. "My poor girl. Are you okay?"

"Why isn't she moving?" Lustra frowned. She sat on the rocker and placed Prisca on her lap, where she analyzed her. "She's cold to the touch."

"May I?" Gabe put his hand out, touching Prisca's head. "You're right. We should get her under the heating lamp."

"You had her outside most of the night," Lustra said, tone accusing. "What were you thinking? It was chilly." She got to her feet and carefully placed Prisca into the aquarium. She flicked on the heating lamp.

"There, there, my little one," Lustra said, running

her finger down Prisca's neck. Her voice was soft, but then her mouth drew into a grim line. "Something's wrong with her."

"It seems she is in a trance." Ace leaned down, studying Prisca. "She needs quiet and warmth. Give her some time."

"This is your fault!" Lustra turned her head, pegging unforgiving eyes to Gabe and then to Ace. "And yours! If anything happens to my baby, I will hold you both personally responsible."

"Prisca was in the vortex," Ace said. "Everyone experiences something different when in this realm. We don't know what Prisca gained, if anything. If she were older, perhaps she could tell us, but she is just a baby. In her human form, she is only a few months old, but Prisca's serpent is far beyond her years in wisdom, as it has already been proven since she had sought out Rachel for help. We don't know what this tiny beast can process or if she even understands the vortex."

"So, what was the point?" Lustra returned to the rocker, utterly defeated. "I thought my human daughter would've returned. Prisca is right back where she started from. She is probably afraid. All my work these past couple of weeks to reassure her has been destroyed by your resolve that she enter the vortex. It was all for nothing."

"We don't know that for sure," Ace said. "Give it time."

"Time." Lustra leaned her head back against the rocker, wiping at her tears. "All you people have is time on your hands and plenty of years to live out your serpent's life. But I am human. My time here is limited and each day that my daughter is in this limbo is one day of hell on earth for me. I am missing all her milestones. We aren't bonding." She closed her eyes, a sob escaping her. "It's not fair. Not fair at all."

"I'm sorry, Lustra," Gabe said. He placed his hand on her shoulder. "Hang in there. We are only trying to help."

"Just go," Lustra said, continuing to cry. "I want to be alone."

"Very well." Ace nodded to Gabe, who followed him into the hallway.

"Now what?" Gabe leaned against the wall. "This is a nightmare for her."

"It's a nightmare for all of us," Ace said, walking away.

Chapter Forty

Ariel stretched out her long serpent's form over a rock overhang. Beneath her, she observed the lights of the city of Reading. Moonlight spread down upon her, but she didn't bother trying to open the vortex. She didn't need to seek answers this night, already knowing her place and her purpose. Such was one of her gifts— the gift of discernment.

She envied the people sleeping in the city below. Their average, everyday lives. They'd get up in the morning and go off to work, off to school, or perhaps just huddle in their beds. Bills would have to be paid, and vacations planned. Some would worship God on Sunday and others would curse his name. Such was the human condition, fragile and self-absorbed.

Ariel lifted her head, pointed it toward the south. Her tongue flickered out. Rain was coming, and frankly, she was glad. She was feeling sorry for herself, admitting her loneliness. Her mind turned toward Gabe. It hurt to have him view her as a traitor, and she was. She'd never denied it. Now she'd lost his respect. She loved him and had always loved him. At one time, they had been close. She'd wanted more than friendship back then and had foolishly hoped in time it would change, but then Rachel came onto the scene, and all was lost.

Ariel had hoped Rachel would fail as a guardian,

choosing another path. It was wrong, she knew, but her human side was weak. As an Ophite, Rachel would've been her natural enemy. But surprisingly, Rachel had chosen to be a guardian and joined their cause, despite her tainted bloodline. With that unification, Ariel had simply been replaced in Gabe's life.

And now here she was, an outcast. Even Michael had been pitiless. He was ignoring her, never bothering to see where she'd gone or if she was all right. Such was her life now. And so now here she lay, just waiting.

Slowly, she roused herself from her musings. She stared at the moon for a long moment, then slithered off the rock into the underbrush. A short while later, she entered the property of Paradise Farms. Being part of Blake Howard's sect had its rewards. She knew her way around the property, the pitfalls and the holes in security.

Deliberately, she shielded her mind from being scanned, blocking it efficiently. She worked her way around the outskirts of the property then followed the stream until she reached the hillier terrain. At the top of a mound, she paused, scanning the trees. There it was. The massive oak she sought. Swiftly, she maneuvered her form up into the branches. The limbs were long, intertwined with adjacent trees in a straight line. She followed the route until she came up to the rear of the mansion. She scanned the property for serpents. No one was within the immediate area. She dropped onto the ground, sped across the yard, and moved onto the porch. Within moments, she had climbed onto the roof, slid across to the front of the mansion, and dropped down onto a second-floor porch attached to her old bedroom.

In seconds, Ariel transformed into her human form and opened the sliding door. She stepped into the dark room, entered the walk-in closet, and flicked on the light switch. She grabbed a pair of jeans and a long-sleeved shirt and put them on. In the rear of the closet, she lifted a piece of loose rug. Beneath the carpet, a hole had been created in the padding. She reached into it and pulled out a large brass key.

She exited the bedroom, scanning her surroundings. It took some time, but she managed to work her way undetected through the second floor until she reached a rear staircase. Stealthily, she managed to get to the first floor. Two human maids were cleaning the foyer area. Most of her time spent at the mansion had been underground. Office and conference rooms were situated beneath the right corridor. But on the left side, underground portals and hidden areas were expansive, including the community hub, the core of Blake's entire world—his access to Lord Talco's realm, a place of worship and sacrifice.

Ariel used every skill she possessed to get to the hub, hiding and retreating, working her way down the corridors. When she reached the center of the passage, she pulled the hidden lever. The pocket door slid open, revealing an empty room. She shut the door and flicked on the light switch. The room illuminated, revealing the altar and replica of Lord Talco's serpent. The mouth of the cave was nothing but sheer rock, only being opened supernaturally from within. A gate across the expanse held a huge, heavy chain and was padlocked.

Ariel pulled out the key and glanced at the clock on the wall. It was time.

Chapter Forty-One

As the moonlight faded behind storm clouds, Gabe returned to the house. It was well after midnight, and the night seemed off. Lustra continued to keep him updated on Prisca, who remained the same. He couldn't explain why the serpent had become unresponsive. It was hard to look at her and not feel guilty. Lord knew Lustra treated him with icy regard. Perhaps, he'd taken Prisca into the vortex too early. She was just too young. He'd rushed things and now questioned his own motives, never gaining any insight.

Gabe needed some sleep, but he couldn't mentally shut down. He entered the kitchen and poured himself a glass of juice. Heavily, he sat down at the table. Although tired mentally, his body desired to be free of his human form. His serpent was restless and needy. But to set his serpent free meant to give himself up to the night and not his bed. Frankly, depression had settled over him. He supposed he liked wallowing in his guilt.

All his research, all his connections, and he still had no knowledge of Lord Talco's mysterious lair. He'd studied the underground maps and the terrain around Paradise Farms. Lord Talco's cave had simply vanished as if it never existed. Supposedly, the portal opened every three years. That seemed an eternity. He could never endure such misery waiting out the time, and there was no guarantee that Rachel would be alive. Perhaps Blake's shaman could be forced to open the portal, but he'd no idea of the identity of the man, if he lived at the mansion, or what powers the sorcerer possessed.

Gabe slid his hand into his pocket, pulling out his wallet. He took out Rachel's picture and laid it on the table. She was smiling, with huge brown eyes both innocent and trusting. She was a beautiful girl with her auburn hair and matching brows. A light scatter of freckles sprinkled her slender nose. If only she could've had more time to remain in her innocent state, but she had been called into service. And now, it cost her freedom. Everything he knew about being a guardian was in question. What did it matter if one chose the guardian path if it could be stolen one day?

Gabe frowned. Perhaps Rachel's freedom hadn't been stolen. After all, she had willingly sacrificed herself to save others, him included.

"Couldn't sleep?" Michael walked into the kitchen wearing a blue sweatshirt and mesh shorts. His blond hair was tousled, face stubbled from lack of a razor.

"Nope," Gabe replied. "I see you're up?"

"I slept for a couple of hours," Michael said. "I was having some really weird dreams. I started paying attention to see if anything was important, perhaps a message."

"And?"

"Nothing. I gave up trying to figure it out. Ariel had been in my dream. She was standing at the foot of my bed, watching me sleep. It was creepy and woke me. I even searched my room for her." Michael grabbed a glass from the cupboard and filled it with the remaining juice. "She's pretty mad at me right now. I haven't been speaking to her."

"I'm done with her," Gabe said. He finished off his drink, stood, and put the glass into the sink. "I don't know what her problem is, but I'd rather not deal with her in the future. I can't trust her."

"Same." Michael leaned against the counter. "I'm not sure how much longer I'll hang around here. I know you're trying to find a way to help Rachel, but sometimes things are just out of our hands. And as for Prisca, I'm not certain she will even survive. Her state of being is unusual. Her life is broken and shattered. What Blake did to her was beyond unforgivable. He altered her life's course. Her spirit is somewhere out there—lost. I'd hoped tonight that we could give her a chance, but she seems now worse off. We failed her. And for whatever reason, divine intervention has chosen not to aid us."

"I know." Gabe leaned back in the chair. "She'd been safe with Rachel, partially protected, and now who knows? Discernment isn't my specialty. That's Ace's leverage. Like Ariel, he is both a warrior and has other gifts, but he can't even find Prisca's missing soul."

"Gabe?" A woman's voice reached out telepathically.

Gabe flinched at Ariel's voice. He hadn't spoken to her since the night they rescued Michael and the others. Instantly, he was suspicious.

"You need to come to Paradise Farms," she said. "Meet me at the altar."

Stunned, he sat up, gripping the table ledge. After a pause, he said, "Another set up?" He couldn't keep the sarcasm from his tone.

"No," she said. "But you need to come. Blake won't be expecting you as at the moment. You have the upper hand and Prisca. He won't suspect you returning here. I will be waiting for you. Be discreet and bring Michael. It's imperative that you both come now."

"And if I don't?"

"I won't be responsible for what could happen."

"And what is that?" Gabe asked.

"Rachel might die."

Chapter Forty-Two

There was no sense of time. Rachel had no idea how long she had been in Lord Talco's realm. Her mind would slip into an abyss, but then memories would return in fragments. Sometimes, she remembered her childhood and at other times glimpses of her former life. Her basic need for food, water, and warmth had left her. Instead, she purely existed, an empty vessel with no usage.

Hopelessness washed over Rachel. She had ceased to feel sorry for herself. Lord Talco played his dangerous games with her mind, and he was winning. It was coming to a point that she just wanted to just surrender and get it over with. What was the use anyway? She'd failed in her causes, failed Prisca.

Prisca. The name jolted her as she suddenly recalled the infant. Where was the baby? Was Blake still in possession of her? She frowned, trying to remember what had happened just before she'd blacked out. Nothing came to mind, just jolts of traveling, pain, lights.

Movement came from the hallway breaking into Rachel's thoughts. She felt him before he appeared. Despite her attempt to appear nonchalant, terror gripped her. Lord Talco came into the room wearing a silver robe, bringing with him a dark energy that penetrated the air. His eyes had taken on an ominous glow as his evil desires washed over her. She moved away from him, her back to the wall. There was nowhere to run or to hide.

"I feel your serpent, Rachel," Lord Talco said. "She longs to meet me."

"No," she said. "You feel nothing. I think she has abandoned me."

He smiled, revealing his jagged and sharp teeth. He had no hair on his head or brows and no ears. Instead, his scalp was slick and translucent like the rest of his flesh with spine-like veins pulsating. She preferred it when he used magic to hide his true countenance, but he had since taken on his truer form.

"Your serpent is still with you, Rachel, but she will soon join me. Have no doubt."

"You can't have her," Rachel said, protective of the beast within her, the beast that had been her salvation on more than one occasion. "She is mine, and I am hers."

"So you say." He moved closer. The veins beneath his terrible white skin pulsed with liquid, and she wondered if it was truly blood. Even his temples pounded in a silent beat. His body stood taut and strained as the beast within him stirred.

In defense mode, she rushed along the wall and headed toward the door. She'd no doubt she'd fail, but she had to try. She had just reached the entrance when his long fingers bit into her shoulder, clamping down in a viselike claw. Pain radiated down her spine as she was spun around. Lord Talco's hand uncurled from her shoulder, only to grab her by the throat. He lifted her in the air and threw her. She fell in a heap by the hot spring, legs folded beneath her. She gasped for air, crawling to her knees. He came toward her, intent in his dark gaze.

"We can do this the easy way, Rachel, or you can just let me take her. But either way, she will be mine."

"No," she said, gasping in pain. She struggled to her feet, backing away from him. Once again, she darted around him. His foot caught beneath her knee, causing her to fall face first into the water. Warm liquid filled her nose and mouth. She sputtered, trying to break to the surface, but before she could get there, Lord Talco grabbed her hair, pulling her toward him on the opposite side. He yanked her halfway out of the water, her back against the edge. His one leg swung over hers, pinning her in position.

"Get off me!" she cried. "You are a disgusting beast!"

Lord Talco's eyes narrowed in on her face as his hand gripped her throat, effectively holding her still. Her wet hair clung damply to her forehead, cold and chilling. She pried at his fingers, but to no avail. She could only watch as his face mutated into a freakish work of art. His nose withdrew and flattened to his face. His brow jutted out, appearing scaley. His jaw thinned and grew elongated, eyes reflective and cruel.

Between his widening lips, his swollen tongue flickered out, long and repulsive. It pulsated in a frenzied beat. It grew longer till it resembled a tube. His jaw grew larger, bonier, stretching his mouth into a wider stance.

Rachel screamed.

"Come, my darling," Lord Talco said, massaging her throat. "Come forth, my beautiful serpent, and meet your master."

Rachel's serpent stirred within. Shocked, she realized that indeed her beast hadn't left her after all. "No," she cried telepathically to her serpent. "Please, don't." But her serpent wouldn't heed her will. Tears flowed freely. Perhaps it was better this way. She could stop fighting this losing battle. Soon it would be all over. Perhaps she'd find peace.

Lord Talco's fingers grew longer as well. His nails curled, appearing razor sharp. His fingers slid over her face, then clamped down on both sides of her head. His cold touch burned her temples as a pulse thumped against her skin. With his face hovering over hers, she couldn't help but be snared by his eyes, which were void of humanity, emotion, and pity.

His eyes narrowed and changed, sometimes elongated, sometimes slanted. Then his tongue slid over her throat. The tube found her mouth, stretched, and sunk down on top of her lips, sealing it as efficiently as any mask. Putrid air filtered from his lungs into hers. She couldn't escape. She tried to breathe through her nose, but the force of the foul chemicals coming from his lungs made it impossible. She could only blink and try to hold her breath. She grew dizzy. Then he was sucking the air from her lungs.

Weakly, she began to pass out, drifting as she began to dream.

Beneath her skin, Rachel's serpent stirred again, but her mind had slipped away, dreaming. She found herself suddenly in her deceased grandmother's bedroom, wearing a white nightgown and standing before a floor length mirror. Her reflection no longer revealed a little girl, but an older, sadder version of herself. She moved closer to the glass, staring into her eyes, which were brown and then turned blue. She squinted, puzzled. Was there a hint of purple? She couldn't break free from her image as her hair billowed around her shoulders. As she watched, her eyes darkened, turning into coal-like pits.

"No!" she screamed into the mirror.

Rachel began convulsing beneath Lord Talco's hands. Her body altered, fusing together, growing in length and size. Her golden serpent emerged even as Rachel watched from a distance, still in her dream state, staring into the mirror. She'd never seen her transformation in such a way. It was frightening and yet captivating. With a start, she realized that on one side of the mirror she was still human, but in her reflection, she was also her serpent. She lifted her hand, spreading her fingers, touching the smooth glass. Her serpent came closer, the sides of her mouth curling.

Her serpent began to fade away in the mirror.

"Come back!" she said. "Don't leave me."

Her image in the mirror became human.

In Lord Talco's arms, Rachel's serpent began to shake violently, still connected to the tube down her throat. Greedily, Lord Talco consumed her offering.

Rachel's serpent grew limp, her heart slowing. In her dream state, she began traveling, now separated from her body. It felt good to be free. This was familiar. Perhaps she was dying or had already died. Such was her purpose. Trees stretched out before her and fields of green. A lake rippled in the distance, a wave of purple mixed with gold.

She found herself by the shoreline, staring at the expanse. It was so beautiful and serene. She could stand there forever. She decided she would stay. No more wars. No more pain. No sorrows or fears.

"Rachel?"

Her name came in a soft whisper. She turned around to find a little girl with dark curly hair, standing in the tall grass. The child's eyes were indeed strange, one blue and the other purple. She knew this girl, but she'd forgotten her name. It was on the tip of her tongue. If only she could remember.

"Hello, Rachel," the child said. She held a boutique of violet flowers in her chubby fingers. "These are for you."

The scent of the lilacs washed over Rachel, bringing back memories of spring. Rachel blinked. She didn't want to talk to this girl; it brought a wave of terror to her heart. She just wanted to remain in peace and in the light. She was so tired. She just wanted rest.

"No." Rachel shook her head, avoiding the child's eyes. "Go away."

But the girl ignored her words, still holding out her offering, her eyes steady. Compelled into doing so, Rachel stretched out her hand to take the offering but as their fingers touched, the girl grabbed her hand and crushed the lilacs into her palm. Their palms meshed together as the flowers disappeared into her skin and then the girl walked into Rachel, becoming one.

A powerful explosion rocked Rachel as a tidal wave of energy rolled over her body. It was fierce, lifting her from her feet. And then her spirit was moving in reverse, gliding, her feet never touching the ground. The beautiful world faded away as the shadows of darkness encroached, pressing against her, but she wasn't afraid, nor was she alone.

Suddenly, Rachel was in Lord Talco's chamber,

hovering over her human body which was lying motionless by the hot spring. Her eyes were open, and she was dead. An eerie light filtered around her form. Leaning over her, Lord Talco waited expectedly.

Rachel saw everything at once and yet was helpless to stop it. Suddenly, she plummeted into her body. Her vision cleared as she saw through her own eyes, realizing her serpent had never altered as her dream had suggested. It had all been part of a ruse, but she'd no time to reason it out as energy traveled through her, blood rushing. She opened her mouth, filling her lungs with air, and then she changed. She had little time to react. Her body contorted, her serpent bursting forward in a loud hiss of rage. The anger was fierce and terrifying.

Lord Talco fell backward, stunned, his tongue recoiling into his mouth. With her serpent's forehead, Rachel slammed it into his face, pressing him down onto the rocky surface. Horrified, he put up his hands in defense.

"I don't understand…"

Rachel's serpent mouth curled, fangs revealed. Her eyes glowed feverishly.

Lord Talco crawled away but then he regained his composure, lifted his chin, and straightened his shoulders. "I am Lord Talco, beast. You are at my command."

"Amm…I?" She hissed, speaking directly to him. "Youuu…want …meee?"

He got to his feet, rushing toward the doorway. He put his hands out, pleadingly. "Join me. We can offer each other much." Fear lay in his features, yet his eyes yielded hope.

Rachel's serpent moved swiftly, rolling her long form around him. "I...I'm tireddd...oof you." Suddenly, she sank her fangs into his right shoulder, dragged him upward, and threw him against the wall. "Let's ffffinnnisssh thiss."

Lord Talco stood, eyes determined. "One last chance to join me, beast."

"Nevvverrrr," Rachel's serpent said.

"Then you will die." Lord Talco's features changed, disfiguring him. He grew longer, thinner. His head grew large. His transformation was ugly—not smooth and graceful like a guardian. His body twisted, rolled, and he grew in size. His tail lengthened, extending out to twenty-five feet.

"I doonn'tt thinnnnk sooo," Rachel said, unimpressed with his reveal. Within seconds, she was on top of him, pinning him with her own additional weight.

Talco rolled, coiled, and flung her off his form. Undeterred, she attacked again. The onslaught continued.

Inwardly, Rachel felt the difference in her serpent. Never before had she experienced such power. Her serpent was strong, cunning, and had never been so large. The realization that she had the gift of warrior hit home. Again, Rachel attacked. Her body rippled with muscle, strength, and agility. They coiled together, mouths opened, each trying to gain the death bite—the strangulation.

Talco managed to drag Rachel's serpent beneath him, grazing her with a fang, but the wound only fueled her serpent's rage. She rolled and flung him against the pool. She attacked again, unyielding, powerful with the skills of her ancient kind.

"Youuu…havvve been ssslack, Talcooo," she hissed. "Weeeaak."

Rachel's words enraged her enemy, who lifted his head, roaring his battle cry, but his display failed in its effect.

Rachel sank her teeth into Lord Talco's proffered neck. She bit deeper, holding him still. Her body twisted around his, rolling his form while her mouth held his flesh in place. He tried to shake free and failed. Rachel became feral, her rational thoughts slipping away into survival mode. When his head dropped heavily to the floor, she released her hold, sliding along his face. When she reached his snout, she opened her mouth wide, then wider still. She placed her mouth over his nose, drawing in his essence, his life force, destroying him in the process. And then he was limp. When she was through killing him, she shoved him away.

Rachel's serpent raised her head to the ceiling, gaining insight and gauging her whereabouts but as she did so, another huge serpent burst into the room, his coat fluorescent lime. His intent to kill her washed over her, but she held no fear. She now housed the additional force of Lord Talco's power, which surged with her own, the very same power he'd tried to take from her.

Two more male serpents entered. She attacked and killed them both, stilling their hearts with her deadly bite. A third beast came, and she repeatedly smashed him into the wall till he lay limp. Angrily, she growled and slithered into the corridor, traveling through the tunnels. Dark serpents were close by. Their thoughts filtered through her mind, distressed, lost, and angry that their leader was dead.

Compelled to abandon the evil compound, she fled, following her instincts. She tunneled through caverns, finding ancient passageways. When she burst into the higher caverns, she moved with alarming speed, slamming into whatever blocked her way. She was oblivious to pain. Oblivious as to whom she was. She was only a beast, simple and pure. Upward she traveled, seeking the night, the moon, and her freedom.

Chapter Forty-Three

Lightning cracked the sky, but the rain refused to fall. The earth grew still as the wind increased its fervor. Gabe, Ace, and Michael studied the mansion's compound, each using their senses to determine what dark beasts were about.

It appeared Blake Howard's followers had indeed dwindled in number. He sensed six serpents in the upper portion of the mansion, three humans, and a canine. Anything beneath the mansion was blocked from detection—of that he could only guess.

Ace agreed to stay hidden in the forest, waiting for Gabe's assessment of the situation. If things went haywire, he'd have the opportunity to seek out other guardian warriors for help.

Gabe and Michael made it safely onto the rooftop of the mansion. Still trepidation held Gabe. Ariel had urged them to hurry. It was a daunting prospect with just the pair of them. How could they expect to succeed if it were another trap?

"Gabe," Ariel said telepathically to Gabe. "Come to me. Hurry."

"How many serpents are in the mansion?"

"There are fourteen in all," she said. "Blake isn't here, but he will be coming."

"How many upstairs?"

"Six," she replied.

Ariel passed his earlier assessment, but Gabe still held no trust.

"Gabe," she said, urgently. "You must come now. The alarm will be going off. The Ophites will all rush to the cavern. There is a porch on the second floor, and the door is open. Use it. Hurry."

"Tell me what this is all about."

"No time. Just get here."

Soberly, Gabe glanced at Michael. "Thoughts?"

"Let's go," Michael said, already moving ahead.

They were off, dropping onto the porch. Inside they were met with no opposition. Outside the door, a dog began to bark. When Gabe opened the door, a small dog ran into the room, barking. He picked it up, put it out on the porch, and closed the door.

A human woman came into the room, saw them, and began to scream. Michael silenced her with a swipe of his tail. She fell to the ground, unconscious. Without further ado, they left the second floor and moved on to the first. Two serpents were waiting. The battle was swift, and Michael and Gabe were victorious. Finally, they trekked into the basement.

Gabe moved down the corridor, heading toward the last place he had seen Rachel—Blake Howard's sacrificial chamber. Emotions struck his core, which he quickly shoved away. He needed to stay focused and on guard.

Gabe reached for Ariel in his mind. Nothing. New doubts set in, but he was in it too deep to withdraw now. He'd follow through, though he may live to regret his decision. Determination overtook his misgivings. If it was a trap, he wasn't going down without taking a few dark serpents with him. Of that, he was certain.

A rumbling noise sounded down the corridor. Something was moving, coming closer.

Gabe and Michael moved toward the source. They entered a lime-scaled corridor, seeking direction. Abruptly, a pocket door slid open. Ariel in human form ushered them inside the worship chamber, now devoid of any occupants. Just then a loud alarm filled the air. Over the doorway, a red light began flashing.

"I need answers, Ariel," Gabe said telepathically. "They already know we're here." He moved toward the altar, the stone serpent above just as evil as he remembered. The gate in front of the stone wall, which had once been used for the entrance to the cave, was slightly ajar. A heavy chain lay in a heap on the floor. Loose dirt lay against the crevice.

Gabriel stood behind the stone serpent, Ariel's blonde hair flowing along her shoulders, her eyes steady and self-assured. Then all hell broke loose.

Blake Howard entered the room in his serpent form. Never beholding the man in this state, Gabe was struck by the size of his enemy, guessing him to be closer to thirty feet. Blake was sleek and silky black. His eyes glowed feverishly red, but it was the thickness of his form that drew Gabe's concern, powerful and muscular. Six more serpents moved in behind Blake, spreading out in a half circle. Each was dark, varying in shades.

"Now what?" Michael said telepathically to Gabe.

"We fight," Gabe said. "They will not take me alive."

Three of the serpents went after Gabe, the other three Michael. Blake remained impassive, seemingly watching the show. Gabe wanted to lash out at Ariel, who stayed in her human form, watching from the shadow of the statue.

Gabe had no time to notice how Michael fared. He was up against three dark warriors, whose skill was akin to his own. Two attacked from the front, while the other attacked his rear. He needed to keep moving, using his agility as his best defense. Gabe managed to injure one beast, but his attack gave opportunity to his other foe, who bit into his tail. Furious, he managed to drag the serpent away, only to be attacked on the other side. He heard Michael cry out in pain.

For one split second, Gabe caught Ariel watching them, a sober look on her countenance. If she'd wanted them to die, then indeed she had led them to their deaths.

Gabe struggled to gain the upper hand, but every time he subdued one beast, another attacked. He bled; superficial wounds opened. The slickness made the floor slippery. Then he gouged one beast's eyes, who roared in pain.

Again, the room trembled as if an earthquake had struck. A loud crack followed. The lights flickered, dimmed, and then brightened. Gabe had little time to react as he was in a battle for his life. When he glanced at Michael, the three serpents were on top of him.

"Why aren't you helping Michael?" Gabe telepathically yelled to Ariel. He turned toward her, but she was staring ahead at the gate, transfixed. He followed her regard. The wall where once the cave entrance had stood was now cracked. Pieces of rocks were scattered about. Earth had fallen through the wall. A small hole was revealed. The rumbling increased as more dirt rolled out.

Gabe's enemies also took notice of the earthquake. Each drew up their heads, tongues flickering, eyes on the bulging wall.

Blake Howard was tilted toward the sight, coiled and mouth aghast.

Ariel was the only one in the room who was quiet and unassuming.

The earth rolling continued. Everything shook. The chairs. The benches. The ceilings. The hole widened as more dirt rolled out, crumbling into a heap. Then a noise came from beyond, a high-pitched roar. Suddenly, a serpent's head burst through the wall. Almost entirely white, the serpent was beautiful in her design. Feathers adorned the rear of her neck, and she had blazing blue eyes. Energy surrounded her and her anger penetrated the air.

"Rachel?" Gabe said telepathically. But this Rachel was altered, bigger, stronger, and unlike any serpent he'd ever seen, but her eyes—those eyes. He knew them so well.

Stealthily, Rachel slithered into the room, fearless and daunting. Her head cocked to one side as a slight smile lifted her mouth into an eerie smile. Then she attacked. In an instant, she was on top of one of the dark serpents who was next to Michael. She grabbed his neck with her fangs, crushing his head onto the floor. Stunned but taking advantage of her attack, Gabe took out one of the serpents near him. Rachel was already onto another serpent, finishing him off, while Michael gained the upper hand against another.

A roar split the room as Blake Howard lifted his head high and attacked Rachel. If he thought she was an easy conquest, he'd been mistaken. The beautiful serpent was agile and cunning. She mocked Blake, always tempting him to strike, but moving just in time before he could hit.

The two battled head-to-head. Teeth gnashed as their bodies slammed into one another. Gabe engaged in battle with another dark serpent, finding the young male skilled and strong. He made short work of his attack, wanting to aid Rachel. He pushed the wonderment of her change to the side, forcing himself to concentrate.

Then the young serpent lay dead. Michael was finishing off his conquest. Ariel watched from the shadows. Gabe then joined in the battle with Blake, but the white serpent wouldn't have it. Rachel roared at him, shoving him out of her way. In an instant, he knew she intended to take Blake out herself, and she didn't need or want his help.

Gabe ignored Rachel's warnings, attacking Blake anyhow. He couldn't just stand by and watch her fight the powerful beast. He couldn't break the need to protect her. Once again, she snapped at him. Using her tail, she flung it into his head, knocking him backward.

"I'm trying to help!" Gabe yelled into Rachel's mind, but there was no reply.

Blake got the upper hand, pinning Rachel with the weight of his body. Angrily, she wiggled her way free but not before he managed to wound her. Blood seeped out of the gash, a vivid contrast to her pale skin. Rachel snapped her head around, slamming it into her foe. The force moved him several feet, and then he fled.

Rachel chased Blake, coming upon him as two Ophite serpents came from the opposite corridor, squaring off against her. With his reprieve, Blake sped off, while Rachel was forced to defend herself against the two beasts. But then Gabe was there, followed by an injured Michael. Gabe overcame his opponent, while Rachel made short work of hers.

"Leaveeee....me," Rachel hissed aloud at Gabe. She snapped her tail at him.

"No!" Gabe said, but she'd shut him out of her mind.

Rachel was already slithering through the corridor. Gabe was stunned at how fast she could move; he was barely able to keep up. She moved through the mansion and burst out the rear door.

"Gabe," Michael called telepathically. "What should I do? I'm hurt and can't keep up."

"Return to the house," Gabe said. "I'm following Rachel. I'm not sure where she's headed or where Blake has gone, but I'm not leaving her alone with him."

"What about Ariel?" Michael asked. "Should I go back for her?"

"No," Ariel's voice suddenly interjected to them both. "I need to close up the cave's portal. It's an access that needs to be sealed to prevent anything else from coming through."

Gabe continued onward, following the trail of broken limbs and destroyed saplings. Ace suddenly appeared beside him, moving along.

"Did you see Rachel?" Gabe asked Ace.

"I did," Ace said. "But I'm not tangling with that dame. She's one pissed off broad."

"I need to follow her," Gabe said. "Michael's hurt and Ariel claims she's closing Talco's portal. I'm not sure where I'm headed yet. Rachel is different, savage and feral. I don't know what she's doing or where she's going."

"I do," Ace said telepathically. "She's going to the house."

Chapter Forty-Four

Despairing, Lustra kept watch over Prisca. The baby serpent was still lifeless. She sang to her, keeping her close to her heart, but all her efforts were failing. Prisca wouldn't respond. Now, she sat and cried. She was so tired. The rain outside lulled her. Her eyes hurt; her throat was parched. Finally, she laid Prisca inside the aquarium beneath the heating lamp. The serpent's head flopped to one side.

"Please, Prisca, come back to me." She kissed her fingertip, placing it against the tiny head. "I love you so much. Please, baby girl. Fight for me. For us."

Lustra climbed into the bed, curled into a ball, and slept. Outside the wind picked up, rain slashing the windows. Lightning streaked across the horizon.

In the living room, David Gilberts and Ron Craig, both guardians, were on guard duty. Both were young and inexperienced serpents, who were a last-minute addition. Both stared down at their cell phones, one playing a game, the other arguing with his girlfriend.

Suddenly, the front door rattled like a runaway freight train had passed. David and Ron both dropped their phones, jumped to their feet, and raced into the foyer.

Again, something crashed into the front door.

"What do we do?" David shouted to Ron.

"Try to reach Ace."

"There's no time," David said. "Change into your serpent."

Both young men altered into their serpents, their clothing flung onto the floor. Lustra came rushing down the hallway, horror on her face.

"What's happening?" she cried.

David whipped his head around, shoving her back toward the corridor.

Lustra, holding her robe against her throat, turned around and sped off. Shutting the bedroom door, she locked it and moved the rocking chair in front of the opening. Outside her door, a crash and splintering of wood wrenched the air. Sounds of grunts and thrashing ensued. Quickly, she scooped up Prisca's limp form, shoved her into the opening of her gown and raced to the window. She tried to pry open the pane, which was secure and locked. Frantically, she ran into the bathroom, shut and locked the door. She left off the light switch, climbed into the bathtub, and pulled the curtain closed. She hunched down, catching her breath, terrified Blake had found them.

More noises erupted. Something moved overhead. Shaking, Lustra pulled Prisca closer to her heart.

"I'm so sorry, little one," she soothed. "Momma won't let him take you." Tears slid from her eyes as she caught back a sob. Then another crash, this one closer. Whatever was coming was now in her bedroom. A great snort shook the quiet. Furniture moved; the floors vibrated. Something pressed against the bathroom door, gently at first and then slammed. The door held. Then came another onslaught, and this time the wood fractured.

"Go away!" Lustra screamed.

Another heave, and the door gave way. Behind the curtain, Lustra could only stare at the serpent's silhouette as it slithered into the room. But the bathroom was small. Only half of its body could fit. As the beast moved toward her, Lustra leaped out of the porcelain tub, shoving past the serpent and running into the bedroom. Screaming, she ran into the hallway, passing one of the injured guardian serpents, who'd blocked the front door with his injured frame. She pivoted around and ran toward the kitchen, hoping to get to the rear door.

With a quick glance over her shoulder, Lustra struggled with the image of a great white, feathered serpent. It wasn't Blake. This beast moved like lightning, pushed past her, and blocked the door. The serpent's head lifted, face level with Lustra's, and snorted.

"What do you want?" Lustra cried. "You can't have her!"

The beast moved closer, its snout inches away from Lustra's chest, which held the hidden serpent. Incredible blue and purple orbs glowed feverishly at Lustra, who froze, mesmerized. Between her breasts, Prisca stirred. Quickly, Lustra tried to still the tiny serpent, hoping the feathered beast was unaware of Prisca's presence. But the small serpent persisted, rising between the folds of her nightgown.

"Prisca, no!" Lustra cried. She tried to tuck the baby's head down, but it shot right back up. A rumble escaped the white beast, whose snout touched against the tiny head. Then the feathered serpent opened its mouth. Lustra screamed as the great beast moved closer. It was going to eat Prisca. Lustra closed her eyes, shaking in horror. If she was going to die, then she'd die with Prisca. At least they'd be together. Silence followed. Lustra opened her eyes, appalled at the sight. Prisca was now in the white serpent's mouth. The serpent turned and moved toward the living room.

"No!" Lustra cried. She leaped upon the tail of the beast, which was like trying to hold onto a moving car. "You can't have her. She's mine. Mine!"

The serpent continued toward the foyer, Lustra in pursuit.

David, in his serpent form, could only watch the female serpent approach. Slowly, he slithered out of the way, retreating.

Rachel's serpent moved outside, onto the front lawn. She coiled and raised her head toward the sky. In that moment, moonlight broke through the clouds. Beams stretched their fingers over the serpent, her white coat gleaming. She rolled her great head around as if luxuriating in the glow, then lowered her face toward the ground, then lower.

Lustra took the opportunity and raced up to the beast, intent on kicking her. She reached for the beast's feathers, which she wanted to rip from the serpent's form, but then a cry stopped her. Not just any cry but a baby's cry. Lustra's heart stilled. Then the great beast's head lifted. On the ground lay a bawling infant—Prisca. The naked infant stared up at the serpent above her and ceased crying.

Lustra scooped up Prisca, pulling her into her arms, against her chest. She froze when the white serpent turned her giant head. Lustra retreated a few steps. The white serpent's eyes were now blue. The beast's head wobbled unsteadily, and it began to tremble, appearing confused. It moved toward the house, paused, and then shuddered. Suddenly, the beautiful serpent crashed to the ground. The serpent's body began wriggling, convulsing. It rolled onto its side, then tried to right itself. Then it changed, shrinking in size. A naked woman lay on the ground. Long auburn hair covered her narrow back as she clawed at the ground.

"Help me." A soft cry came from the human.

Lustra woke from her shock. She moved toward the woman and knelt with Prisca in her arms. Maneuvering the baby, she yanked off her robe and dropped it over the woman's shivering form.

"I take it that you are Rachel?"

"Yes," Rachel replied, then there was silence.

****

Gabe arrived at the house just in time to witness Rachel transform into her human form. He rushed up to her, just as Lustra covered her with the robe.

"Rachel," he cried, sinking down beside her. Hearing her name, she lifted her head.

"Gabe," she said weakly.

In reaction, Gabe pulled her into his arms, holding her against his chest. His hands touched her hair and face. She was here. Rachel was home. She felt so fragile and thin. Violently, she shook. He lifted her in his arms, carrying her into the house. Inside, he took her into the living room, gently placing her on the couch. He smoothed her hair from her brow, marveling at the miraculous vision.

David and Ron appeared in the doorway, human and sheepishly avoiding Gabe's glare.

"Sorry, Gabe," David said. "The situation got out of hand. We didn't know she was Rachel. Her serpent came in here and was unstoppable. We feared for Prisca, but she threw us aside like rags dolls."

"As warriors, you've a lot to learn," Gabe said. "We'll speak about it later. You can go for now."

Alone with Rachel, Gabe paused. Prisca was crying in the next room. Lustra soothed her, crying and talking to the baby.

"Rachel," Gabe said, returning his attention to her. Her beautiful eyes were now brown. She was pale, tired, and all too thin. "What can I do to help you? "

"Nothing." She stared up at him, touching the side of his face. "Seeing you is all that I need. I love you so much."

"I love you." Gabe leaned down and kissed her. "I know I don't always show it, but I do love you, Rachel. Right or wrong, you're everything to me."

Rachel clung to him again, her body shaking. Their mouths met. When Gabe lifted his head, she softly smiled at him. Rare emotion hit him like a thunderbolt, the sensation shaking him to his core. They were both guardians, designed and ordained to protect the innocent, be it human or changelings, but this woman was part of him, the very essence of his being.

"There's so much I want to know," Gabe said. "Your serpent is incredible. You should've seen her."

"I sort of did," she said, remembering her odd dream and the mirror. "But she wasn't just my serpent. She was Prisca's as well. Somehow, in Talco's realm, we came together. Our gifts intertwined. Prisca's soul force was still with me. Somehow, her serpent was able to connect with mine and helped protect us. It was so incredible. In her own way, Prisca led me home—led herself home. She is my sister, and we have an eternal bond."

"I don't understand your physical changes though," Gabe said. "You're also part warrior?"

"It was an incredible experience," she replied. "Prisca has the gift of warrior, not I. I don't know how much of the warrior part will remain or if I've been given a great gift. I will have to wait to see what happens when I next transform. If it's not to be, then I've still learned a few new tricks along the way from Prisca's serpent." She paused, smiling coyly. "But I also received another gift in my bondage—the gift of discerning spirits. With this gift, Lord Talco couldn't seduce my serpent with his illusions, though he tried."

"How did you escape him?"

"I killed him," she said. "As a human, Prisca is fragile, but her serpent has many gifts. Somehow, Blake woke Prisca's serpent from her dormant state before her natural time at maturity. She went into a protective mode, knowing Blake's evil intentions. So, she took charge and brought me into the picture, most likely because we are sisters. I was meant to stop Blake and free Prisca, or so I thought. Instead, Lord Talco took me. I was the device for Prisca's serpent to gain access to his lair to destroy him for good, thus ending Blake's access to the underground lord. Prisca merged with me in battle. Together, we fought. If her serpent has one flaw, it's her impatience. She likes to get things done. Destroying Talco had been my real mission, our real mission, and it was fulfilled. As awful as it was, it was also an incredible experience."

"How does Ariel play into this?" he asked, brow puzzled. "She knew you were coming back and had me come to the mansion just in time. Did she know what was going on?"

Rachel paused, thinking for a moment. "Yes. It was Ariel's job to ensure I'd arrive at Blake's mansion to be the sacrifice. She was to ensure it would happen. She did her job very efficiently, perhaps even enjoyed it a bit, but in the end, Ariel is loyal to our cause. At least, she is loyal to you. You know she loves you. She tries to hide it and grieves over losing your friendship, and she blames me."

"I had my doubts about Ariel," he said, shaking his head. "After all, she betrayed me and Michael. We were locked up."

"She would've rescued you." Lightly, she cupped his jaw. "Eventually, she did as it was planned. She made it possible for your serpent to return to you, knowing you'd free yourself."

"Interesting," Gabe said, thinking over her words. "I never really thought about how I escaped. I thought I did it on my own, but now it makes sense. I've been pretty cold to her."

"Well, it is expected, considering the circumstances. So now you know what part she played. Ariel couldn't reveal her mission or her sources. For in doing so, we might've all tried to undo what was happening and stop it. It turned out the way it was meant to be."

"I suppose," he said. He leaned his face into her palm and closed his eyes. "I thought I lost you forever. It haunted me wondering where you were and what was happening to you. I never want to lose you again."

"There's no guarantees, Gabe, for any of us. We live in the now. Each day is special. We live to serve others."

"Right now, I'm serving myself," Gabe said. He lowered his head, kissing her lips.

Chapter Forty-Five

"It's nice to know where I fit in with the scheme of things," Michael said, limping into the room and noticing the embraced couple. A large gash was noticeable on his head. His clothes were dirty and wrinkled. Behind him, Ace stood, watching the pair on the couch.

"I was just coming back for you," Gabe said, moving away from Rachel.

"Sure, you were," Michael said, shrugging. "I see you have been doing something more important."

Gabe rose from the couch, turned to Michael, and gave him a hug, pounding him on the back. "I knew you were safe, and Ace would take care of you."

"That I did," Ace said. He also embraced Gabe, scanning Rachel. "Welcome back, young lady. You sure know how to make an entrance."

"Thank you," she replied, returning his hug and then Michael's.

"Where's Prisca?" Michael asked.

"With her mom," Gabe said. "I'd like to see how she's making out."

"I'll come with you," Rachel said, sitting up.

"Maybe you should rest," Gabe said, concern in his gaze. "You've been through so much."

"So has she," Rachel said, smiling. She held up her hand, which he took, helping her to stand. "I want to see her."

Rachel, Michael, and Gabe stood by Lustra's shattered bedroom door. Gabe knocked softly against the broken frame. "Lustra, would you mind if we came in for just a minute?"

"It's fine," Lustra said, her voice soft. "She's asleep."

Prisca, now dressed in a warm sleeper, was asleep in her mother's arms. Her dark hair curled around her head, face serene and angelic. One tiny hand was tucked up against Prisca's cheek.

Rachel reached out and touched the baby's downy hair. This was her sister. Despite their age difference, it seemed like they'd already spent a lifetime together.

"Thank you, Rachel," Lustra said, eyes brimming with tears. "For returning my daughter to me. I will forever be indebted to you."

"I will forever be indebted to Prisca's serpent," Rachel said, bending down to kiss the baby's brow. "For she'd brought two sisters together; it is a special bond, and I love her so. If you ever need anything, just ask me."

"I will," Lustra said. "For now, I just want her to hold her and for her to be safe."

The men never said a word, just watching the interaction. After a moment, the onlookers filtered out of the room.

Chapter Forty-Six

In the waiting area at The Norris Recovery Center, Rachel anxiously sat. When her mother walked into the room, unexpected emotions filled her with intense pain. An uncertain, hesitant smile hovered around Leah's lips. She moved toward Rachel, who stood.

"Hello." Rachel gave her mother an awkward hug, noting her frail shoulders. In that moment, she detected the sickness in her mother's body from her many years of substance abuse. Leah's liver was in failure, and she wouldn't have long to live. She doubted her mother knew of her condition, but it was only a matter of time before it was revealed.

"You're so beautiful," Leah said, placing both palms against Rachel's face to stare at her. "And tall. How tall are you?"

"Five seven," Rachel said. "That isn't that tall."

"You've got five inches on me," Leah said. "And that thing you turn into...what's that, about fifteen feet?"

"It's more like twenty feet or so but I've grown a bit and have never really measured myself." Rachel glanced around the room, worried someone would overhear their awkward words. She grabbed her mother's hand, leading her to a chair in the corner. She lowered her voice. "You mustn't talk about it, Mom. People wouldn't understand, and they don't need to."

"You're telling me," Leah said, eyes dancing. "I did tell some folks in the past, but people thought I was nuts or it was the drugs talking."

Rachel lowered her head, swallowing hard. She loved her mother, but forgiveness was hard to find. The seemingly mundane visit was more out of duty than anything else. The connection she once held to this woman had been broken but still, she was going to try.

"How's things going in here?" Rachel asked. "You look like you put on a little weight."

"Yes, ten pounds," Leah said. "But not where I need it. It's all in my stomach and not my skinny chicken legs." She laughed, slapping her thigh.

Soberly, Rachel quieted her thoughts. Her mother was eccentric and always had been. The drugs had only made it worse. In the past, her mother had been cruel while under the influence and very hurtful to her daughters. She remembered every vile word.

"Do you ever see Stacey?" Leah asked.

"No," Rachel said. "I do write to her now and then. I don't want to intrude into her life unless she wants me to. I suppose when she's an adult, it will be her decision, not mine. She is living in New Jersey and is happy, loved, and safe. I intend for her to stay that way."

"She's just a human like me, right?" Hope filled the woman's large eyes.

"Yes," Rachel replied. "She has a different father. I still don't understand how you ever gotten tangled up with a man like Blake Howard."

"It was easy," Leah said. "You've seen him—so handsome, so charming. Oh, it was romantic. I fell in love with him, and he'd swept me off my feet. When

I'd gotten pregnant, things began to change." Leah paused, eyes clouded. "Blake put me up in a townhouse and paid the bills, but he became mean and controlling. What I thought was love was really a sabotage of my life. He monitored every part of my day and became abusive. Daily, he had me watched. I could never go anywhere without being spied on…"

"Serpents?"

"Yes," Leah replied. "I was their pet project. They were only interested in my baby to come. They'd drop by the house and give me weird drinks. Blake wanted me to see some doctor of his but because I wouldn't go, he came to visit me. Oh, that day he was in a foul mood and really nasty. I told him I wanted nothing more to do with him. At that point, I just didn't care anymore. I…I slapped him…big mistake."

Fear entered Leah's eyes; a tremor shook her frame.

"He changed right into that…that beast right in front of me. I was horrified and scared. He coiled his body around me, and I thought I was dead." Her gaze filled with unshed tears. "He released me and changed into a human. He threatened me not to tell. I didn't know what was growing inside of me. I was so scared."

"I can imagine, "Rachel said. "So, you ran?"

"I ran," Leah said. "And kept running, moving from place to place. I thought I was so smart. I sold the jewelry he gave me and my fancy clothes—anything to survive. Still, they tracked me down, but for the most part left me alone. They were just waiting me out."

Leah glanced at Rachel, smiling. "I gave birth at the hospital. I was so relieved you appeared normal, or at least I thought you were. Blake showed up and told the nurses he was your father. He held you, but it was to see if you had the mark, and you did on your wrist. He was so happy. He told me I could keep you for a couple of years, and then he'd be back to take you."

Leah glanced down at Rachel's wrist. "Do you still have your mark?"

Rachel rolled over her wrist. "Yes. It has healed."

"I thought if I could get rid of your mark, it would keep Blake away," Leah said. "That maybe it'd keep you from becoming a beast. I was so afraid. I could hear Blake speaking to me in my thoughts and dreams. It was horrible to be owned by him. I brought in a natural healer to take the mark off of your skin. I had no idea he'd burn you. You were so young, and I didn't think you'd remember it. I started drugs to block my mind from him. I know you think it's an excuse but believe me, it worked. Blake couldn't find me for a while."

"The drugs took over your life," Rachel said, cringing at her words. "In some ways, just like Blake had done. You do have some serpent blood, Mom, though not enough to change into one. Blake could've tracked you just because of that."

"So I was told," Leah said. "I guess that's what drew Blake to me in the first place."

Rachel thought about her words. Indeed, the man was her father, and she barely knew anything about him. In time, she'd confront him again and then end his reign of terror on unsuspecting women.

"But he didn't fool my Rachel." Leah rubbed Rachel's arm. "You outsmarted him. I'm so proud of you."

"Thanks, Mom," Rachel said, the word mom so

foreign. It had been her belief that her mother had no hold over her, and now she knew it had been a lie. She supposed she was starved for a mother's love—this woman's love, as warped as it seemed at times.

"I'm going to have to go." Retreating from her thoughts, Rachel rose to her feet. "Please finish out the program. How long do you think you will stay?"

"It's a three-month program," Leah replied. "I'm going to make it this time. I swear it."

Rachel doubted her mother's words, but the woman would soon be dealing with more health issues, which she was obviously in the dark about. It was a depressing thought, but one she'd have to deal with when the time arrived.

"You can do this." Rachel leaned down and hugged her tightly. "I know you can. You just need to believe in yourself and make it happen."

Leah nodded against Rachel's shoulder. "I'll try."

"Don't just try. Do it. I love you, Mom."

"I love you, Rachel." Tears spiked Leah's gaze, trembling on her lashes. "When will I see you again?"

"I don't know," Rachel said. "I will be in Pennsylvania for a while to regroup. I never know from day to day what might come my way but don't worry about me. I'm good at taking care of myself."

"I know you are," Leah said. "You're a strong woman."

Rachel smiled, kissed her cheek, and exited. She thought about her mother's words. She wasn't feeling strong. She almost bawled her eyes out and for once, it would've been nice to have her mother comfort her, instead of it being the other way around.

****

Outside the rehab, Gabe observed Rachel walking through the doorway. Her brown hair held blonde highlights, hanging loosely over her shoulders, stirred by her graceful movements. Her big brown eyes were clouded and sad. Her emotional stress of dealing with her mother washed over him. Her inner pain snared him. Leah had caused her daughter a lot of grief, but Rachel was stronger because of it, a true survivor. She had a natural way of dealing with children that were in similar circumstances based on her own experiences. Most guardians had troubled pasts, for that reason alone, to help them aid others.

"Hey, beautiful," Gabe said. Rachel lifted her gaze to his. He smiled, trying to brighten her mood. "I hope you're hungry. I'm starving and want a Philly cheesesteak."

"That sounds good." She stood in front of him, toying with the front of her leather jacket. Finally, she tugged it down over her jeans.

"How'd it go in there?"

"It went as expected." She avoided his discernment. "My mom only has months to live. She doesn't know it yet. I had a premonition, and it makes me sad and mad. She ruined her healthy body, and it can't be repaired. Now she will die and there's nothing I can do about it."

"I'm sorry, Rachel." Gabe slid his arms around her waist, pulling her into his arms. She tucked her head against his shoulder, clinging to him. "I wish there was something I could do."

"There's not," she said, lifting her gaze to his. "What will be, will be. There is no stopping it. This gift of knowledge and spiritual awareness that is now part of me has its drawbacks. I will visit her again and be there for her. At least we were able to have a real conversation and not some warped version of one."

"I'm glad you did," he replied, linking hands. They stopped at Vinny's steakhouse, ordered their steaks, and sat by a window, watching pedestrians move by.

"So now what?" Rachel asked.

"Ace found a place for Prisca and Lustra to live. It's in Maine, close to him. It's suitable and Prisca can go to school, hopefully leading a normal life till she's mature enough to learn of her serpent. Hopefully, she will have no recollection of what had occurred, though her serpent probably will."

"Sounds good," she said. "I'd like to visit her. After all, she is my sister."

"You could do that, if you're careful," he said. "You wouldn't want to attract any attention Prisca's way, not that you would do so intentionally."

Soberly, Rachel swallowed her food. She couldn't be part of Prisca's life. How awful to have to stay away from another sister, the exact reason she stayed away from Stacey.

"Cheer up, Rachel. Things will work out."

"I suppose," she said, hiding her pained gaze. "But we still have to deal with my father. Prisca will always be a target if I don't."

"I agree with you," he replied. "He might not want to wrestle his warrior princess."

"I'm not a princess."

"To me you are," he teased. Beneath the table, he playfully pressed his foot against hers. "After all, you have ancient blood from a fierce warrior queen."

She thought about his words, coyly searching his

features. "I do, don't I. I kind of like it. So watch it or you might not like the taste of my bite."

"You can bite me as long as it's done in love."

She laughed at his serious tone, love swelling her heart. "Yes, only in love."

A word about the author...

With a passion for writing, award-winning Tamera Lawrence likes to entertain readers with edgy thrillers and mysteries. Tamera draws on personal experiences to bring to life interesting characters set in today's complex world.